A SHIMMER OF ANGELS

Lisa M. Basso

D1292319

For John and Jackie. Without you two, I never would have put words to paper. You are loved and missed every day.

A Shimmer of Angels
All rights reserved. Published in the United States of America by Month9Books, LLC. Month9Books is a registered trademark, and its related logo is a registered trademark of Month9Books, LLC. www.month9books.com

Summary: Sixteen-year-old Rayna pretends she doesn't see angels, until students start showing up dead, forcing her to reveal what she's seen and what she knows.

ISBN 978-0-9850294-3-2 (tr. pbk)
ISBN 978-0-9850294-2-5 (e-Book)
1. children's 2. fiction. 3. fantasy. 4. A Shimmer of Angels. 5. Lisa M. Basso. 6. young adult. 7. Paranormal. 8. Angels.

For information, address Month9Books, LLC, PO BOX 1892 Fuquay-Varina, NC 27526.
www.month9books.com

Cover design: Stephanie Mooney
Cover art copyright©: Month9Books, LLC. 2012

Praise for A SHIMMER OF ANGELS

"Basso's first entry in her Angel Sight series is guaranteed to please. From her independent but troubled heroine to the two tempting heroes and an unusual paranormal aspect, readers will love the slightly dark feel, and eagerly anticipate the next book."
— RT Book Reviews

"Rayna is a courageous heroine who finds herself in the middle of two gorgeous angels and a fascinating world. I look forward to more from Lisa M. Basso!"
— Karen Mahoney, author of The Iron Witch

"The characters were so engaging, the dialogue snappy but expository, and the actual plot so engrossing that I read the entire book in just a few hours."
— BadassBook Reviews

"I enjoyed the storyline, the characters and I would most probably read this book again at some point."
— Katie's Books

"A Shimmer of Angels is one of those books that I just couldn't set it down."
— Girl With a Laptop and Books

"When I finished reading this book, my first thoughts were 'Wow, this is just totally amazing."
— Girl In the Woods Review

Acknowledgements

Writing a novel is a journey the likes of which no one can truly be prepared for. It's so much more than sitting at a desk alone. So, in honor of that, there are a few (dozen) people I'd love to thank.

First of all, I have to thank Georgia McBride for falling (pun intended) in love with this story and believing in it enough to take a chance on it and on me. These words would not be on this page, and this story may never have been shared with so many if not for you.

To my incredible editor, Mandy Schoen, who is, simply stated, a genius. Our long, back-and-forth e-mails helped keep me sane, and your incredible insights kept me afloat and pushing forward. Thank you for understanding my twisted characters and finding ways to make them shine (and lose their $#!*).

I also want to thank Courtney Koschel, Rachel Bateman, Ashlynn Yuhas, Brittany Howard, and Kelly P. Simmon. And to all of the Month9Books family, including the generous, talented, amazing up-and-coming Month9Books authors whose books I can't wait to get in my hands and devour: thank you.

I couldn't go on any further without thanking my mom for loving me so fiercely and showing me how far a hard-working woman can go in life. Even though we live so far away now, no distance will ever be too great for us. (P.S. so sorry for those pesky teenage years, but without them I wouldn't be so dead-set on writing for Young Adults.)

Thanks Dad, for taking care of me, always being there, and for passing on a seriously unique (and sort of messed up) sense of humor.

And, of course, Randy, for encouraging me to take that big step and finish my first novel, for pushing me when I need it and letting me work when and where ever the muse strikes. Thank you for being my rock. You truly are the love of my life, and I still can't believe how lucky I am.

To Lesley Jones, my unbelievably awesome, go-to writerly friend who is always there when I need an ear no matter how busy you might be. For all the e-mails, chats, brainstorming sessions, hours of gaming and giggling, and most importantly the crazy cat-lady silliness. Never, never change, and keep reaching for the stars.

I'd also like to thank my fabulous critique partner, Katee Robert, for helping me along on this crazy writing journey, and for letting me share in those thrilling, smexy stories of yours.

Terry, Danny, and Katie Gripton, my second family, for taking me in so long ago when I felt lost, and for letting me keep coming back (and not just for a summer or two).

My dear Andrea Creighton, the truest, most dedicated friend any girl could ask for—the kind that freaks out (in a good way) when you tell her you're going to be published, and inspires me to be sillier every day.

A huge thank you to the readers. Without your extreme good taste, I wouldn't be here in this amazing position. To my blog and Twitter friends, my breaks revolve around you and your crazy antics. To everyone I may have forgotten, and everyone to come, thank you, thank you, thank you.

A Shimmer of Angels

Lisa M. Basso

Chapter One

Doctor Graham said I was in remission the day he signed my release papers, and I believed him. God knows, I wanted to believe him. Armed with three prescriptions and an outpatient schedule requiring weekly visits with a counselor, I'd left, because anything was better than that place.

The thing about beliefs? Even the strongest can be shattered by the simplest of things.

Hallucination-free. I should have expected it wouldn't last. And judging by the golden-haired boy across the street—the one sporting the curved wings— remission had just become a fond and distant memory.

I squeezed my eyes closed. *Please don't be real. Please don't be real.* My heart sputtered and cold disbelief coiled around my lungs, reminding me that pleading never worked. So I sucked in a breath and opted for common sense instead. *Angels don't exist. They never had.* Dr. G had made me see that during our therapy sessions. And yet, three months, twelve days, and fifteen hours after my release, there they were. Again.

I used to see them all the time—winged beings, walking around. They were the cause of my frequent stints at the Sunflower Serenity Mental Health Clinic—

or the SS Crazy, as I called it—over the past three years. But they were just projections of an unstable mind. I understood that now. I pulled in a slow breath and forced my eyes open.

I felt stupid relieved to find the wings gone, the guy they'd belonged to swallowed up by the crowd outside the window. I would have laughed at my foolishness had my pulse not been jumping. It was a slip, nothing more. The first in months.

A plastic cup bounced off the black-and-white checkered floor, pulling me back to the hectic shuffle of the diner. Waitresses scrambled to talk, shouting over the louder patrons. Exhausted-looking parents wrestled with squirming kids, shoveling food down their throats before dropping them at school. It was Heaven compared to the silence of a mental institution's single-occupancy room, and nowhere near as … colorful as mealtimes with the clinically insane.

"This place is crazy busy." Lee leaned across our table, his bony elbows bumping the salt shaker on one side, his empty hot chocolate mug on the other. "Are you sure you want to work here?"

Leland Alexander Kyon—spiky-haired beanpole and geek extraordinaire—was not only a total dork, but the best friend I'd ever had. He knew me better than anyone, and if he thought this was a bad idea, I probably should have listened.

"Well, I need a job. My dad says kids today should learn the value of a dollar." I laid the back of my hand over my forehead and sighed dramatically, mostly to distract him from the way my knee kept bouncing against the underside of the table and the trembling of my fingers set against my own mug of hot chocolate. "So Laylah and I are destined for a life of diner servitude and bad tips."

It wasn't a total lie. Dad's tech job paid well, but

my stints at the SS Crazy had resulted not only in my restored sanity, but also huge medical bills. Dad swore it hadn't affected our financial situation, but I knew he wasn't being straight with me. It was the little things: the off-brand cereal, the badly patched uniform skirt Laylah had worn every day for a week, even the way he emptied the swear jar every Saturday morning before we'd get up. My family was hurting, and it was my fault. Besides, there was college to think about. I couldn't let Dad take out loans for me. Not after everything I'd put him through.

Too bad neither Dr. G nor Dad agreed with me that I should have a job. Something about the risk of stress-induced relapse. But Dr. G didn't have to worry about college. He'd already put his son and daughter through grad school.

I probably could've chosen any old job, but I wanted something that would make me feel normal again. And what's more normal than a waitress at the all-American Roxy's Diner?

I straightened the silverware over my folded paper napkin, making sure the bottoms of the fork and knife lined up, even as I inched the spoon up to balance the difference in length. A toddler in a highchair across the aisle screamed and flung his chocolate milk at the floor, dousing a passing waitress in a wave of brown, milky rain. I tensed, my fingers knocking the silverware askew.

Lee and I watched the mother send the poor waitress scampering for a milk refill. He shook his head. "Whatever, Ray. It's your sanity."

I froze, cutting him a shocked glance. I'd never told Lee about the sanitarium. His mention of my sanity was merely Lee being Lee. Unless he suspected … but he wasn't looking at me, turning instead to dig some cash from his book bag. *He doesn't know how messed up you are,* I reminded myself. *And he won't if you just breathe, act normal.* I hated keeping the truth from him, but I hated the thought of him knowing it even more. He was the only friend I had, and I intended to keep him.

Lee tossed a five on the table. "Just remember what I told you: stay positive." He leaned back in his seat and crunched down on a dark piece of sourdough toast. "Perky wouldn't hurt, either."

I speared him a glance. "Perky? Really?"

"Darlin'?" Our waitress called, her voice grating like sandpaper. Weathered laugh lines and crows' feet defined an otherwise pretty face. "You still interested in the job?"

I nodded and murmured, "Wish me luck."

Lee shot me a double thumbs-up.

I followed the waitress to a booth by the window. She angled for the seat facing the back of the building, which would leave me the seat with a clear view out the front window, where angel-guy had been. There was no way I'd let the possibility of seeing another set of imaginary wings doom this interview. I moved quickly, sliding in behind the waitress to claim her seat.

The back wall of the café was blissfully wing-free. I let out a small breath. *See? You can do this.*

"Have a seat," the waitress invited, her voice sharp with sarcasm as she took the seat across from me. My face flushed with embarrassment as she examined me, much the same way Dr. G had so many times. Like there was something not quite right with the person across from her.

Nerves turned my stomach, and I wrung my hands together under the table. During my time at the facility, I'd learned that when you're wearing a smile, it's easier to pass yourself off as happy. As *normal.* As someone other than the girl who'd tried to end herself. Twice. So I flipped the happy switch I'd been perfecting. The corners of my mouth fluttered as I tried to hold a smile that wasn't as convincing, or as solid, as it used to be.

Pull it together, Ray. Normal kids hold down jobs, and you're normal now.

The name tag pinned to the waitress's pink-and-white frilly uniform read "Daphne." She leaned across the table to flick a crumb to the floor, and I noticed the dark line of a hairnet behind her ear. And I'd thought the nude stockings and white nurse's shoes were the worst part of the uniform.

"Can you tell me about the job?"

Daphne slapped her notepad down on the green-and-pink speckled tabletop. "We open at six every morning. We close at ten, midnight on weekends. The work is hard, the tips are crap, and the neighborhood gets rough after dark."

I was sold.

Daphne tilted her head, propping it up with her hand. A dull sheen coated her hooded eyes, mirroring the luggage and yellow-tinted concealer beneath them. "We pay minimum wage, offer flexible hours for students, and we're desperate." She leaned in closer, dropping her arm. I waited, wondering if her head would fall without the support. "What's your name, darlin'?"

"Rayna, but I go by Ray."

"You know, Ray, you have to be at least sixteen to—"

A siren cut through the air. I jerked my gaze to the window in time to watch an ambulance squeal around the corner and out of sight. Daphne was still talking. I knew that, but I couldn't make myself hear the words. Couldn't tear my gaze from the corner of the building, where the ambulance had disappeared.

Couldn't quite make myself believe it wasn't coming back for me.

Daphne's cigarette-etched voice rose above the fading wail, a note of suspicion lacing her next words. "You're not one of those runaways, are you? 'Cause I'll need a parent or guardian's signature for the work permit."

I dragged my attention back to the interview. *It's just an ambulance*, I told myself, willing my shaky hands still. At least they were under the table, out of sight. I dug my nails into my palms to keep myself in the moment.

"I'm sixteen and definitely not a runaway. Just new to San Francisco." A dish crashed to the floor. I flinched, immediately hating myself for it. The time away from the SS Crazy hadn't made me any less jumpy. But there was little difference between the sound of that dish breaking into a million white pieces and that of a fellow schizophrenic throwing the contents of her dinner tray at my head.

A waitress with way too much cleavage stooped beside the counter to pick up the pieces. The bell above the cook's station chimed, and a man at the table behind Lee bellowed for service. Daphne and I turned toward the yelling customer, totally busting Lee, who was watching Cleavage Waitress a little too closely.

Daphne squirmed to the edge of the booth. "Glamour calls. Jot down the hours you're available and any previous references you have." She slid her ordering pad and pen toward me and climbed the rest of the way out of the booth, her joints popping as she stood. "I'll be right back."

She shuffled toward the pick-up window. I watched her balance five omelet specials across her arm, dropping them off at the table behind Lee. She returned to the counter and shoved a broom into the clumsy waitress's hands. I looked down at the blank ordering pad in front of me.

Previous references. I cradled the pen in my hand, waiting for it to write something—anything that would make me appear experienced, confident, and sane. Somehow, I didn't think library apprentice or gardening instructor at a mental health clinic would accomplish that.

Daphne returned much quicker than I had anticipated. Her hands popped up to her hips, and she quirked her lips, waiting.

"So," I began, determined not to let my anxiety get the best of me. "I don't have any previous references and I can be here by three thirty, but I have a standing appointment on the second Wednesday of every month." My monthly check-in with Dr. Fritz, the local psychiatrist who monitored my meds—not to be confused with the school therapist I met with once a week—could not be missed. Ms. Morehouse, my school therapist, was the only reason Dad was letting me attend public school again.

Daphne drummed the table with her fingers, her droopy eyes peeling back the layers of my psyche. "Hmm. You've got a sweet face."

I bored the toe of my Converse into the linoleum. I didn't like her examining me like that. She had no idea what lay beneath the "sweet face."

"It's a good face," she continued. "The kind that could bring in more business. So do you want the job or not?"

My first big decision on the outside. I had to do it, if only to show Dad and Dr. G that I wasn't some fragile girl afraid of her own shadow. Determination welled in my chest. I straightened up and pulled back my shoulders. "You've got yourself a new waitress."

She tugged a thin stack of papers from her apron pocket. "Fill these out and bring them back in a day or two." She shook a finger at me. "Don't forget a parent's signature."

Yes, yes, yes! "Great, no problem."

Daphne's shoulders relaxed, and she smiled—she seemed almost as relieved as I was. She shuffled off to a table closer to the counter, stockings sagging around her left ankle. My lip curled as I took one last critical look at the uniform. I'd been dressed in worse.

I rolled the papers between my hands as I walked back to Lee.

"Did you get the job?" Lee asked between clicks of his phone.

I pulled my backpack up from the floor by its purple handle and tucked Daphne's papers into my English binder.

"I think I did."

He looked up from his tiny screen long enough to offer me a smile. "That's great, Ray!"

Yeah, it's great now, but wait until Dad and Dr. G find out. Then, the opposite of great. Potentially disastrous.

And what if Dr. G and Dad were right? What if I really was too fragile to hold down a job, to interact with a demanding public, to pour coffee for low-caffeinated patrons? I tucked my hands behind my elbows. What if I wasn't really better at all?

Movement in the window caught my eye. I checked my breath and dragged my gaze up from the table, forcing myself to look out the window. Throngs of people passed through Union Square daily for the shopping and world-famous cable cars. Today was no different. The corner of Powell and Sutter bustled with business men and women and tourists toting cameras over their shoulders. But not a wing in sight.

My heart slowed to a normal pace, and a relaxed smile crept across my face. I could do this. I was stronger than the madness. I grabbed my backpack, hoisting it over my shoulder. "You know, Lee, I think today might just be a good day."

Chapter Two

"A good day, huh?" Lee meticulously wrapped up his ear buds, wiped down his phone's screen, and tucked them into a cloth-lined case. "I did just beat my high score in *Die, Zombie, Die!* So you could be on to something."

Dr. G always told me to celebrate the small victories, and Mom had taught me to dance like no one's watching. My happy dance—a wiggle to the right, then two bounces left—caught him off guard. He snorted a laugh.

I let Lee's smile infect me and grinned back at him. It felt good, until I caught my warped reflection in the metal napkin holder. What a sorry excuse for a smile. My eyes showed a bit too much white, my lips a fraction too wide to pass as normal.

Tightness crawled up my throat, and my smile died a quick death. I looked over my shoulder, surprised that no one was staring at the crazy girl. Just to be sure, I checked over the other. I took a deep breath, smoothing the end of my ponytail down, the way my mother had when I was little.

Normal. Be normal and everything will be fine. Today will *be a great day.*

Lee checked his watch. It was his father's watch

and hung so loose on his wrist I was constantly worried he'd lose it. His smile faded. "Oh, Tardis!" Despite the morning I'd had so far, my lips twitched into a smile—a genuine one, this time, and a side-effect of having a best friend whose curses consisted of *Doctor Who* references. "We're gonna be late for school!"

"Not today. Today is going to be a good day." The zippers on my backpack clinked together as I yanked the heavy bag out of the booth and shrugged it over my shoulder. Dad would never agree to let me work if just the interview made me late for school. Then again, if Dad had his way, I'd be homeschooled and never allowed outside.

Lee and I bolted from our booth and out the door, the diner doorbell chiming as we left. A fall wind whipped around me, lashing the ends of my hair across my cheeks. I pulled my jacket's faux-fur hood over my rumpled tresses and glared enviously at Lee's spiky, over-styled hair. It never so much as quivered as we dashed across the street in defiance of the yellow traffic light—a dangerous feat in this city thanks to the wild drivers and bold bicyclists.

We passed one of those Halloween superstores halfway down Powell Street, and I knew what Lee meant to say before he opened his mouth.

"I almost forgot; the Halloween Dance posters went up yesterday. We're still going, right?" He popped a piece of peppermint candy he'd swiped from the diner into his mouth.

When Lee and I first met, I was so excited to have a friend—one I could make future plans with beyond stringing bead bracelets in Arts and Crafts hour before the meds wore off—that I had jumped at the idea of a school dance. Now that the dance was a few short weeks away, I was having second thoughts. And third and fourth ones.

One look at how excited Lee was, and I knew I'd try. For him.

"Are you sure you can keep up with *this*?" We stopped at a streetlight and I busted out another happy dance, just to hear him snort again.

"I don't know if I've ever told you this, but when you *dance*," he threw up air quotes, "you disgrace dancers everywhere." The light changed, and we maneuvered through the dense traffic still crowding the crosswalk.

"Oh, I'm sorry," I said. "Do my awesome dance moves embarrass you? Or maybe they secretly make you feel inadequate?"

Truth is, that really was my only dance move.

I turned to Lee and found him staring at a girl in a miniskirt. I shook my head. "That's two."

"What? Nuh-uh. That was only one." The peppermint candy crackled as he chewed.

"Nope. Cleavage Waitress at the diner was one. Miniskirt makes two. And it's only ... what time is it?"

"8:03."

Crap. Two minutes until first bell, and we were still three blocks away. Without another word, we ran through Union Square's busiest streets, dodging cars, dog walkers, and packed sidewalks. We skirted around the corner of Ellis Street just in time to hear the bell ring. We exchanged "Oh, shit!" looks, raced halfway down the block, flung open the fingerprint-smudged glass door, and trampled up the steps of Stratford Independence High School.

"See you at lunch," I said, half out of breath. Lee saluted me at the second floor, and we parted ways. Maybe I'd make it to class on time. Maybe if I didn't, Dad wouldn't find out.

Stillness settled over the third floor. I pressed forward, fear of getting caught mounting with each step. The buzz from inside my classroom slashed through the hallway the moment I opened the back door. All eyes turned in my direction. I stopped breathing. In an instant, being late to class became the least of my concerns.

It was like stepping into quicksand. I felt myself sinking slowly down into something I knew would not be easy to climb out of. I dug the nails of my right hand into the palm of my left to steady me.

Because there, standing in front of my Honors English classroom, was a boy with brilliantly shimmering wings.

Chapter Three

*I*t's happening. Again.

"Rayna." I barely heard Ms. Cleeson's voice over the panic bubbling up inside me. "Can you please take your seat?" I pulled the door shut. It slammed, making me jump. Ms. Cleeson barely glanced in my direction. As if signaled by the door slam, she and the class collectively turned their attention back to the boy, all of them acting like *I* was the morning's unwelcome interruption.

"Cam ... Cam-el, is it?" She leaned over her desk, rifling through the paperwork beneath her baby bump.

"Cam is fine," the winged boy corrected her politely.

I couldn't move my feet, which was a problem because I wanted to run as far away as I could. Sweat started at my temples, trickling down the sides of my face. If anyone had noticed his wings or my panic, I guessed they would have said something by now. I turned away, but I couldn't escape the light emanating from those enormous wings.

Ms. Cleeson thanked him. "Rayna, our new student was just introducing himself."

That was pretty obvious. What was not so obvious was what a boy with wings was doing in my classroom.

I closed my eyes, squeezing them tight until the colored spots dancing in the darkness faded. When I reopened them, I saw the residual imprint of wings. The wings shone, their feathery tips moving in a slow rhythm as they floated up and down.

Unable to move, I muttered through clenched teeth, "I, uh, I … forgot my book." *Nice save.* I spun around, envisioning a seamless escape, and slammed into the door instead. With sweaty fingers I fumbled for the doorknob, unable to perform the simple act of grasp and twist.

Oh, God.

My breath came short and sharp. I pressed my body into the door, willing it to open. The inevitable chuckles from my classmates rang in my ears.

Just then, a hand swooped in and swallowed the doorknob—and my hand—whole. A high-pitched scream from deep within me drowned out the snickers in the room.

I glanced over my shoulder to confirm what I already knew: the fingers belonged to the new kid. He twisted the knob, and the door groaned open. His hand released me. I bolted down the hall, into the one place I hoped he wouldn't follow: the girls' bathroom.

The sharp sting of lemon cleaner and bleach invaded my nose. I flung my backpack against the wall. It hit with a satisfying *thwack* and crumpled to the floor. Frosted glass windows above the stalls suppressed the clamor of cars and pedestrians on the busy street below. I paced the short length of the bathroom, but it didn't seem to help the constriction that tightened my chest until it hurt to breathe. My lungs burned. *Breathe.* I forced in a sharp intake of air.

Angels aren't real. They are figments of an over-active imagination that craves assurance there is such a place as Heaven, so it can believe your mother is in a good place. Dr. G had explained the light anomalies as hallucinations, common to someone with Schizoaffective Disorder.

But those wings had been so bright. How could an imagined vision sear my eyes with that glowing intensity?

Stop it, Ray!

I stumbled to the nearest sink, curling my fingers around the basin rim. I fought the urge to rock, only to realize my body was already teetering, the thighs of my jeans damp as they met the basin, over and over again.

Focus, Rayna. On something. Anything. Don't slip back. You can't go back.

My gaze found the scratched mirror above the sink, and I concentrated on my reflection, willing myself to think of anything but the image I couldn't purge from my mind. Brilliant, shimmery wings, the color of falling snow on a bright day …

Stop. It.

Reflection. Focus on that. It's all you have.

My eyes gazed over skin so pale even the flaking cream walls held more color. My brown hair was flat, except for the fly-aways that curled wildly around my face. My skin had once been bronze from the sun. My more-green-than-hazel eyes had been bright with happiness, not with fear. That single glance at my reflection confirmed it: I was crazy again.

An eerie quiet settled over the room. The tiled wall snagged my hair as I slid down to the floor.

The winged men in Arizona had only ever touched me to defend themselves. I'd flown off-the-handle a few times and attacked the things I saw. To be fair, I'd been in a dark place then and blamed the hallucinated wings—and the men they were attached to—for everything that had gone wrong in my life. Still shaking, I examined my hand. The boy's phantom touch still warmed my skin. His hand felt real; he felt human, with flesh and muscle and bone ... *and wings.*

I raced to the sink. Turning the hot water on full blast, I shoved my hand under the water, burning his touch off of me.

Dr. G would be so disappointed. After three years, he still hadn't managed to cure me. I'm not sure what was worse: the thought that I had failed him, or the realization that I was going back.

My backpack lay in a heap in front of the farthest stall. Inside the smallest zippered pouch, three amber pill bottles peeked at me from under the tiny flap. My hands trembled as I palmed them, the pills rattling in their respective bottles. Antipsychotics and mood stabilizers. I swallowed one of each, never bothering to stop for water.

It had been stupid of me to quit the meds cold turkey. I knew that now. *Stupid, stupid, stupid.* Every part of me shook as I scooted back to the wall, dragging my backpack along. I closed my eyes and waited for the crazy to subside.

The bathroom door squeaked open. I jerked, bumping the back of my head against the wall. Pain rattled my vision. Gina Garson darted in just in time for the door to miss her as it slammed closed.

Busted.

Her brown eyes pinned me to the floor. I stared back, with my backpack curled up in my lap and three pill bottles lying beside me.

So very busted.

It just had to be Gina Garson, volleyball championship MVP. She stopped short at the sight of me and cupped a hand over her mouth. One of her eyebrows popped up in such a judgmental stare that I shrank away from it.

"It's not what it looks like." I began shoving the

bottles into my backpack, but my hands shook so violently the stupid bottles dropped back to the floor. I scrambled to collect them.

"Sick." Gina's muffled accusation was clear.

Yeah, okay. Maybe it was what it looked like. "Not like you think. I swear. Please. Don't tell anyone."

Her stomach gurgled, a loud rumble, and she ran for the farthest stall. The door banged closed a second before the world's most horrible sounds came from inside.

Without thinking, I dropped my backpack on the pill bottles and stood up. "Are you okay?"

Another round of loud, gross noises. "Peachy." She spit. "Stomach flu."

I braced myself against the wall, my own stomach turning end over end. Somehow, I had to talk Gina into forgetting she'd seen me.

Or I could just run. I was good at that. The second floor girls' room had to be less … populated.

I grabbed my backpack to leave and sent one of the pill bottles rolling into the center stall.

Shit. Oh Shit.

Gina's stall quieted into short, shallow breaths.

I dumped my backpack on the floor and lunged into the stall beside hers. The tip of my middle finger teased the smooth plastic. I breathed a sigh of relief. *Safe.* I flicked my finger to reel it in, but it slipped, sending my anti-psych meds spinning smack-dab into Gina Garson's jeggings.

I'm sure somewhere outside this bathroom the normal world continued, but not here. Here, Gina and I had both stopped. Stopped living. Stopped breathing.

The pills rattled as she picked up the bottle.

The stall door opened, and Gina walked right by me without so much as a glance. I spotted the bulge of a pill bottle in her cardigan pocket. She rinsed her mouth three times and then peered at me through the mirror while the faucet ran. She reached into her pocket. "You look like you might need these more than I do." She tossed the bottle to me.

I shoved it and the other two bottles into my backpack and let go of the breath I'd been holding. "Uh, thanks."

I should have left then.

Gina wiped her face and turned around, leaning against the sink. "So what's your deal?"

My muscles seized. "What? What do you mean?"

"You ran out of class like a freak on fire. Now you're in here, popping pills. Need I say more?" She tossed her paper towel in the overflowing trash bin.

The difference between Gina and me was not only that she was popular and I wasn't, or that she was great at volleyball, while I was great at nothing. The biggest difference was that no one would know about Gina's sickness because I wouldn't tell them; I'd bet good money, however, that everyone would hear about my crazy, pill-popping freak-out before lunch.

I picked at a loose thread on my jacket sleeve. "Just forgot something, is all."

"Okay. Whatever. But, when I asked to go to the bathroom, Ms. Cleeson said to bring you back if you were in here." I watched her pull a tiny compact and lipstick from her pocket and begin working her lips like a super model.

I couldn't go back to class. Not after what I'd done. What Gina had seen.

The bell rang. Gina snapped her compact shut and turned to me. "I didn't see anything if you didn't."

This was too good to be true. Not that I could trust her to keep her word. Not that I had much choice. "Deal," I said past a dry throat.

Gina nodded and left the bathroom without so much as a backward glance.

I, on the other hand, waited for the tardy bell to ring and the hallway to quiet before I left. Not a single shimmer tormented me on my way to Science class.

Bald-headed Mr. Ratchor greeted me with a terse, "You're late." He marked it on the role sheet to show he meant it, and I took my seat.

I pulled out my book and spent the next fifteen minutes burying myself in the finer points of photosynthesis. I had almost managed to push thoughts of first period away when there was a knock on the classroom door.

"Miss Evans, can you come with me please?"

I looked up from my textbook.

Ms. Morehouse, the school's counselor-slash-therapist, stood at the door. "Rayna?" She called again.

No, no, no.

I'm not sure why I was surprised that Gina had lied about keeping my secret. I gathered my things, mindful of the curious stares following me to the front of the class.

Today was definitely not a good day.

Chapter Four

The second I set foot in the cafeteria, I knew everyone had heard about my first period freak-out. The cheerleaders arched their brows and whispered as I passed their tables. The jocks eyed me while steamrolling me to be first in the lunch line. The back-row clique from Honors English class nudged each other and laughed when I jerked to a stop.

Stratford Independence was overflowing with kids who were good at something. Some excelled at sports, others were more into academics, after-school clubs, social climbing. The list was endless. My particular brand of talent was blending. Apparently, I'd lost my touch.

Right before I turned to run, Lee came from behind and dragged me to our usual spot. He straddled the bench next to me and whispered conspiratorially in my ear, "Wanna tell me why you're the talk of the school this morning? What the hell did you do?"

Great.

"It was nothing. People love to exaggerate." I picked up my sandwich, but didn't take a bite.

Lee popped one of my veggie chips into his mouth, then immediately spit it out. He took a long swig of his soda and regrouped. "From what I hear, you slammed into the classroom door, fell on your jellybaby, had to be picked up by some new kid, and disappeared. That doesn't sound like 'nothing.'"

"Jellybaby?"

He tilted his head to the side, as if to say, *you should know this* Doctor Who *reference, Ray.*

I rolled my eyes, ignoring the look that normally spins me into a fit of giggles. "I didn't fall!"

"And then Ms. Morehouse came for you in second period."

Not only had Ms. Morehouse pored over my thick file while I sat there, but then she'd insisted Ms. Cleeson's call to her was concerning. So concerning, in fact, that we had a nearly three-hour impromptu session right there in her basement office. Gina *had* kept her promise, at least.

"So if you know everything, why bother asking? I should just ask you what happened, Mr. Know-it-all."

He tore into his bag of "real" chips—Lee was always teasing me for eating "that fake stuff"—but stopped just short of crunching down on one to glance at me. "Just tell me if I should be worried about you. That's all."

I might have been able to fool Ms. Morehouse into thinking nothing was wrong, but Lee wouldn't be so easy. I didn't want him to worry. I didn't deserve a friend who got me the way he did. Maybe I'd overshot when I found Lee. I should have picked someone who didn't care so much, someone who would have been easier to lie to. "I didn't feel well, so I spent first period in the bathroom. And yes, I saw Ms. Morehouse. But I'm fine. I swear."

"Were you going to tell me?"

I let my head roll back. "No, because it was nothing, Lee."

Lee looked like I had just told him his favorite Sci-

Fi series had been canceled, and I was sorry I'd snapped. God, I was such a crappy friend.

"Lee, I—"

"Well, well, well," a throaty voice breathed against my ear. I nearly jumped out of my seat. My sandwich tumbled out of my grip, onto the table. Luke Harper, the hottest guy in school—if you listened to gossip, which I tried to make a habit of not doing—stood only inches away, his hand braced on the table beside me as he leaned in. "When are you finally going to give in and let me get a kiss?" A sexy smile rode the right side of his peachy lips. He eyed Lee suspiciously.

Cute, and a complete meathead, I reminded myself.

I swallowed and lumped up enough courage to say, "I'm, uh, not."

Good one.

He straightened, and his hand dropped away. "Aw, loosen up, Evans. I'm just kidding. Sort of. But seriously, if you need a date for the Halloween dance, I think I might be persuaded to drop Gina and take you."

Pissing Gina Garson off seemed like a bad idea after what she'd seen in the bathroom. So far, it seemed that she hadn't told anyone, and I'd like to keep it that way.

"You and Gina should go together," I said. "I'm sure you'll win king and queen or something."

Lee cleared his throat. Luke jutted his chin at my best friend, his eyes slightly narrowed. Anyone else might think Lee had an issue with Luke ditching his date, but I knew better. I'd never figured out what the deal was between them, but Lee never felt much like talking about Luke, so I'd learned to leave it alone. Tony DiMeeko came up behind Luke and clapped him on the back. "Have it your way, Evans. Catch you later." Luke spun around, rubbing the top of his shaved head. Tony nudged him in the ribs with an arm so large

I questioned the school's steroid-use policy. The two moved through the less important people and followed the lunch line.

Not to be outdone by Luke Harper, Lee launched into a speech about his Crush of the Week, Jenna Lancaster, the lanky cheerleader who had said all of three words to me since the start of school, despite the fact we have four classes together. *Four.*

Lee droned on about Jenna's legs as hints of light brightened the dull cafeteria yellow. *Sun?* Hope burbled up in me. I twisted toward the far end, where windows lined the top of the wall. The sky remained the same muted gray of low-lying fog. Something almost golden hit a water bottle on the table beside us, throwing bright light at me again. I caught the reflection of a wing in the rippling water. Even my thoughts froze.

Lee was still talking, his lips moving in the fast rhythm he got when he was lost in his own thoughts and couldn't get everything out soon enough, but I couldn't hear his words.

This can't be happening.

I turned around to where the reflection should have been, near the caf doors. There was no one there. Why did it still seem so bright?

Another flash. I followed the light to the new kid crossing the room, his wings dipping through people and chairs as he strode toward us.

Stay calm, I told myself.

Stay calm? The kid with the wings is following me! English class is one thing, but here in the cafeteria in front of two hundred other kids?

No, he was having lunch. We only had one lunch period. And those wings? Not real. He was just a boy. Calm down.

But I didn't. Couldn't.

The new kid walked through the crowd of students, his movements slow and confident. His wings were tucked behind him, and the curves peeked out over his shoulders while the tips feathered against his calves. The shine bursting off them created a halo effect. As the wings passed through people, chairs, and tables, they dissipated, reappearing as white smoke before solidifying again. No one seemed to notice them but me.

"Lee, did you have the new kid in any of your classes?" My words bled together, eyes trained on the winged intruder.

Lee twisted around, practically bouncing out of his seat. "Nope. Please tell me it's a nice Korean girl. My mom's been on me to start dating. If I don't find a mom-approved girlfriend soon, I'm going to come home one day to find one of her co-workers from the consulate standing in my living room wearing an engagement ring!" He shuddered, oblivious to the fact my own nightmare was across the cafeteria, and closing in on us.

"Sorry, Lee. Not Korean. Not a girl." I swept my uneaten sandwich into my bag and rocketed off the bench. The pounding in my chest vibrated through my voice. "Maybe we should eat outside today."

"Out front, with the smokers?" Lee sounded dubious.

"I know, but it's stuffy in here. And I can't stand being stared at like this." I grabbed Lee's arm, pulling him up and toward the side exit.

As the door closed behind us, I looked through its small glass window. The golden-haired boy settled himself at our empty table.

If my subconscious was intent on giving the new kid wings, then that only left me one option. I'd avoid the hell out of him. It might be difficult, especially with him being in my English class, but in order to maintain my sanity—or as close to sane as I could get—then I didn't have much other choice.

He glanced at me through the tiny window and held my gaze. This was going to be so much harder than I thought.

Chapter Five

I made it through the rest of lunch and fifth period Music class without incident, unless you count flinching at bright lights because they might be wings, checking over both shoulders every fifteen seconds or so, and generally falling back into my old habits. I should have known better than to get my hopes up.

I nodded politely at my sixth-period teacher, who liked to stand in the doorway and greet students as they entered the classroom. Posters of former presidents and handmade timelines of important dates in world history lined the faded yellow walls. My shoes squeaked as I slammed to a halt. Too-bright light danced through the classroom, like sun off of still waters.

The new boy was seated at my table, straight across from my chair. Once I sat down, nothing but the table would separate him from me. Other kids bumped into me, pushing me forward. I walked toward the table on lead feet, my backpack knocking into a chair. The resulting *thunk* made me jump out of my skin.

I took my chair and grasped onto my remaining composure, which was deflating like a life raft on choppy seas. To avoid another look at the mass of feathers sitting across the table, I lobbed my History book and spiral notebook onto the table, then buried my face in them.

Despite my heart's pounding warning, I couldn't resist a good, long look at the boy. I'd never seen wings on someone so young before. I noticed the curve of his mouth, the soft angles of his jaw and cheekbones, and the fair color of his eyelashes. He lifted pale eyebrows. A comfortable-looking smile pulled at his lips. *Damn.* His face was nothing less than angelic. *Figures.*

"So, we meet again."

His voice chimed like heavy bells. I'd talked to the men with wings—these hallucinations—before, more like cursed and shouted at them for ruining my life, but it's hard to hold a conversation when all you can think is *wings, wings, holy crap, he has wings.*

Count to ten. I wrung my hands beneath the table, jamming the nails of my left hand into the palm of my right, attempting to ground myself in the now.

After a slow breath, I replied, "Yeah. Small world."

Small world? Ugh.

"You seem … nervous." He leaned one shoulder over the table, his right side pulling back slightly. His wings followed the lines of his body.

Ignore the wings. They're not really there. He's just a boy. Don't look at the wings.

"Normally, people are very at ease with me, but I seem to have the opposite effect on you."

I looked up, blinking to cut the glare bouncing off his wings, the feathered ends tucked tight to his body. "W—what makes you think that?"

His eyes narrowed, leaving only a small amount of gray. "You left English class this morning …"

Something about the way his voice trailed off tugged at me, drawing me in. His lips parted, and the tiny muscles along his jaw tightened. I clenched my sweat-drenched hands into fists, hoping to gain some control over my body's ticks and twitches. Which meant my meds—and their glorious side effects—were already starting to kick in.

"...Then again in the cafeteria."

"Yeah, I forgot some stuff in my locker." *Smooth.* "Both times." I squeezed the words in before the second bell announced the start of class.

"Seats, class. We're jumping in at chapter five." Mr. Barnes slapped his hands together and rubbed them excitedly.

Cassie, a girl with the same long, blue-black hair and blunt bangs as this week's pop-princess, quickly took her seat next to the new kid. "Does he have to get so excited about history?" she mumbled. Like her pop-star idol, she too dressed in a style that Laylah's favorite fashion show called "goth-glam." Today, her shirt was ripped and pinned strategically. She even wore those weird fishnet, fingerless gloves.

"Right?" Jeremy, a musical prodigy and low man on the band-clique totem pole, peeked at Cassie from beneath his overgrown curls. I hadn't noticed him when I first sat down.

"Rayna Evans."

Startled, I glanced up. What had I done now?

Oh. Roll call. Right.

I started to answer. A simple "here" would have done it. But the weight of a classroom full of curious eyes stuffed the words back down my throat. Apparently, lunch period wasn't quite enough time for people to forget the scene I'd made that morning. Funny, it seemed like forever ago to me.

"She's here, Mr. Barnes," Cassie said. I shot her a grateful look as heat rose to my cheeks and I sank down in my chair.

Mr. Barnes moved on, and eventually the curious stares drifted away. All except one.

"Cam-el Wright."

Was his name really Camel? Like the animal?

Honestly, his name should be the last thing about him that bothered me.

"Cam," the new kid corrected.

"Great." Mr. Barnes closed his attendance book, then slid the coveted teacher's copy of our History book over it. "The Civil War is also known as the War Between the States, or The War of Northern Aggression, as my southern-raised Grammy calls it." A few snickers rang out in the classroom at the mention of Mr. Barnes's Grammy, but no one from our table seemed to be paying enough attention to care. Mr. Barnes smoothed his shoulder-length ponytail, starting at the thinning top, working his way down. When the last of the giggles died down, he continued his lecture. I tried to listen, but was distracted by the soft, rhythmic breathing across the table. The sound resembled music: smooth, graceful, and free.

That no one else seemed to notice it pushed me that much closer to the edge.

I buried my head in my textbook and pretended not to notice how still he sat, how he didn't take a single note, or even bother to pick up a pen. As time ticked by, I gripped my pencil tighter and tighter.

When his foot brushed against mine, I stabbed the pencil into my notebook, snapping off the tip. Jeremy tore his gaze from Cassie long enough to raise a thick eyebrow at me.

The new guy's shoe tapped against mine again, definitely on purpose. No one is that clumsy.

Except maybe me.

I jerked back. Too hard. My chair tipped over, taking me with it. I smacked Jeremy in the mouth on my way down. My head bounced off the floor, and Jeremy let out a nasty curse, checking his lip for blood.

Gasps and smothered giggles erupted from all around. Stars fluttered across my vision. I tried to blink them away, but realized they were really the light from his wings. His *nonexistent* wings. He was standing, hands braced on the table, watching me.

Mr. Barnes rushed to help. "Are you all right? That was quite a spill." His southern drawl spiked at *quite a spill*.

"I'm fine," I brushed his hand away with shaky fingers and climbed to my feet. "Something's wrong with that chair. The legs got stuck when I tried to push back and ..." I didn't bother to finish. Everyone knew I was a freak.

Just sit down and shut up.

I righted my chair. Cam tilted up a ridiculous looking half-smile. I pressed my lips into a line and angled my chair away from the table, away from Cam, and toward the front of class.

My head throbbed with the beginning of a lump and an unsettling awareness. He was still there. Watching me. What was I going to do? I went to work on my nails, biting them to nubs.

When the bell finally rang, Cassie and the new boy were the first ones up. I held my breath until his wings disappeared through the door. An air of freshness loomed in his wake, like the scent of earth and fresh cut grass. Strange that I hadn't noticed it before. Odd that he smelled so earthy, but looked so heavenly.

I kicked my stupid chair. Three years of intensive therapy and I was still stark-raving mad.

Chapter Six

I swept a pale-blue stroke across my canvas. Sky. Blue sky. Loving the idea so much, I curved it around the entire painting. Mrs. Pheffer had asked for abstract. What was more abstract than fluffy white clouds in a brilliant blue sky? I could hear her making her way around the room, asking questions to those of us already working and helping the others to choose a direction.

Art was the one class I could truly embrace. Even in the SS Crazy, Arts and Crafts hour was one of the only happy times I'd had, second only to gardening. It also helped that Art was the last class of the day.

I filled in the rest of the canvas with blue, switching brushes to drop in a few white, puffy clouds, completely losing myself in the expression it allowed.

A shout scattered my thoughts, and something slammed down on the floor. I jerked at the noise, my concentration—and serenity—shattered. My brush cut a harsh, white line through my painting.

I looked across a room crackling with tension.

Allison Woodward—a mousy-looking girl I'd teamed up with once for a group art project—jumped from her stool and stomped her foot over her fallen easel, ripping part of her painted canvas right off its frame. "There! Now you don't have to tell me what's wrong with it." Her chin and bottom lip quivered, competing with her stern brows and tight eyes.

Mrs. Pheffer pressed her hands down in the air. "Allison, please calm down. I only asked what your painting depicted."

Allison didn't move. Mrs. Pheffer looked toward her inspirational painting of the week, propped up beside her desk. It was an abstract mess, if you asked me. She placed her hand over her chest, as if the boldly colored shapes would give her the strength she needed to resolve the escalating conflict.

Tears welled in Allison's brown eyes. "It's stupid. This whole thing is stupid! Screw it. Screw everything." Her voice cracked. "I don't even care anymore!" Her hands sprang up to cover her face, and she ran out the door.

What was wrong with everyone today? Maybe my lunacy was contagious.

Mrs. Pheffer gasped. "Oh, no." She jogged toward the door, but Alison was already gone. With trembling fingers, she knelt to gather the pieces of Allison's work. The concern never left her face, but she feigned a small laugh. "I'm sure she'll be right back. We'll just give her a few minutes."

Two of the Soccer Insiders beside me whispered and giggled; gossiping was their other sport. Across the room, four girls I recognized from Ms. Cleeson's Honors English class chatted in high, bubbly voices. Two emotionally charged students fleeing a classroom in one day, they probably couldn't believe their luck. The boys—there were only five of them—either lifted their eyebrows and returned to their paintings or whipped out their cell phones. A major no-no in Mrs. Pheffer's class.

It was surreal to see a freak-out from the other side of things.

My gaze fell on Allison's smudged painting. At first, all I saw was a mess of dusty blues and harsh blacks. I narrowed my eyes at it, and slowly, the painting began to make sense. Clouds of gray and blue surrounded a blurry figure etched in black. There was something else too. Something extending out from behind the torso, blocking the light. Something long and so dark, almost black. Feathery. Coming toward me.

I brought my hand to my mouth and gasped, nearly tipping off my stool.

Allison had painted an angel.

***

By the time the final bell echoed twenty minutes later, Allison hadn't returned for her things. If I was her, I'd wait until the halls fell quiet.

With my thoughts jumbled, I tried desperately to fix the painting I'd wrecked, making me the last student to leave. Mrs. Pheffer was still there, staring at the inspirational painting she'd brought in for today's assignment.

On my way out, I spotted a faint mark on the floor. I almost mistook it for a scuff mark, until I caught the faintest hint of blue. The paint from Allison's canvas must have transferred to her shoe when she stomped on it.

I followed the smudges out of the art room, through the nearly empty hall, and down the back staircase. The prints began to fade by the second floor. The paint had to be wearing off. At the first floor landing I caught sight of another faint smudge of blue, stamped into the floor in front of the basement steps.

I hesitated, remembering the dark colors of the wings in Allison's drawing. It wasn't my place to check on her. Allison and I weren't even friends. I had no idea what was going on in her head, or if she'd be pissed at me for following her.

The front door was only a few feet away. I could leave now. I *should* leave now. The painting's dark lines and misty figure waited for me when I closed my eyes. The empty hallway was eerily silent, adding to the apprehension churning in my stomach. I sank down onto the steps and tucked my head between my knees.

My left shoelace stared back at me, its loose bow mocking me. I took it for as long as I could stand, then frantically untied and retied it two, three, four times, until it was right. After that it didn't match up with the right one. I tied the right one again and again. Three times. Now it was right. But three and four didn't match, so I had to do it one more time, slowly pulling the bunny over, around … *through*, just enough. It had to match up. It had to be perfect.

Beside me on the step, Allison's paint practically screamed at me. I was wasting time, in the hopes of being able to get up and walk out the front door without any more angelic hallucinations.

This is what happens when you take yourself off your meds, Ray.

I could go to Allison, though that could be risky. She could be upset enough to lash out at me. I twined my fingers around each other, the OCD taking over while I thought. I knew how she felt; I'd been there just this morning. And at lunch. And in History class. It was one of the worst things in the world, feeling all alone. I had to let her know she wasn't alone, to prove to myself there was nothing to be afraid of, and possibly ask her why she'd painted a figure with wings.

I forced myself down the last flight of stairs and into the basement.

The dull buzz of the florescent lighting greeted me

before I stepped out of the stairwell. Many of the lights had burned out, leaving the basement in half-lit abandon. Beneath the haphazard, flickering bulbs, the unused lockers that lined the walls cast strange shadows in the corners.

I crept passed Ms. Morehouse's office, where fully-working lights shone through the bottom of her door and dispelled the shadows. Explaining to her that I was tip-toeing around the basement because Allison Woodward had drawn an angel and ran out of class didn't sound like a winning way to end my day. I edged past the office and down the hall.

The footprints were almost impossible to see now. By squinting, I was able to spot one last, faded paint smudge outside the girls' bathroom. A chill coated my skin.

Guess I'm not the only one who runs to the bathroom to hide.

I rapped lightly on the doorframe. "Allison?"

No answer. I pressed my ear to the door. No noise.

I pushed against the weight of the door. It stuck a little at first, then opened jerkily, as if the hinges weren't lined up properly. Pink-tiled walls, a silvery basin sink, and three cream-colored stalls made the bathroom identical to the one on the third floor. Except for the liquid oozing beneath a stall door. It crept toward me in a puddle of bright, bold crimson.

Chapter Seven

A heart-stopping shriek rose up my throat. I took two steps, then fell to my knees by the stall. My jeans sopped up the thick, warm liquid. So much of it.

From behind me, someone tugged my arm. I screamed, twisting and pulling myself free. I scrambled back against the wall, my chest filling with too-quick breaths. Ms. Morehouse wrenched me from the bathroom and dragged me out into the hallway.

She yanked a cell phone from her pocket and punched in three numbers, her hands shaking with the same convulsions I fought. One last beep and she handed me the phone before rushing back into the bathroom.

"Nine-one-one. What is your emergency?"

"There's blood. In the bathroom. A girl—she needs help!"

"Can you tell me what happened and where you are?" The man's calm voice helped me a little.

"I don't know what happened. She's in the girls' bathroom—in the basement. San Francisco. Stratford Independence High School. One, uh, one twenty Ellis Street." My hands shook almost as much as my voice. I blinked and found myself on my knees.

"I'm sending a response team to you. They should be there soon. Try to remain calm. Do you know where she's hurt?"

"No." I tried to stand. Collapsed, my knees liquid beneath me.

I needed to go back in there. To help Allison and tell the operator what I could. But I couldn't move.

The calm man's voice hummed through the phone, but my vision tunneled and my arm became too weak to hold the phone up. It tumbled to the floor.

I stared at the phone. Blood. It covered my hands, filled the lines of my palms. Deep red, almost-brown. It was everywhere. The bloody imprint of my hand, every small line and crease, had transferred to Ms. Morehouse's phone. Wide circles of it had sopped into the knees of my jeans. I gagged, scrambling back, desperate to run from the feel of it. But I couldn't escape it, no matter how far I ran. Warm and sticky, the blood soaked through my jeans, onto my legs. Into my skin. I clutched my head and rocked. The drying blood matted into my hair. My thoughts jumbled in red.

Ms. Morehouse emerged from the bathroom an eternity later, red staining her hands and the front of her shirt. Tears dripped down her pale cheeks, tacking the ends of her bob to her chin. Her movements were as languid as the pain in her eyes.

She sat against the lockers beside me. "Are you okay, Rayna?" She didn't look at me, her stare fixed on the door. Her voice was high, but whisper soft. Disconnected.

Was I okay? That was a question I couldn't answer without repercussions.

"Allison?" I managed to squeak out.

Ms. Morehouse shook her head. "Is the ambulance coming?"

I glanced at the phone again. The call was probably still connected. I nodded.

"Good." She pulled her knees up to her chest and wrapped her trembling arms around them.

Shivers tore through me. I forced myself to look at her face.

I used to room with a girl on the inside who'd been stabbed to death with a spork. I knew those tears well.

***

I stared out the half-inch the policeman had cracked the window for me, wishing it would let in more fresh air. The car reeked of doughnuts, stale coffee, and soiled leather. It made me feel confined, like I was locked up again. The sheen in my eyes reflected off the window's glass.

A white car pulled up in front of my abandoned police car. The man who stepped out closed the door and placed a brown Stetson over his dark hair. He turned in a half-circle, surveying the group of fifty or so students, faculty, and onlookers drawn by the yellow police tape. His eyes stopped on me.

When the police had first arrived, they'd questioned me in the basement. Once the space became overcrowded with officers, they moved us near the front door. As soon as Ms. Morehouse had confirmed I was the one who'd found Allison, they'd put me in the car. Told me it'd be quieter there, away from the stares and flashes of camera phones, but it didn't take a genius to know that when they'd brought Ms. Morehouse back inside, she'd shown them my weighty file.

Sickness rumbled in my empty stomach.

Another car stopped in the middle of the street. A woman in her early forties ran out of the passenger seat, wailing, her face twisted with more pain than I think I could ever bear. A tall, stoic man with thinning brown hair left the driver seat and joined her, his movements slower. She cried while his red eyes looked too far away, his hand absently clenching the buttons on his shirt. *Allison's parents.* Chills that had nothing to do with the surrounding fog and cool air had me clutching my jacket closed.

The police shuffled the crowd farther back, and the man in the Stetson helped Allison's mother inside. Mr. Woodward slowly followed.

Tears welled in my eyes, and I looked away. I didn't want to think about Allison. About what I'd seen. Otherwise, I'd lose it too. I stroked the ends of my hair and tried to wipe it from my mind. *Think about something else. Anything else.*

The painting. Not exactly a safer subject, but the only one that could compete with the image of her body lifted onto the gurney in the bathroom, wrists sliced into a bloody mess. It was the same way I tried to go, my first attempt, three years ago. The one that landed me in the SS Crazy to begin with. I took a deep breath and forced my thoughts to the painting. To the dark wings she'd drawn. I'd never seen them look anything but bright, attracting the sun the way they do. Of course the painting had nothing to do with my hallucinations. Angels weren't an uncommon theme in art. No way her painting had anything to do with her death. Thinking they might, even for a second, proved just how crazy I was again.

I clutched my backpack, eager for dinnertime, when I could take my meds again. I needed my dinner meds.

Outside, Stetson man reemerged from the building with Mrs. Pheffer. A uniformed officer trailed behind them with a ripped canvas painting in a large, clear bag marked "evidence."

Stetson man stepped aside to allow the medics room to carry a gurney out the front door. The matte black bag strapped to the top must have held Allison's body. The crowd watched in stunned silence as the EMTs loaded the body into the ambulance. A single head in the crowd turned to look at me. I blinked at the sight of the gold rays that fired out from behind him. The new kid.

I cringed at the sound of the wheels cracking against the ambulance floor.

I quickly turned, hands over my eyes, and lowered my head against the front seat.

No, no, no, no! Not again.

The ambulance doors clicked closed. It wasn't him. It couldn't be. I had to check again, so I used the ambulance's distraction to peer at the crowd again. Not a single glimmer of gold in sight. He was gone. Or he was never there in the first place.

Stetson man exchanged keys with a uniformed officer and headed my way. He tipped his hat back and slipped into the driver's seat. His cologne reminded me of something my dad had worn—only on Father's Day, and only before Mom's death. Its scent was musky and all kinds of god-awful.

He checked his leather-bound notepad. "Rayna." Our eyes met in the rearview mirror. His were the color of cinnamon. "I'm Detective Carl Rhodes." His tone wasn't nearly as firm as I'd expected. It was as if he knew he was talking to someone fragile. Breakable. He turned, looping his arm behind the front passenger seat, and arched his brow. "Why don't you tell me what you saw."

So I did. I left out the part about the wings in Allison's painting, but he still watched me carefully, as if he knew there was something about me that wasn't quite right. He took down a few notes, but stayed quiet until I was done. It didn't take me long. There wasn't much to tell.

When I finished, he said, "According to your records, you have no classes in the basement. Why were you down there? Were you following Allison?"

"Allison's paintings are—were," I corrected myself, my voice dipping lower, "beautiful, light, even her drawings ... she worked with pastels. We did a project together once. The girl refused to even outline in black. And then today ... I saw her painting, how dark it was. How ... hopeless. And I know what it's like to feel like that. When she ran out of class, well, I did the same thing earlier today. It wasn't my place to check on her, but ... I thought if anyone could help ..."
I shook my head, tears welling in my eyes again. "I ... I didn't know." It was all I could say.

Suicide.

Poor Allison. No one deserved that end. My heart ached for her family.

I'd seen girls get better. Hell, I'd been one of them. She could have gotten help.

I wrung my hands together and forced myself to look out the window, to look at anything but the detective.

"If you haven't yet told me everything, now would be a good time to say it."

"I told you what I saw. Everything." Or maybe I hadn't. *They didn't know I picked today to see a boy with wings.*

What if ...

Stop. It.

I mashed the heels of my hands against my eyelids, trying to blot out the insanity tumbling around my head. The detective looked me over. "Officers tried to get a hold of your father, but since there was no answer—"

"He's home! He's probably working; that's why he didn't answer the phone. But he always gets home before we get out of school. It's not far from here. Please, I'd really like to go home."

He started the car and pulled out into traffic. "Fine. We'll stop by. If he's not there, I have to take you to the station until an adult can come pick you up. Where do you live?"

"2036 Sacramento Street. Across the street from Lafayette Park."

I squirmed in my seat, desperate to get home and strip off my bloody clothes. I scratched at my skin. Allison's blood. It would be my undoing, not the hallucinations. The hallucinations of a boy with wings. My body begged me to rock, to let the insanity in again. It was knocking at my door, scratching at walls I'd erected around it. But I couldn't give in, couldn't let one hellish day implode everything I worked toward. I bit back the urge to tear through my skin with my fingernails. I forced my eyes on the road, breathing deep and erratic, sure, but still breathing. I just had to get through this. Just keep breathing.

Chapter Eight

O ur house is a Victorian, the color of a typical, San Francisco sky. Most days, the gray matched the mood of its inhabitants.

"Home sweet home," I murmured as the detective parked the cruiser at the curb and circled the car to open my door for me. I was almost alone. Alone I could break down. A little. Only a little.

We climbed the front stairs, each side covered with my potted flowers and plants. Pale pink and soft lavender asters interspersed with the more substantial sage-green, fuzzy lamb's ear, while coral bells added height and brought in traditional fall colors. My attempt at making this place feel more like a real home and less like a stop between psychiatric wards. I dragged in a deep breath of earthiness. None of the flowers held much in the way of floral scents, but the moist dirt always reminded me of home.

The forest-green door swung open before we could knock.

"What did you do now?" Laylah glanced at the detective, then glared at me, like I was the reason for everything wrong in her life. Her superior smirk cut her glare short, the kind of artificial pull of the lips only a sibling could give.

Even with her intolerable attitude, my twelve-year-old sister was nothing less than beautiful. Her eyes favored Dad, reminding me of the Nikko Blue hydrangeas I used to tend when I was locked up, and her blonde hair shone just like our mother's used to. No hair products, just healthy, naturally shiny hair.

Detective Rhodes followed me into the foyer, closing the door behind us. To the right, the living room TV buzzed with life. In direct contrast, the dining room in front of us sat as unused as the day we'd moved in.

The smug look on Laylah's face dropped off, replaced by alarm. Her gaze fell to my blood-soaked knees. "Oh my God, Ray. What did you *do*?" She grabbed my hands, pushed up my sleeves, and inspected my wrists.

"Miss Evans is fine. I need to speak with your parents. Are they here?"

I yanked my arms from Laylah's grip. How could she think I would do that again? And yet, I wanted to crawl into a corner for being responsible for putting that look on her face again.

"My mother's dead," she said in a flat voice. I winced. "Dad!" She shouted through the dining room and into the kitchen behind it, then spun around and returned to the living room, where I could hear her friends whispering. Her weird, Musketeer clones dressed alike, even on the weekends, and never seemed to have an original thought or homes of their own, since they were always here.

Dad emerged from his office behind the kitchen. When he wasn't at work, he spent most of his time there, studying, working on side projects, and escaping. His tired-as-a-zombie look changed the moment he saw the blood on my clothes and the detective by my side.

"Mr. Evans?"

Dad moved faster than I'd seen in a long time. He wrapped his arms around me so tight, even my pancreas hurt.

I hadn't been fond of hugs since Mom's death. It's Dad's form of group therapy. When one of us was caught crying—grieving—it was group-hug time. It didn't matter where we were: living room, hallways, kitchen, even the middle of the mall. Hugs don't make me feel any better, and they wouldn't bring her back, so what's the point? Hugs are torture.

Maybe torture was the wrong word, but Mom used to say, "Go with your gut." And my gut was telling me to run the other direction.

"Are you okay?" He released me. I could breathe again. "What happened?"

"I'm fine, Dad." I hedged the truth, hoping the detective's presence would distract Dad enough not to notice.

"Detective Carl Rhodes." He tucked a bag he'd grabbed from the car under his arm and removed his Stetson with one hand, offering his other to my dad. They shook. "We tried both of your contact numbers, but couldn't get through," Detective Rhodes filled in.

I would have rather crawled into a hole than be here for this conversation.

Dad stuttered for a moment. "My youngest was on the house line, and I was on a business call." His voice was racked with guilt. "What the hell happened?"

"Can we speak privately, Mr. Evans?" Detective Rhodes asked.

"Of course." Dad gestured toward his office.

"Rayna." The detective handed me the plastic zip bag tucked under his arm. It looked large enough to hold a Cocker Spaniel. "I'll need your clothes for evidence."

Dad spun his wedding ring around on his finger and

cast an uneasy glance at me. Worry wrinkled his brow. And I knew Dad was seeing me the same as he always had: as a victim, as poor, crazy Rayna.

I accepted the bag. *It's just standard procedure*, I told myself. *It was a suicide, and you discovered the body. They can't think you had anything to do with it.* I jiggled the bag in my hand nervously, trying hard to believe my inner self's logic. My shaking knees called me a liar.

I blew through the living room as fast as I could, passing Laylah and her two friends dominating the couch. Their eyes were glazed, their mouths wide, as they took in MTV's newest pop-princess.

I fumbled up the stairs and burst into the bathroom. Instead of being alone with my thoughts, I riffled through my backpack for my iPod and jammed it into the small speaker Laylah and I argued over every morning, cranking up the most upbeat album I could find. I turned the shower knobs, letting a few drops from the showerhead wet the soil of my favorite orchid before I moved the purple phalaenopsis back onto the windowsill.

My jeans stuck to me in the places where Allison's blood had dried. I sat on the brown, fuzzy toilet seat cover and peeled them off, then shoved them into the evidence bag. He didn't expect me to include my backpack, did he? He'd said "clothes." Nothing about my backpack, though it, too, was bloodstained. I didn't want to have to ask Dad for another backpack. I'd cost him enough already.

The stain was small enough for me to wipe the spot of red off with a towel. No one would notice. The black and red plaid jacket Aunt Nora had made special for me as a recent release day present back in July, however, wouldn't be so lucky. Into the bag it went.

Once everything was shoved into the bag, I set it

down in the hallway so I didn't have to look at it again. Then I stepped into the shower, eager to scrub the stains off my skin. The hot water stung my eyes. I welcomed it—anything to keep from looking at the pink pooling at the bottom of the tub. Eventually the water ran clear and my shaking eased, small shivers returning only in short bursts.

"Rayna, can I talk to you when you're out?" Dad's voice carried over the music.

I stepped out from the shower. Steam clouded the mirror and dripped a foggy veil over the sky-blue walls. Dad would have a thousand questions. If I couldn't keep it together, if Dad found out about the hallucinations returning ...

Things felt like they had before, when the wing sightings were at their worst. For the better part of the year after Mom's death, I'd seen at least one a month. Dad had reached his wits' end. When I began to notice how much it bothered him, I'd tried hiding it. The lying had killed me a little inside every time, and in the end, I couldn't keep it up. I never could.

The last thing I wanted was for life to go back to that, to ruin everything the three of us had worked toward since Mom's death, and my first hospitalization.

I wrapped a towel around my hair and threw on my fluffy lavender bathrobe, the one with a monkey embroidered on the back. I took longer than I needed, pulling on all the reserves of strength I had left. The walk back to my room was a long one, the hardwood floor in the hallway cold beneath my feet. I rolled my shoulders, preparing for a fight I knew I couldn't win.

Chapter Nine

Dad paced the flower-shaped rug beside my bed. With my eyes down, I shooed him out so I could get dressed, buying myself more time. Time I needed desperately. Even with the door closed, I could hear him in the hallway. His heavy footsteps, working back and forth.

I sank against the door.

Get a hold of yourself. Your freedom depends on it.

After a few false starts, I stood and pulled on a pair of heather-gray sweatpants and a white, long-sleeved top, spinning around to check that everything in my room was in order before letting Dad back in. Of course everything was in order. My room was spotless. When I was inside, the first thing they drilled into me—besides that I needed help—was neatness. They said a routine would help keep me focused and made daily inspections. Even now, if something here was out of place, it was because I'd done it purposely, to allow myself that little sliver of rebellion. To truly taste freedom. I still couldn't stand it, but I was teaching myself to live with one book being askew or one pencil not quite lining up with the others.

I took a deep breath, wiped my palms on the sides of my sweats, and opened the door. Dad whooshed in like a tornado, hands behind his back, still in pacing mode.

"Before you say anything, Dad, I'm fine."

He canceled pacing mode and shoved his hands into his outdated jean pockets. Uh oh, Stern Dad mode. I swallowed.

"Are you?" he asked.

I forced myself to meet his gaze. I'd learned the hard way that eye contact was important when someone questioned my sanity; crazy people either avoid it altogether or stare too long. So I looked him in the eye as I said, "Yes, Dad. I'm good." Waited a moment. Two. And then I looked away. Before he saw the lie in my eyes. That was another thing the SS Crazy had taught me: it's hard to convince someone you're not crazy when you wear a lie as openly as I do.

"What happened? Detective Rhodes wasn't very forthcoming."

"Allison Woodward. I ..." I swallowed. "I found her. I saw cuts on her wrists when they took her away. Deep ones." The sight of all that red flooded back to me, and I had to swallow again.

"Oh, sweetie." His fingers slid up his forehead, covering one of his eyes. More grief. I swallowed back a grimace, hating the sympathetic sheen of his uncovered eye. "Do you remember seeing anything else ... or any*one* else?"

I darted a glance at him again, wondering for the first time what he and the detective had talked about downstairs. "No." The inflection in my voice was too high. "Why?"

"The detective asked me to contact him if you start to recall anything else." He dropped his hand from his face. "This is all so awful. I'm so sorry you had to see that, sweetheart. Are you really okay?"

Hysteria bubbled up my throat. "I told them

everything already. I don't know anything else. You believe me, don't you, Dad?"

A long silence followed. The muscles in my face tensed, holding me together.

Finally, he said, "Sometimes the mind plays tricks on us, and we can see things more clearly when we've had some rest, some time to think rationally. Tomorrow, I think we should take a drive up to see Dr. Graham."

He must have seen the horrified look on my face. I knew it was there, but I couldn't control or stop it. I knew speaking to Dr. G was probably the best thing for me, but seeing him, at that place, going back there ... *I can't go back. I can't. I* can't.

"This *does* call for a session. I never said you had to stay. You don't—have to stay, I mean." His hands wiggled in his pockets, like he'd rather be fixing computer chips. He'd probably rather be anywhere other than where he was now.

"No." My voice was steel; it had to be, so he'd know I meant business. "I won't go back there. I'm fine. I swear. You put me in there, so many times. I lost three years in-and-out of there. Three years of my life." I avoided his eyes, my legs shaking. "I won't be like a prisoner again. I haven't seen any wings in a long time."

Please, don't make me go back there. I locked my knees so I didn't sink to them.

Dad's never been very observant. If I could just keep calm, he might never know I was lying. The man knew technology, not people. Before Dad sent me inside the first time, Laylah and I had hidden a pregnant cat, soon followed by a mewing litter of kittens, from him for four months. Laylah had him convinced the noises coming from her room were her latest TV obsession, Animal Planet.

"*I* think it's a good idea, something preemptive. You're supposed to be avoiding stressful situations, remember?" A frustrated noise rumbled in his throat, and he turned to look out my window. "I knew sending you back to school was a mistake. I never should have let you talk me into it. We'll find you another tutor so you can finish your junior and senior years here, at home, away from all the stress."

He meant away from real life, anything that could awaken the hallucinations. Working at the diner would most definitely fit into that category.

A steady breath, hot with frustration, flared my nostrils. *Keep it together.* "Dad," I said as calmly as I could, "I told you when I left last time that I would never go back there. I meant it."

He turned to me. "Everything's back to normal. *I'm* normal, and will *never* need to go back there." I clenched my teeth again, using that tension to keep me from breaking apart. "I'm not seeing things that aren't there like before. If you send me back there for something that's beyond my control, my trust in you will be broken. And this time I will *never* forgive you."

He squeezed his eyes shut, a grimace pulling the corners of his lips down. Transparent regret. "Rayna, the last thing I want is for you to have to go back there again. But if Dr. Graham can help you face this and work through it, wouldn't it be worth it? Why would you want to put yourself at risk for a relapse? Seeing a friend, a classmate, hurt in that way. I don't know if *anyone* could get through it without some kind of help."

My stomach clenched, feeling tight and hollow. "How about I promise to talk to Ms. Morehouse tomorrow?"

I was begging. It made me hate myself a little more.

"You can't seriously be thinking about going back to school."

"I'm okay, really. School will be better for me than sitting around here all day." I gestured to my perfectly clean desk, to my bed made so well you could bounce a quarter off of it—or a dime, which is what the nurses at the SS Crazy had used. "It'll keep me busy. Plus, I can talk to Ms. Morehouse."

The two dark caterpillars above his hydrangea-blue eyes crawled back into resting position, which let me relax a little too. He sat on my bed, wrinkling my floral bedspread.

My fingers twitched to pull him up so I could straighten it. Instead, I tugged at the ends of his hair, which brushed the striped collar peeking out beneath his navy sweater-vest. It was so thin at the temples. *Focus. Calm.* "I haven't been taking very good care of you. You're in desperate need of a haircut." The tip of one of my fingers accidentally brushed his cheek. "And a shave," I added to lighten the mood, pretending to examine my finger for blood.

"I'll go to the barber tomorrow if you promise me something. If this *incident* interferes with your recovery, you'll let me know right away." He didn't add *so we can see the doctor*, but he didn't need to.

I took a deep breath and raised my hand, pinky and thumb tucked in, the three remaining digits standing at attention. "Scout's honor." Good thing I'd never been a scout.

"Deal." Dad leaned forward and placed a kiss on my forehead; his chin stubble was even rougher than his cheek had been. On his way out, he said, "Oh, I almost forgot. Lee called while you were in the shower. But in light of recent events, I think it would be better for you to speak with him tomorrow."

I didn't have many friends, so I was usually grateful

that I didn't have a cell phone. Today, for the first time, I wished I did. I could explain the afternoon's events to Lee, hear his voice, and laugh with him. Any voice that wouldn't talk to me in that slow, deliberate, I-won't-push-her-off-the-deep-edge tone. "I've got homework to do, anyway," I said, shrugging. I was too tired, and my mind was too full, to think about anything else.

"And, Ray?"

I didn't like lying to him.

I drew my eyes up as innocently as I could while feeling like dirt inside. "Yeah, Dad?"

"If you need to talk, about anything, I'm here. Okay?"

I stretched my lips in the widest smile I could, hoping it didn't look as forced as it felt. He nodded and ducked out, closing the door behind him. I pressed my ear to the door, listening to his footsteps descend the stairs.

At least he hadn't asked about my meds. If he knew I'd stopped taking them, he'd have driven me to see Dr. G right then, no discussion.

I slid the chair over from the desk and angled it under the doorknob. The absence of locks on my door couldn't be avoided thanks to my stints at the SS Crazy. But I had the backup system, also thanks to my time on the inside. It wouldn't hold if someone made a serious attempt to get in, but it would buy me a few necessary seconds.

I removed a thin marker from the top desk drawer and, battling the quilted dust ruffle, reached under the bed for my black-light flashlight. Then I pushed past two racks of clothes to the back of the closet. It was deeper than it was wide. I carefully removed a piece of tape from the corner of my *Across the Universe* movie poster.

A noise from the other side of the wall snatched the

breath from my lungs. Muffled chattering from Laylah's room. Those damn Musketeers never went home.

I shook my head, uncapped the marker, and clicked on the tiny flashlight. Its purple glow displayed the psychedelic colors of the poster. I pulled a second piece of tape and watched the poster float down.

Twenty-seven hash marks glowed on the white wall. My recreated record of the number of wing sightings I'd had in Arizona, after Mom's death. Getting a replacement copy of the poster and reconstructing the tally was the first thing I'd done after my release. I used it to remind me where I came from, and where I never wanted to return to.

Never was coming sooner than I thought.

Using the special black-light marker, I drew a line beneath the twenty-seven other sightings and began a new tally. My hand shook as I drew a single, new mark.

I remained there for a long time, staring at the new line, letting the truth of my life weigh down my soul like rocks to my earthly body. How many more would accumulate before I got caught?

Chapter Ten

I didn't sleep that night. The upside—and only upside—to not sleeping was catching Dad before he headed out the door. I needed his signature on my work permit. Dad didn't like the idea of me working, but he caved when I promised that a part-time job wouldn't derail my fragile post-insanity mind and reminded him I needed to stay busy to keep my mind off Allison. Before he could think better of it, I grabbed an extra notebook and zipped out the door.

The extra notebook was an idea that had come to me in the early morning hours. I needed a place to unleash the thoughts circling in my head like vultures, instead of waiting for them to strike at the worst possible moment. The notebook would keep my secrets when no one else could. Most importantly, it was something I didn't mind tossing before heading home for the day, just to make sure I didn't get caught.

The weight of my backpack battered me as I inched down San Francisco's hills, past a massive mural of the orange-painted Golden Gate Bridge and the famous Painted Ladies—a specific row of spectacularly well-kept Victorian homes.

Lee and I met at Roxy's Diner for a hot chocolate fix every morning before school. Today I got there early, so I could get out all of the thoughts crowding my mind since yesterday morning. I started by journaling yesterday's hallucination of the wings outside the diner and worked my way up to discovering Allison's body. Writing about it was almost as bad as seeing it firsthand.

Daphne slipped into the seat across from me— Lee's usual spot—and slid a mug of hot chocolate across the table. I slammed the notebook closed. "Guess you were serious, after all."

The waitress's mussed hair resembled a bird's nest in both the way it was constructed and the overall messiness of the finished product. I pulled the work permit out of my bag and ironed it flat with my hand before pushing it across the table. Her index finger tapped the edge of the paper while her droopy eyes centered on me. "Now, you really want to work here? Lots of girls apply, but when they hear about mopping the bathroom floors, taking out the trash, and dealing with the more *eccentric* customers, they never come back. I think we'll start a pool on how long you'll last."

If there was one thing I loved besides gardening, it was proving people wrong. "I was hoping to start after school today."

"We're too short-handed on Wednesdays to train. If you want, you can start tomorrow instead. I'll have an extra waitress you can shadow." Daphne rose from her seat and pulled out her order pad, already moving on to the next thing.

"Tomorrow's great," I said after her, already thankful for the added responsibility, hoping it would drive my thoughts away from Allison. And a certain winged boy. He could be gone today. I could very well walk into class today and find no wings—or no new kid at all.

I was sure that Allison Woodward was gone. I

swallowed a mouthful of rich hot chocolate and allowed myself to think the word I'd been trying to avoid: dead. She was dead. I *felt* that. Dr. G always said, *you know it's real when all five senses receive it together*. I could still summon the metallic scent of her blood and feel it soaking into my evidence-tagged clothes.

Lee plopped into the seat across from me, startling me out of the memory. "You never called me back last night."

I pushed my mug toward him in apology.

He greedily gulped up the rest. He smiled at me, but his eyes were rimmed dark and his whole demeanor drooped. I thought to ask him what was bothering him, but it was getting late. I paid the check, and we walked toward school. "Did you hear about Allison Woodward?" he finally asked.

Of course he would have heard about it. "Yeah. I, uh, found her."

"What?" His voice cracked. "You *found* her? Holy Daleks, are you all right?"

Daleks. If he hadn't insisted on last week's *Doctor Who* Wednesday marathon, I would have missed that one.

"I, uh, kind of have to be. It sucked. It was … horrible. One of the worst things ever, but I'll be okay. I have to be."

Why. He was going to ask why. And I had nothing to tell him. No one wanted a schizo for a BFF. And I couldn't lose him.

"*One* of the worst things ever? Wow, Ray. What have you *been* through?"

"A lot." I tugged nervously on my backpack's straps.

"Losing your mom must have been hard. I don't really know, because my dad died when I was still a baby. Whatever happened to you in Arizona, that's all over now."

Oh, how I wished that was true.

"Thanks, Lee. You really are the best friend."

Neither of us said another word until we got to school. We trudged up the stairs toward our first period classes.

"Do you think they'll, uh, make a big announcement about Allison?" Lee asked, his shoulders slumped and his head low.

"Probably." His sadness echoed so sharply, I had to ask. "Did you know her well?"

"Had a crush on her since fifth grade." His defeated sigh tore me in two.

We paused at the second floor landing. I reached out to him, then hesitated. The way he adjusted his glasses didn't hide the hurt on his face. I grabbed him and pulled him into a quick hug. I hated hugs, but Lee looked like he needed one.

The corner of his lips twitched up. "Thanks, Ray." He sounded like he meant it. "See you at lunch."

I climbed the remaining flight of stairs alone, ignoring the churning in my stomach, and steeled myself. Missing class wasn't an option. Not after I'd skipped it yesterday. Besides, being here was better than staying home. The more time I spent around Dad, the more likely he was to notice I wasn't quite right, not anymore.

Two girls passed on either side of me, one muttering a semi-polite "excuse me." I followed them into Honors English, head down, feet shuffling.

The new kid was already in his seat. And he still had wings. The tiny specks of light that struggled through the October clouds headed straight for him. His wings didn't disappoint, amplifying their radiance, shimmering across the faces of our classmates.

It wasn't until I took my own seat—more like fell into it when my knees gave out—that it dawned on me: we were neighbors. Of course he would have been assigned the only free seat in class, the one next to me. It was a pattern: any free seats in my classes were next to me, emphasizing just how much of a freak most of the school thought I was.

He acknowledged me with an entrancing smile. His wings shifted slightly, the tips of his feathers curling under like a cat's claws.

I returned an uneven smile through dry lips.

If I stretched my hand out, it would pass right through them. I wondered if I'd feel anything. Ghosts are said to give off cold spots when they touch or pass through people. If that's true, would these wings give off warmth?

No, I reminded myself, *because they aren't real.*

"Is everything all right?" he asked.

His voice pulled me from my unnatural daze. Had he noticed me staring at his glorious, non-existent wings? *Stupid, stupid, stupid.* "What? Yeah, fine." My pulse thrummed in my ears. Suddenly, all I could think about was the way he'd stared at me while they took Allison's body away.

Ms. Cleeson arrived and closed the door behind her. She placed a hand on her third-trimester belly and announced Allison's death. Most of the students already seemed to know.

"Grief counselors will be available all week for those of you who would like to talk to someone."

I glanced out of the corner of my eye. The boy with the wings didn't seem as upset as the rest of the class—probably because he didn't know her—but he wasn't stoic, either. His brows, which were a half shade deeper than his blond hair, wrinkled together and stiffness gripped his upper lip.

The classroom door opened again. "Ms. Cleeson?" Ms. Morehouse peeked her head in. The new boy turned to look at her and caught me staring. I quickly looked toward the door, too. "May I borrow Rayna?"

Everyone's eyes shot to me. I stiffened, repressing a yelp while my cheeks burned red-hot.

"Of course," Ms. Cleeson nodded, taking a seat behind her desk.

Back to the basement for more therapy. I wondered if my dad had called her. My teeth clamped down, biting back the pang of trepidation hammering against my chest. All eyes remained on me as I gathered my things. The new boy's slate-gray stare pierced more intensely than everyone else's combined. I headed to the door. I would deal with him later; right now, I had to lie to my therapist.

Chapter Eleven

L ee plunked a family-sized bag of pork rinds and a liter of Jolt Cola down on our lunch table. At least he would make the day worth fighting through. Talking with Ms. Morehouse and Jeremiah, the visiting grief counselor, had taken up the entire morning. I had no idea if I'd been convincing enough, but at least there were no questions about wings.

"I forgot to tell you this morning, I met the new kid. He's kinda cool. Really friendly, ya know?"

"Where?" I cast a glance around the cafeteria, but didn't see the winged boy in question.

"Yesterday. We have fifth period Bio together. His name's Cam."

So they'd met right after he'd tried to join us for lunch. "That guy gives me the creeps." The words slipped out before I thought to censor myself.

"What are you talking about? He's super chill." He chomped down on a pork rind. The smell of fried pig skin turned my stomach. "And he's smart. I'm stoked I won't be stuck doing all the lab work by myself anymore."

Throat suddenly dry, I pushed my veggie chips aside and sat up a little straighter. "Why would you work with him?"

"Cam's my new lab partner. At the beginning of the year the class was uneven. Natalie Cruz and that stuck-up Rose Kim can suck it now. We'll see how far they get next lab without me."

"You can't work with him."

His brows furrowed. "Why not?" He laid down his next rind. "What's your problem with him?"

I couldn't let Lee get involved with the new kid. If they became friends I'd have to stop hanging out with Lee, or I'd slip. There was no way I could be around those wings for too long without breaking. But I couldn't lose Lee, either. He was my best friend and one of my few, precious links to the world of sanity. I'd do anything to keep that from happening. Including planting ideas in his head. "Don't you think it's weird he happens to show up," I lowered my voice, "the same day Allison dies?"

The ends of Lee's lips turned down. "Wow. That's … wow. That's some conspiracy theorist stuff. What would make you even think that?"

My shoulders slumped. I was a selfish, horrible person, and a terrible friend. I looked down through the small, circular holes in the blue cafeteria table at my sneakers. "Well, think about it," I prodded, pinning my arms against my stomach. "It's a pretty big coincidence. And he just happened to be in the crowd outside when they took her body away. Convenient, right?"

"If there was a crowd then there must have been plenty of people outside the school then."

"Yeah, but … still."

The din in the cafeteria carried to our corner table, reminding me we weren't alone. Yesterday he had tried to join us. What if he tried again today? I checked over my right shoulder, and when I didn't see shining, I turned and looked over my left one. Nothing. He wasn't in the cafeteria. Where could he be?

Lee scoffed at me.

"What?"

"Nothing. It's just that when you do that, the looking over both shoulders thing, you prove my own conspiracy theory right."

"Which is?" I had to know what he believed, so I could make sure it was nothing close to the truth.

"That in Arizona you were some cool teenage super spy and you and your family moved because things got too *hot* there for you. And not temperature wise. So since you're hardwired with all this cool Kung Fu knowledge, you're always looking over your shoulder, watching and waiting for the next attack."

I almost laughed, but I couldn't afford to let him take me off track. I was determined to keep him away from the new kid. "You're not even giving it any thought. There's something … off about him."

"Have you even tried talking to him?"

I pushed my sandwich away for the second day in a row, worrying my lower lip between my teeth. I'd never tried to get to know one of the winged hallucinations before. I'd spent most of my time trying to avoid—or attack—them. Maybe that was the problem. I'd never seen wings on someone I knew personally. If Lee was going to make friends with the new kid—with Cam—I had two choices: quit being Lee's friend, or find a way past the wings.

Dr. G had told me the key to my sanity was knowledge. He was right. It was time for me to get to know the boy with the wings and face this thing head on. I was done running.

Chapter Twelve

After lunch and Music class, I sat across from Cam in History. He focused on note-taking. His wings dipped up and down with every breath he took.

"Is there something I can help you with?" His gaze locked onto mine before I could pretend to be studying anything but him. His tone was inquisitive and curious, while his eyes invited the truth.

My fingers tensed beneath the table. When I spoke, there was far too much inflection in my voice. "Uh, no."

I flung my gaze down to my notebook. Several tortured minutes later, when I finally managed to convince myself he was refocused on class, I glanced up.

He was focused all right. On me.

The hypnotic flow of those remarkable wings drew me in again. His eyes narrowed, a question tightening his forehead. "What are you looking at?" He whispered.

"What do you mean?" I kept my voice low, covering almost flawlessly this time.

He frowned at me, then turned his attention back to class. Mr. Barnes scribbled several dates on the chalkboard, linking them with names of famous Civil War generals, I think.

This was stuff I should probably know. I copied everything down, noticing I was two pages behind in the textbook. I flipped the pages and looked away. I'd always hated history. So boring. Mr. Barnes droned on and on.

A shaft of sunlight drew my eyes toward the window. Actual freaking sun! I sat back in my seat so I wouldn't rush off toward the window and get detention or something. Shimmering gold, like light off a sparkler, pulled me back to Cam's wings. The sun made them glow.

His wings jerked, their immeasurable wingspan opening so quickly I didn't have time to look away. The breeze they created shifted my hair into my eyes. I looked up at him from beneath its cover. With trembling fingers, I reached up and pushed my dark hair aside.

Surprise jolted him. His eyes grew wide and round, spoiling his angelic face with absolute awareness. His jaw slackened and his fist clamped down onto his pen, snapping it in half. Black ink splashed over his hand, white t-shirt, and well-fitted, green plaid over-shirt.

Oh, God.

I scrambled for my books, sweeping them into my bag. My chair skittered into the kid sitting at the table behind me. I didn't even get out a "sorry" before fleeing the classroom.

"Rayna," Mr. Barnes yelled after me, followed by something else I couldn't quite hear before the bell rang, ending sixth period.

I didn't look back as people piled into the halls, simply dodged them, ran up a flight of stairs to the third floor, and took solace in the girls' bathroom.

What the hell just happened? They couldn't be real.

They were real, I felt *the air rushing pass me. But, no. No, no, no, no, no, no. How else do I explain that?*

God, could he be a real angel? Could they all have been real?!

A hysterical bubble of laughter burbled up my throat. I swallowed it down.

Angels—real ones—don't exist. Maybe. Or not.

My back pressed up against the same tile wall I'd used for comfort yesterday when he'd first arrived, and I slid to the ground.

I couldn't crumble now. There was too much to do, too much still to figure out.

The toilet in the second stall flushed, startling me to my feet. I pulled it together enough to splash water on my face and run into the hallway. The last thing I needed was another episode of "tweaker girl's hiding in the bathroom."

Twenty-six quick, but measured, steps brought me to the Art room for my last class of the day.

Just make it through the day; hold it together.

A streak of gold skimmed the thinning group of students in the hallway, catching my eye. I stopped just outside the classroom. Turned very slowly toward the odd light.

Cam watched me, half in the hallway, half in the stairwell. The very stairway where Allison had taken her last steps. Confusion and anger marred his face. His lips parted, as if to speak.

No.

I turned and ran into the classroom, my heart throbbing in the back of my throat. But he didn't show up in the doorway.

Good. That was good.

I pulled my knees up to my chest—difficult to do on a tall stool—hoping no one would notice how much I was shaking. Real. Those wings were as real as the sweat coating my forehead, neck, and palms.

Chapter Thirteen

An eternity later, the bell rang, signaling the start of Art class. My odd posture attracted a few stares. But I couldn't look crazy. If I got sent to answer Ms. Morehouse's probing questions, I didn't think I'd be able to think straight enough to lie my way around them. Slowly, I lowered my legs to the floor and reached for my backpack. Sun glinted off something. I tensed, dropping my bag. Nothing. It was nothing. Just sun.

How can those wings be real? For so many years they told me they weren't! I've been fooled. Or lied to.

Real. They were real. But they couldn't be.

Someone was speaking, distracting me from thoughts I shouldn't be thinking. At the front of the classroom, a woman in a long floral dress unveiled an abstract painting. A sub. Mrs. Pheffer probably couldn't handle what had happened to Allison, either.

The sub wrote several words on the chalkboard. Colors. Blocking. Surrealism. Like I needed anyone to explain *surreal* to me. Her words faded, lost again to my own internal shouts.

I saw Cam. He saw me. Maybe we saw each other for what we really were.

I swallowed, hearing the swish of saliva slide down my throat.

Slow down, I told myself, reaching for an anchor.

Dr. G's "knowledge is power" speech soothed me somewhat. *Start with what you know as fact, then discover and uncover the rest. The more you're sure about, the less confused you'll be.*

So you felt something, I began, trying to break it down rationally. *You saw the wings. You felt them blow wind into your face, but there was no physical touch.* That meant there were still three other senses that haven't been tested. Yet. I thought I could pull off a sniff test, but I didn't much feel like trying to taste his wings. What would I even say? *Oh, don't mind me, Cam. I'm just going to be back here, licking the air behind you back. No biggie.* I barked out a hysterical laugh.

Every head in the classroom turned in my direction. I slapped a hand over my mouth and forced my eyes down. The rhythm pounding in my pulse belonged at a rave. I was losing it.

I forced my thoughts back on track. Had I really felt anything? That breeze could have come from anywhere—an overzealous air duct, a window some rebellious student had cracked open—and here I was convinced that it had come from Cam's wings. *Wings. It was just wind, Rayna.*

So, if taste was out, touch and smell were left. The boy smelled like a damn lawnmower—which I loved— but was that his wings or just him? No way would I get close enough to touch them—not now, and probably not ever, if I wanted people to believe I was still sane.

There had to be another way.

When I looked up again, determined to keep up with the normal kids, I noticed my classmates had gathered their materials and were already hard at work.

I fought myself out of my stool and to the supply room. Where it was dark—no sun to glint off anything, no people around. I wedged myself into the corner and sank to the floor. I needed a minute. Just one. I pulled my knees to my chest and hugged them, but wouldn't let myself rock. The beginning of tears stung my eyes. I couldn't let myself unravel. Not here. Not now.

I shot up to my feet and bumped into the shelf beside me. Tubes of white, green, and blue paint smashed to the ground. I wiped my eyes and scurried to pick them up before someone came in. Scrambling, I picked up a palette and squirted a few colors on it, grabbed my set of brushes from my cubbyhole, and raced back to my stool.

The sub was safely making rounds. Everyone was engulfed in their work like nothing had happened yesterday. Like Allison hadn't been in pain and run out of here, never to be seen alive again.

I gripped the largest brush in my hand and let my eyes drift closed. The image of Allison's painting kept springing to mind. Even though the glance I got yesterday was brief, I was sure there were wings. Allison had drawn ... an angel.

The image faded in my mind. I opened my eyes. The sub loomed over me.

She knelt. "Is everything all right here?" Her hair was wild and, up this close, her stout features were prominent. In her dress, the short woman resembled a tree stump.

I swallowed, pretending my mind hadn't just been on the verge of breaking completely.

Get a grip, Rayna. Allison's painting couldn't have had wings. Everything these past two days had to be stress manifesting in unexpected—or, for me at least, very much expected—ways. It had to be. My craziness had taken over, devoured every rational thought.

Even if they weren't real, I'd been seeing wings again for almost thirty-six hours. The relapse had already begun. This was the worst, feeling real life slip through my fingers while everyone watched. Nothing could be worse than that. Nothing.

The sub simply stood there, looking up at me. I made my shaking lips move. "Fine, just imagining what to paint."

The wide-eyed sub nodded, but didn't move along to the next sorry soul. What did she want from me? My pulse hammered. Maybe subs got the same general warning about me the regular teachers did: *keep an eye on that one.* If I didn't do something soon, she'd call Ms. Morehouse.

I smeared my brush in the green paint. Before I could think, I streaked a thick, diagonal line across the canvas. *Good one.* Now I'd have to struggle with how to finish this assignment.

The sub tapped the tips of her fingers on her lips. "Bold choice," she said, then moved to my left.

My head whirled like a centrifuge, spinning out of control. I needed an anchor, a way to put these thoughts away before they exploded out of me. With shaking fingers, I dropped the paintbrush and smoothed my hair back, then dug into my backpack for my secret notebook. I roughly sketched the image I remembered from Allison's canvas with the edge of a dull pencil.

Around me, each brush stroke, footstep, and whisper set me on edge. Every few seconds I peered over my shoulders. No one could know how much I was slipping. No one could see the thoughts in this notebook.

My original idea of throwing out the notebook before I got home, erasing any trace of these thoughts, was beginning to unravel. It had already become a part of me, as important to my sanity as any of the lessons

I'd learned from Dr. G. Detaching from it now would be like using Miracle-Gro to get rid of weeds; stupid and so not logical.

The final bell rang while I was still in deep thought with my notebook. I washed my brush, packed up my notebook, and ran to the main stairway, hoping to disappear in the faceless crowd.

Through the glass front doors, I spotted Lee in our usual meeting spot, right out in front, leaning against the black handrail. The gray afternoon seemed brighter than usual. I blinked and looked again. The unmistakable sparkle of wings cast a sort of halo around Lee.

The slow gulp of cool air I took lodged in my throat. Two minutes ago I'd wanted nothing more than to disappear into the crowd. Now, as the rush of students pressed into me, forcing me toward those wings, I was wishing I'd gone down the deserted back staircase. I pushed past the glass doors with numb fingers.

It was as if Lee was standing with the devil himself—assuming the devil looked like he'd stepped out of an Abercrombie and Fitch billboard.

"Ray!" Lee straightened, waving his hands to get my attention. Cam stared at me from over Lee's shoulder. I clenched my fists around the straps of my backpack and weaved over to them. "This is Cam." Excitement never left his voice. "He's gonna walk with us."

The blood from my face drained. *Not in this lifetime.*

Cam didn't look at all surprised to see me. His smile was meant to look casual, but muscles ticked in his jaw, warning me there was something barely contained lurking beneath that cool exterior. His gray eyes studied me just as deeply as I studied him.

I inched closer to Lee and swallowed. "Actually, I forgot. I'm supposed to pick my sister up from school." The lie tumbled out before I realized I'd be leaving my best friend with Cam ... and those wings.

I slid my gaze to them. Almost every spectrum of light shimmered from his feathers. Outside they were prismatic, even now that the fog had returned. His face gleamed slightly, like his skin had been infused with gold powder. He squinted at me, obviously mistrusting.

Ditto, buddy.

"Oh, that's kinda great, 'cause I'm meeting my mom at her work today." Lee's tone dripped sweetness, like his tongue was made of taffy. With all the candy he ate, it was a serious possibility. "Should we go?" He angled around us and started walking.

Out of excuses, Cam and I followed, keeping the same pace alongside Lee. Him to one side, me on the other.

Lee glanced at me. A toothy grin widened across his face, only it didn't crinkle his eyes, making them shrink the way his smiles usually did. No, this smile was much more intent. What was he up to?

Oh God. Was he trying to set me up?

Out of the corner of my eye, I saw Cam watching me. Maybe he had manipulated Lee. Could he do that? No, of course not. Hallucination, remember?

My face contorted at the thought. The heat of his gaze zapped through every pore of my skin. Inside I was screaming, crumpling, and fighting. Laylah's school and the Korean consulate were in roughly the same direction. Once I got Lee alone, I could question him to see if Cam had somehow manipulated him. Or I could throttle him for trying to set me up.

I couldn't leave Lee alone with him. I wouldn't.

We trekked up the Powell Street hill in silence. Cam hung back, two paces behind Lee and me.

Probably to keep a better eye on me. He hadn't said a word, but he didn't need to. His watchful eyes and tense wings said everything. He was on edge, as unsure about me as I was about him.

When we reached the corner in front of Roxy's, home of my future paycheck, Lee stopped. "See you guys tomorrow."

I wanted to call Lee out. He hated taking the bus, hated visiting his mom at work, but I was just glad he was leaving, so he got away from Cam.

Lee and Cam exchanged some sort of complicated male handshake. I narrowed my eyes. So, what, they were friends now? Not good. I closed my mouth around a protest; there would be plenty of time for Lee and me to talk tomorrow, when Cam wasn't around. I didn't even wait for Lee's bus to come, just turned on my heel and headed out.

Cam's lighter-than-air steps fell in behind me, catching up as I made my way to the steepest part of the hill. I could feel the tension rolling off his shoulders. Not more than ten seconds passed without one of us eyeing the other. My pulse was off the charts. He could have grabbed me, or shouted at me, but he chose to wear me away slowly by flicking his wings out, reeling them back in, and casting them out again.

Death by insanity.

One of San Francisco's world-famous cable cars eased down the hill, dinging its bell as it passed. Cam pulled his wings in close and swung his head around to follow it. To keep him from starting up again, I used the distraction.

"Not from around here?" I asked suspiciously. If I was stuck with him, I might as well learn as much as I could stand. What I really wanted to ask was, *are you real, or am I truly losing it?*

"I, uh, just moved here." He trained his eyes on me.

"What about you?"

I didn't answer, too afraid it might give him some leverage over me.

We climbed higher up the hill. The hotels stretched fewer and farther between, giving way to just-as-tall apartment buildings. Almost all the exteriors had the first floor built in brick, some painted in white or gray, and some left their natural golden color. The foot traffic thinned, until we were alone.

"In History class today. You ..."

I ran my nails up and down my palms. I couldn't have this conversation. My mind wasn't untangled enough for it. Not now, not ever. "I have to go," I blurted.

His hand snaked around my upper arm, and he tugged me behind a tall bush alongside an apartment building.

"You *saw* me."

My heart slammed into the back of my throat. My knees nearly gave out. I braced myself against the building behind me and tightened my lips. Sparkles in the dark concrete shone like gemstones, playing off the sunlight of the winged one who had me cornered.

I had two choices: lie, or tell the truth. Now it wasn't so easy to tell the difference.

I stalled, searching for the right answer. "What are you doing here?"

He studied me for a long moment, his forehead wrinkling. "I thought I was walking you to your sister's school."

Hmmm. Not exactly what I was asking.

"What I mean is, it's awfully suspicious that you show up at school the same day Allison Woodward bleeds to death in the girls' bathroom." The edge in my voice sharpened when I looked up at him. I wouldn't let his enticing scent weaken me. Or the fact that his hand was still around my arm. *No turning back now.* "Did you kill her?"

"No." His answer was quick. He was so close, our noses were only inches apart. "Why would you think that?"

"I, um."

"Why?" His fingers tightened around my arm. "Who are you?" His eyes narrowed as they searched mine.

I was out of my league. Alone. Stupid. What made me think I could confront my fears, today or ever? My hands trembled against the wall behind me. Space. Space would help me think. I gathered my strength and jerked my arm away, getting the impression that he let me. "I'm no one."

His shoulders lifted in a think-what-you-want kind of shrug, but as they fell they seemed more weighted than before. His wings flicked outward, as if shaking something off.

I pushed off the building behind me and dodged him. And his wings.

Either he'd follow me or he wouldn't. A small, reckless part of me hoped he would come after me. Would tell me I wasn't crazy. That I never had been. Which was the craziest thought of them all.

He was beside me before I reached the end of the block.

I deviated from my usual route, rounding the corner. I couldn't lead him to either Laylah's school or my house. I didn't know what to believe about him, but either way, I wouldn't show a stranger where I lived. Even the insane had their limits.

Instead of thinking more about him, I focused on the only other subject that had seemed able to compete with him today: Allison. "Why would a sweet, cheerful girl like Allison take her own life?" I mumbled to myself.

"I'm sorry." He cleared his throat. "For the loss of your friend."

My breath shook, and a pinhole of weakness punched through my defenses. "She wasn't my friend, not really."

Why was I telling him this? Friends close, enemies closer.

"She wasn't your friend, yet you're upset about what happened to her?"

"Just because I didn't know her that well doesn't mean I don't care. She was nice, smart, a human being. How can everyone be so sad this morning, but by this afternoon no one cares anymore? It's like they just forgot about her because she's gone."

"You're compassionate."

And that surprises you? I wanted to ask, but kept my mouth shut.

He swallowed. Hard. "The situation is more complicated than you need to know, but trust me when I tell you I had nothing to do with your friend's death." His voice remained so even. It was distracting.

But not distracting enough. I thrust my hands into my pockets while we waited for a car to pass at the next corner. "Where were you yesterday at the end of last period?"

He took his time answering, waiting until we had crossed the street to reply. "I was in class."

"All of last period? You didn't sneak out early to, say, use the bathroom?" I thought about the men towing the gurney down the stairs and loading the body into the ambulance.

"No." This time he didn't hesitate.

I glanced at him, but all I could see was his face in the crowd yesterday, watching me as I sat in the cop car. "Why were you in front of the school so late? Why were you watching me?" Paranoia bubbled up inside me. With nowhere else for it to go, I tapped my fingers on my thighs and chewed my lower lip. He knew I could see his wings. Real wings. Wings I *thought* were real. That old, familiar tightness in my chest returned.

He eyed me warily. A look I was used to and sick of. "Are you all right?"

"Fine," I bit out. "Just answer the question."

"Which one?"

I could have stabbed him right then and there. "Both of them."

"I can't. Secrecy is … important to my kind."

I channeled my frustration into my feet and stepped up my pace, continuing to attack my lower lip with ferocity.

He didn't keep up. Good. I hoped he left. I didn't turn around; if he was somewhere behind me, I didn't want to know. Right now, I just wanted to shake him off, go home, and forget the last few days had ever happened. Forget *him*. And his stupid wings. And that irritating, half-smile thing he did when he thought I was being amusing, and I really wasn't.

The stretch of sidewalk in front of me was long, broken only by the spill of a driveway into the street. I closed my eyes and breathed in the scents of the city, allowing my fingers and jaw to unclench. A breeze stirred the late-blooming roses that lined the planter beds along the block's large apartment building. The sweet scent invaded my nose, lightening my steps and reminding me of wonderful, long-forgotten summers. I almost felt better. Until I remembered it was October. This was the roses' final hurrah before they died off.

Halfway through my next breath, fingers clamped around my upper arms, jerking me backward. My hair spilled into my eyes and I fought to keep my feet under me.

"Get your damn—" A large cargo van zipped out of

the garage I'd been standing in front of. Its undercarriage scraped the dip of the sidewalk before it zoomed up the street. "—hands off me."

My voice withered away. I could have been a road pancake—would have been, if it wasn't for him. The boy who I thought would be the end of me had just saved my life. I can't say I saw that one coming.

Chapter Fourteen

"Are you all right?" Cam tested my stability before peeling his fingers up, one at a time. I whirled around to face him, fighting my hair aside. His wings were half-open, the ends flowing carelessly in the breeze. His face was carefully blank.

"You … you could have …" I fumbled over the words and tried again, lifting my gaze up his shirt and into his eyes. "I know what you are."

He straightened, tensing up. He'd saved my life. Confirming his suspicion seemed the least I could do.

"Wouldn't it have been easier to let me keep walking?"

His face shifted into a look of childlike innocence. "Let you walk in front of a moving vehicle? Why would I do something so openly vicious?"

I could feel the disbelief touch my face and fill my eyes. "To make your life easier."

A slow grin lit up his face.

The large building beside us sheltered the narrow street, and for a moment, everything was quiet: the world, even my mind. Time seemed to slow, and it felt like the two of us disappeared into this little pocket of the world. A pocket where an outsider and a boy with wings could share a safe, unshielded moment.

Inside, the horserace in my heart slowed to a trot.

It was unexpected. Weird. And *so* not like anything I'd ever experienced. What was going on with me?

I took him in. Tall, handsome, and angelic. For the first time in three years, the angelic part didn't make me want to run back to my room at the SS Crazy. I'd had insanity drilled into me for years until I believed it, but now, standing with Cam, I didn't know what to believe anymore.

"I wouldn't—couldn't—let you be harmed for my own personal gain. It's … against everything I believe." His brows knitted together; worry spiked inside me again, and he zeroed in on my face.

What? What did he see?

"Are you hurt?"

My heart hammered in my throat as his hand came up, toward my face. His fingers, soft but firm, curved around my chin and tilted my head up. His thumb swiped along my lower lip.

"Blood." His head tilted as he examined the smear on his thumb.

"Blood?" I licked my lips self-consciously. Metallic tang blasted my palate. I must have chewed my lip while we were arguing. Until it bled. Again.

"You should sit."

All I could do was nod.

His fingers brushed my shoulders as he slid my backpack off, bearing the weight for me. With one hand on the small of my back, he guided me up the street, his touch stiffening my spine, even as my knees felt too weak to carry me.

A block and a half later, we reached Huntington Park, a gorgeous little block complete with playground, fountain, and a picture-perfect view of Grace Cathedral across the street. A tiny slice of Heaven. Cam led me to a bench. He sat beside me, his wings tucked back, careful not to touch me.

I wasn't the best judge of character, but Cam seemed sincere, and he had saved my life.

He parted his lips to say something. To deter him, I said the first thing on my mind, something that—probably—wouldn't cause more tension between us. "Is your name really Camel, like the animals with humps?" I tapped my Converse against the concrete, my cheeks heating at the way the word *humps* sounded coming out of my mouth.

He blinked rapidly, his mouth relaxing into a soft smile. "The name I was blessed with is Camael."

My lips mimicked his as I repeated each syllable. "Cam-ay-el."

"Cam, for short." I didn't understand how he could be so at ease with me knowing his secret. If anyone found out mine, I'd … well, freak. But, then again, someone did know now, and he was one of *them*. Typical.

A small, white, fuzzball of a dog bounded up to us, bouncing around Cam's feet and shoving its wet nose into the shimmery wings. Cam laughed, a lyrical sound, and reached down to pet it. The dog's little pink tongue unleashed slobbery horror over his fingers.

"I'm not the only one who can see them," I said softly.

A whistle sounded from the opposite end of the park. The pup turned and scampered away.

Cam nodded, his lips creasing with ease. "Animals who are clear of heart can see us as well."

The weight of it all settled over me. More proof that he—all the … wings I'd seen—were real. I swallowed. "Clear of heart?"

"Those who have not deceived or harmed in any intentional way."

He might look my age, but sometimes, when he said weird things like that, I couldn't shake the feeling he was much older.

"Now that you have your answers, may I ask you something?"

"I don't get the feeling I have much of a choice here."

An amused smile sealed his lips. "You always have a choice. You're human. Free will is the greatest gift, bestowed on your kind before you're sent to Earth."

I scooted away from him, toward the end of the bench, to collect myself. "Fine. You get one, but I'm not guaranteeing an answer if I don't like the question."

"How are you able to see me in this form?" The muscles in his neck were strained.

We were back to this again. The uncomfortable elephant in the park. I licked the dried blood from my lower lip, tension creeping up my back. How would it sound if I were to tell him the truth? That I had no idea?

The longer I waited to answer, the more I studied him. His fists were balled now, and I thought I saw a muscle tick in his jaw.

The late afternoon sun dipped behind a tree, dissipating the shine from his wings.

"We'll … save that for another time." I worked to keep my voice even as I reached across him for my backpack, but when my arm grazed his chest—which was firmer than I ever wanted to imagine—my heart beat sped up. "It's … getting late."

He didn't seem to notice my nervousness; not even his wings changed position. Friction electrified the air between us. "I can't let you off that easy. What are you?" He asked again.

I shook my head and lowered my gaze, unable to watch him any longer. "I have no idea." I braced my hands against the bench, curling my fingers around the bottom. I half-expected him to burst, to call me a liar. All that tension had to go somewhere, and I knew I hadn't provided the answer he was looking for.

He sighed. "We'll talk more tomorrow. I hope I haven't made you late to pick up your sister."

My shoulders slumped, and I had to remind myself he wasn't done with me yet. The idea both scared and intrigued me.

I pushed off the bench. He followed. "I never had to pick up my sister. I lied. Obviously, I'm not *clear of heart*."

I took a few steps, but had to glance back at him, had to get another look at him. He stood with his arms crossed, watching me go, contemplation stamped on his features. The glance didn't ease the tension circling the thin springs of my sanity like I'd hoped.

I rushed home, knowing I was going to be in the deepest trouble with Dad. My suspicions were confirmed the moment I stepped through the front door.

"Aunt Nora called to check up on you," Laylah shouted from the living room. Her voice prickled like the thorns of a stinging nettle. Good to know we were getting along again.

I wished I'd been around for Aunt Nora's call, though. Sometimes, if I closed my eyes and concentrated, she sounded like Mom.

Dad loomed in the kitchen doorway, shaking a tiny screwdriver at me. "Where on Earth have you been, Ray? It's almost five. By my count, that makes you nearly an hour late for your curfew."

Sweat built up in my palms, and my stomach flip-flopped.

"Sorry, Dad. I, uh, took a new route home and … got a little lost." The fire of my half-truth stretched across my forehead, where sweat beaded. "But I have good news." I thought about my secret notebook hidden within my backpack and hiked it up higher, looping my thumbs possessively through the straps. "I start at Roxy's Diner tomorrow after school." I rushed through the living room to the stairs. "Which means I'd better get those chapter questions for Anatomy done tonight. I'll be upstairs if you need me."

He followed me into the living room. "Not so fast, kiddo," Dad said, his tone very *dad-ly.* "How was school today?"

I stopped with my foot on the first stair. "Fine. Can I go now?"

"Not yet. Any news about that girl's funeral? I've decided we should go. After talking it over with Dr. Graham—"

My mouth dropped open. I turned on him, ready to strike. "We talked about this. I don't want to see or talk to Dr. G. You put me there over and over again for three years! It *won't* happen again. Just 'cause you don't know how to deal with your adolescent daughter—"

"He hasn't had any problems with *me*," Laylah interjected from the couch. It was the first time I'd seen her detached from her friends, the other Musketeers, since we'd moved. "Not everything revolves around you, Ray."

"This has nothing to do with you."

She hopped off the couch and stomped toward me, reminding me of the nine-year-old Laylah who had visited me *inside* the very first time I was admitted. It was the first time we'd ever been apart. Separated for three days. She'd changed in that short amount of time, and I couldn't believe how much she'd looked like Mom. Then, and now.

She'd run into the SS Crazy's visiting area, arms wide, tears streaming. I'd never felt like more of a failure than I had in that moment. I was the big sister. It was my job to protect her. Instead, I'd made things harder.

I'd stayed with her the night of my first release. I lay in her bed, stroking her hair as she drifted off to sleep. That night I had promised her I'd never go away again.

The memory overshadowed the present, where Laylah yelled and screamed, pointing her finger in my face, but I'd heard none of what she said. I replayed the slow, painful memory, so vastly different from the way she advanced on me now.

Dad's voice roared over Laylah's. "We're supposed to be a family, girls!"

I cupped my hands over my ears to muffle the shouting and lost myself to another flashback. This one was cold, frightening—a memory of a time when even through my room's walls, I could hear the screams of other patients, girls crazier than me. Anxiety built up inside me, spurring my heart to beat faster. "This isn't the right environment for me."

A blanket of silence covered the room. My hands hovered an inch from my ears before I dropped them to my sides. The constriction in my chest loosened to let me breathe again.

Laylah crossed her arms and hoisted her chin. "Then maybe you should go back to the crazy house where you belong. We don't need you here. Dad and I were doing just fine without you. They should've never released you, then we wouldn't have had to move. For you. *Again.*"

"Laylah!" Dad scolded.

She kept going. "First we left Arizona to be closer for your treatments in Sonora, then we had to leave to move to San Francisco so you would feel better! No one wants you here, Ray. You're still as crazy as the first day you went in." She stormed back to the couch and snatched the remote off the coffee table.

I could barely breathe through the horrible lump in my throat. I felt like I'd just gone ten rounds with a garbage truck.

Dad said nothing, proving just how right Laylah was. The sound of channels changing assaulted the still room.

I needed to make it up the stairs before the ground came out from under me. "I've got loads of homework." My voice was low and soft, but the tears never came.

Once upstairs, I slammed my backpack onto my bed. My things spilled across the white and lavender bedspread. I waded through the new mess for my iPod. Anger boiled away my usual need for neatness. I jammed the earbuds in my ears and cranked the music, but even at full blast, it couldn't drown out the screaming in my head.

Chapter Fifteen

I straddled my bedroom windowsill, hesitating. I'd tried everything I could think of to get my mind off Laylah's words—music, homework, drawing, even conspiring in the secret notebook that shouldn't have come home with me—but nothing worked. This seemed the only way. Though I had no idea what *this* was.

My walls were closing in, and all I could think of was getting out. I didn't know if I was escaping, jumping, or crying out for help.

If I got caught, I'd probably be taken back to the SS Crazy. But the way things were going, I'd be shipped back there soon anyway, especially after Laylah's accusation. If my sister really wanted me gone, Dad would pick her happiness over my own. If roles were reversed, I wouldn't blame them. Dealing with someone like me couldn't be easy.

Dad could walk in at any moment, push past my wicker chair barricade, find my room empty, and call the police, but it probably wouldn't happen. Dad was predictable enough to shy away from his feelings, which—thanks to me—included his crazy teenage daughter.

I carefully stretched a leg over my planter box. The

copper, purple, and pink mums sprouted around the front edges of the white box, with the bright pink sedum dazzleberry filling in the back. I wondered if anyone would water them if I didn't come back. If anyone would watch the butterflies flock to the sedum before it died off for the season. Maybe if I left a note for Laylah … No. She'd probably dump them over the window just to spite me.

Out. I just needed out for now. I could figure out the rest later.

The tree branch was a finger's length out of reach. I grabbed the molding around the window and stood on the ledge of my planter box, careful not to crush any of my flowers. The two-and-a-half-story fall could probably kill me if I hit the ground wrong. I ignored my fear, held my breath, and jumped for the tree.

My hands grated against the rough bark of a branch. For a moment, I just dangled there. Across the street, the faint illumination of dusk circled Lafayette Park. A halo of light broke through the tree from the streetlight above.

I shimmied toward the trunk, the sweat on my palms slicking the bark. The trunk was only one or two short scoots away, but my fingers burned with the effort. I summoned my strength and reached forward— driving my palm into the point of a broken branch. I cursed, yanking my hand back. Blood coursed down my palm.

My balance wavered as I held on to the tree with one hand and my knees. When I reached forward to grab the branch again, sweat and blood made the branch impossible to hold on to. My grip slipped and I fell. The ground rushed toward me.

The feeling of falling was both terrifying and freeing. I closed my eyes and waited for the hard landing to come.

It didn't. Instead, the tug of gravity disappeared, and I found myself wrapped in a cushion of arms. I peeked through one eye and looked directly into a set of midnight-black feathers.

I squirmed, struck by a sudden sense of familiarity. With the halo of light bursting through the tree's canopy and those dark wings opened wide, it looked exactly like Allison's painting. Even his face was obscured by the lighting.

His hold around me constricted. "Relax." The dark-winged man's voice was low and gruff, but somehow smoother than I'd expected—for a creature with black-freaking-wings.

Trepidation slithered up my spine, and I kicked for dear life. "Let me go!"

Several heart-stopping moments passed until I swore he'd hike me over his shoulder and fly away. I'd never be seen again. Never found. Just another girl on a lost poster stapled to a telephone pole. My squirming made no difference.

After half an eternity, he lowered me.

The moment the toe of my Converse touched the ground, I scrambled from his arms, drawing back until my spine matched up against the tree trunk.

"You don't make that escape very often, do you?" he asked. "Your landing could use some work." His dark eyes were the only visible part of his face. A bar of light slanted right across them. Everything else remained cast in shadows.

My feet itched to move, to run. But I forced myself to stay calm. "I don't typically need saving, but today doesn't seem to be my day."

Maybe Cam wasn't the winged creature I should be worried about.

"Something the matter?" His words were slow and measured, the pace and tone of a man who never needed to speak up to be heard. He inhaled deeply. The sound set me on edge, like he was savoring my scent.

"No," I said too quickly. Shivers racked my body.

The shadows covering his face lightened just enough to reveal one corner of his mouth, drawn up in a daunting curve. It wasn't a smile, more a show of teeth. It was nothing like Cam's smile.

Fear twisted my insides, but I wouldn't scream. I wouldn't scream. I wouldn't—

I gasped and sat up in my bed. My pulse thrummed. Sweat tacked my hair to my face. Daylight trickled in through my lilac-colored sheers. I pushed my hair back and looked at my hand. Not even a scratch marred my skin. It should have been bloody from the broken tree limb. My escape, my fall, the black-winged man, it was all a dream.

I fought the sweaty sheets down. Books were strewn around the bed. I must have fallen asleep doing history homework.

The bedside clock read eight thirty-four. Still shaken, I scrambled out of bed, rushed through a shower, and packed my book bag on my way out the door.

I crept through the back door ten minutes into second period, only to be met by a slew of teary-eyed faces. An unfamiliar man handed out neon-green leaflets. He scribbled an eight hundred number on the chalkboard behind him, followed by the words "suicide hotline."

As I slid into my seat, the man at the front of class with Mr. Ratchor started discussing the signs of suicidal thoughts. Since I could probably write a book on that particular subject, I tuned him out.

Guilt clawed at me, again, for the third day in a row. I should have recognized some of the signs in

Allison, but I'd never seen any. She'd always seemed so happy.

Except for that painting. Was it what I remembered seeing, or was I imagining wings where there were none?

I looked around, making sure no one was paying attention to me. More tears; nobody cared about what I was doing. Maybe they had been in shock yesterday and were in a better position to mourn her loss today.

I pulled my secret notebook and a set of colored pencils from my backpack and sketched the dark-winged figure I saw in this morning's nightmare.

When I was done, I almost closed the notebook, but stopped myself. I flipped to the sketch I drew in Art class yesterday. Then I folded the pages between it and today's drawing, so I could see the two side by side. The same dark wings stared back at me from both pages.

Black wings. I'd never seen one with black wings before, only annoyingly bright ones like Cam's. Maybe I could ask Cam what was up with this dark-winged guy. He seemed intent on talking to me; maybe we could go for another walk together after school, get to know each other a little better, and then I could ask him—

Stop. Conspiracy theories about a dark-winged man being involved in Allison's death, then finding his way into my very vivid nightmare wouldn't do anything to help my case. Neither would talking to Cam. I couldn't let myself go down that long, insane road. It led directly to the SS Crazy.

These drawings had to be a coincidence, right?

I looked closer at my drawings. I knew better now than to dismiss anything this similar as coincidence. My subconscious must have made me dream about

Allison's painting. That's all. There couldn't be a real man with dark wings out there somewhere.

With that dismissal, an odd feeling tugged at me, not allowing me to let it go. Still, I fought it. I'd just gotten the unbelievable gift of my sanity back. No way was I going to jeopardize it again.

Chapter Sixteen

"**Y**ou thought all this was for Allison?" Lee popped a handful of M&M's into his mouth.

We'd made it almost to the end of lunch before reverting to gossip, which Lee soaked up like a sponge.

"Isn't it?" I pushed away the other half of my turkey sandwich, my appetite slipping at the thought of Allison's death.

He grimaced. "Nuh uh. Tony DiMeeko died last night."

Oh God. That's what I'd missed by being late to class this morning. The cafeteria spun. I felt almost too sick to ask. Almost. "Do you know what happened?"

"Word is he hanged himself in his closet."

My stomach bottomed out. It wasn't just another death; it was another suicide.

Tony DiMeeko had been a star of the varsity basketball team, and that didn't even compare to his skills on the pitcher's mound. Last I'd heard, he'd been accepted to college on a baseball scholarship. He had everything going for him.

"Why do you think he did it?" I asked Lee.

He rolled the half-empty bag of candy between his

hands. "Beats me. Maybe all that sports pressure got to him."

The bell rang, clipping our conversation short.

"We'll talk after school." Lee dumped the rest of his M&M's into his mouth and left.

I waited until the cafeteria had cleared out some, then walked to Music class.

Two of my classmates were dead within days of each other. I stopped in the stairwell to tug my secret notebook from my bag and see if anything I'd written down about Allison also applied to Tony. The idea was stupid. Crazy.

Either that, or *I* was crazy. Still.

I didn't know what to believe. Except two of my classmates were dead. I couldn't bring this to Cam; there was no way to know if I'd be able to believe him. Trusting myself was becoming pretty unreliable, too.

I turned the corner on the second floor, leafing through the notebook for the sketches. I'd been flipping the pictures so many times the one in full color had begun to tear from the book.

The image brought me back to my nightmare. So terrifying. So real.

I shook off the memory and kept walking. If I let myself relive that one again, there was no way I'd be able to make it through the day.

Focus.

Tony had died last night. Last night around what time? I swallowed, allowing the next thought to fully develop before I wrote it down.

Could Cam have had enough time after I left him at the park yesterday to find Tony and follow him home? Opportunity? Yes. Motive?

I lifted my quivering pen from the notebook.

Could Cam have killed Tony? I mean, he did save my life yesterday.

I slammed into someone. The notebook tumbled and skittered along the glossy, peach tile floor, and I fell on my ass.

In hindsight, navigating the halls with my head buried in the mysteries of those wings wasn't the brightest thing to do.

"Sorry, Rayna. Didn't see you there." Luke Harper helped me up, then bent to retrieve my notebook. I watched, frozen in horror, as his fingers rolled the notebook into a tube and squeezed.

The neat-freak in me wanted to scream, and every other part of me wanted to rip the notebook from his hands. But then I saw his absent stare, pricked with red-rimmed eyes. His fingers worried my notebook into submission again and again.

"No," I finally said. "It was my fault. I wasn't looking where I was going. But—is everything okay, Luke?" I focused in on my notebook again.

"What? Yeah. Fine. Why, if it wasn't would you kiss it and make it better?"

Even with panic rising up my throat, I saw through his blatant attempt to distract me. I pulled my gaze away from the notebook and leveled the best glare I could dig up at him.

"Yeah, okay, I'm freaking out. One of my best friends is dead. How am I supposed to deal with that?" He choked my notebook harder. "We just hung out two days ago. Tony was so happy, gushing about some new private-school girlfriend."

Luke lifted his black-and-orange Giants hat and scrubbed the back of his bald head. "Everyone's sayin' he offed himself, but he had a life—an awesome one." He glanced down the hall behind him and lowered his voice. "The new girlfriend even put out."

Holding back a grimace, I reminded myself he was grieving.

Luke sighed and wiped a hand over his eyes. "It doesn't make any sense. The cops came by last night, asking me all kinds of questions. It sounds like it's a mystery to them, too."

"I know you and Tony were close. I'm sorry. It's hard to lose someone."

God, was it hard.

He forced a brave I'll-be-all-right smile. "Thanks, Evans."

I lifted my hand to his shoulder, meaning to comfort him. Halfway there, I stopped, with no idea what I was doing. I pulled back a little, struggling. I'd never been good with this stuff, and in the last three years, I'd gotten a lot of "good little schizos keep their hands to themselves" reminders on the inside. Finally, I let my hand drop onto his shoulder. He looked up at me, startled. Our eyes met, and held, for a moment too long.

The bell rang, sealing my lateness to Music class with a red check in the tardy box.

When I pulled my hand back, it hit the notebook, which tumbled to the ground. One of my sketches ripped free from the book. I lunged for it, but Luke beat me to it.

He straightened up slowly, looking at my dark-winged sketch with sudden fury in his eyes. "What the hell is this, Rayna?" This boy was miles from the flirty Luke I'd come to know.

Play it off. He can't know the truth. "It's just a picture, Luke. What's the big deal?" Dryness snatched up some of my words.

"I've been seeing it in my dreams."

I froze.

"I ... copied Tony's notes the other day. I haven't been able to get it out of my head since then. Tony died before I could ask him about it, and now it's here, in your notebook. What am I supposed to think?"

The beginnings of hyperventilation knotted my throat. My body trembled in fear of being discovered, called out, then taken away.

Before I could spiral down into a place I likely wouldn't climb out of, a tiny spot of light caught my attention. Cam readjusted his wings to tuck them closer to the set of lockers he was hiding behind. His face was stone, his eyes serious.

My fingers went cold. How long had he been standing there, listening to us? "It's nothing, so, we should, uh, get to class."

Luke looked at me like I was crazy, a look I knew all too well. He said nothing else as he walked away, brushing by a poster in the hall advertising the Halloween dance, taking my drawing with him. I watched him enter his class, then turned back toward the lockers. Cam was gone.

I wanted to curl up in a ball, hugging myself tightly. *Okay. Calm. Breathe.*

This was too much at once. Maybe I was even crazier than before, like my mind was cracking because I couldn't handle the real life stuff.

Luke had been dreaming of this picture. The same one Allison *and* Tony had seen. That didn't mean Luke was somehow magically destined to kill himself, too. No, maybe Tony had seen Allison's painting somehow, and sketched it in his notebook, just like I had. There. Simple explanation. And maybe Cam was following me around because ... now that one was difficult to explain. Maybe Cam was as crazy as I was.

Knowing I wouldn't be able to concentrate on anything now, I spent what was left of Music class hiding in the bathroom. Again. I'd be in it deep if Dad got wise to my skipping classes, but I needed time to process.

I opened the notebook, trying to press it flat—I'd never get it back to normal again after Luke's assault on it—and started writing again, hoping to once again expel all wild thoughts so I didn't have to deal with them anymore.

By the time the bell for sixth period rang, I had a plan. I waited around the corner from Luke's class. I was going to prove to myself that Luke wasn't in any danger, even if that meant being a creepy stalker.

I held my breath and peeked around the corner. Luke ducked out of the classroom. His head was down, his steps slow. Gina Garson was beside him, her usually smooth face pulled into a tight, worried mess. They both moved their hands as they spoke, in short, frustrated gestures, neither of them making eye contact. This was it, I'd finally cracked. I was stalking a classmate—the most popular guy in school, no less—waiting for him to up and off himself.

Sun shone through the windows on my left. I tensed, hunching my shoulders up toward my ears. I looked again, hoping the warmth wasn't a set of wings standing beside me.

Nope. Sun. Actual sun. Two days in a row. Maybe luck was finally on my side.

I glanced back to Luke and Gina. They were closer to my corner, only five lockers away.

"What do you mean you can't handle this now?" Gina hissed. "How the hell do you think I feel?"

Luke pinched the sleeve of her sweater and veered her over to the side of the hallway, closer to me.

I should have left, resumed my stalk-age after school, but I couldn't pull myself away. Who knew watching a couple argue would be like watching a car crash?

"Can we talk about this later? I'm not having the best day."

"Oh, and my day's been a big ball of sunshine and daisies? This stuff is really creeping me out."

Luke exhaled, hard. "I get it, I do, but in case you haven't heard, one of my boys is dead." His eyes took on a watery sheen. "I don't think school is the best place to have this conversation, G."

"You've known for weeks." Gina's body language changed, softening, either to Luke or the topic. "You didn't want to talk about it then, either."

He reached out to her, wrapping one arm across her shoulders and pulling her into him.

Watching their exchange somehow felt wrong, invasive, especially after I'd endured all of Luke's half-hearted attempts to make a move on me. I turned away for a moment, allowing them their privacy, but couldn't let Luke out of my sight for too long. I looked around the corner. Their embrace was over, and tension edged their shoulders again. Whatever the issue, it hadn't been resolved so easily. Huh, turns out life isn't like the movies, after all.

One of Gina's tagalong friends made a bee-line for her. I think the girl's name was a month, April, May, June. Something like that. She ignored Luke completely and cupped a hand by Gina's ear. She whispered for a good thirty seconds, Luke's obvious irritation increasing by the second.

I strained forward. Maybe she had more information about Allison or Tony. This calendar girl was one of those social butterflies who flitted from table to table in the lunchroom.

She pulled back before I could devise a plan to pretend my locker was near them. Gina swallowed like she'd received bad news. My shoulder twitched—damn meds—and the girl zeroed in on me. "What's that freak up to?" She asked Gina.

Both Gina and Luke turned toward me. Anger

sparked in Gina's brown eyes. "Were you listening in on our conversation?"

My pulse created a punk song drumbeat in my chest. I quickly shook my head, but my wide eyes must have given me away.

"Stalker much? You tweaker-freak."

Her words hit me like a physical blow. Only two days ago she and I had shared a secret in the bathroom. I should have known she wouldn't be able to keep that secret for long.

Gina turned with her friend and stormed away toward the stairs without another word. Regret turned my stomach. I managed to pull my gaze up to Luke's.

More hurt than anger marred his face. His brows were furrowed, his lips tight.

I'm sorry, I mouthed to my almost-friend. I had no idea what he and Gina had been talking about, but these suicides, Cam, and Allison's painting were turning me into someone I didn't want to be. Someone I thought I'd left behind at the mental hospital. The worst part? I didn't plan to stop.

Luke shook his head and yanked his backpack up from the floor before he walked away. He didn't forgive me. He didn't trust me. And he'd probably never talk to me again.

This was bad. And annoying. What was I thinking, standing there, so obvious? Don't. Get. Caught. It was like, Stalking 101. This just got so much freaking harder.

Chapter Seventeen

I raced to History class after my huge oops moment with Luke and Gina, even though I dreaded what—or who—I'd find there. But I had to be stronger, so I swallowed and put my best tougher-than-nails face on.

Blinding reflections from wings covered the walls and faces in the classroom, mirroring the almost cheery afternoon sun. I shielded my eyes with my hand and heard my classmates' giggles. It probably looked like I was allergic to sunlight or something. I lowered my hand and walked to the back of the room, painfully aware that my feather-tipped friend had beaten me there.

"Nice to see you." Cam flashed a grin almost as bright as those wings.

"See? Really? Can't see much of anything right now." The sun had intensified his wings to almost blinding status.

The light dissipated much the way it does when clouds brush over the sun. "Sorry. I forgot they … affect you."

I dropped into my seat, feeling too many things all at once: apprehension about being near Cam, shame for spying on Luke and upsetting Gina, and awful crazy—

either from the meds or a relapse, I hadn't decided which yet.

A new set of whispers started at the table behind us. I could imagine them talking about the cool new guy talking to tweaker-girl—yeah, that nickname had caught on fast. If only that were true, that he was merely interested in me like *that*, things would be so much simpler.

I glanced at Cam, trying to picture him without his wings, as just a boy. Under different circumstances, he'd be pretty darn perfect. Smart, friendly, attractive, willing to save a girl's life. Without those wings, things would definitely be different. Almost normal. God, to just be normal. I shook my head and pulled myself out of that train of thought. No way any of that was going to happen.

"Rayna." His voice sent ripples down to my stomach. Whether they were good ripples or bad ones, I couldn't tell. "I have something important to ask you. It's about my reason for being here."

Bad. Yep, definitely bad.

"Luke Harper may be in danger."

The softness of his whisper sent a shiver up my spine, in a way that I immediately scolded myself for. I didn't need any more of those ridiculous fantasies. "Luke? What? No he's not."

"He might be. I wouldn't ask you if it wasn't important, but I think you might be able to help."

My jaw slackened, but I pressed my lips together to keep from saying anything else. If Luke was in danger, how would I be able to help?

"Can we talk after school?"

I looked down long enough for the bell to ring. *Finally.* Our tablemate, Cassie, took her seat, saving me from a response. She eyed Cam in a way I hadn't noticed yesterday, like he was the newest purse in the

Hot Topic store window. If she looked any harder, I swore drool would dribble down over her plum lip gloss.

I surveyed her low-cut sequined t-shirt, then compared it to my own deep-purple, crew-neck sweater. The dark sweeps of green eye shadow and eyeliner made her eyes stand out in all the wrong ways. And that huge, trendy purse wasn't doing anything to help her style. Still, Cassie sure looked fancier than usual today.

"I don't know how I didn't introduce myself yesterday. I'm Cassie." Her smile was the essence of just right, not too big, not to small.

Cam returned her smile with a polite one of his own. Cassie extended her hand. She was either being too formal or just wanted an excuse to touch him. Cam took her hand in his and shook it, while Cassie beamed at him.

Mr. Barnes started his lecture. Cam turned away from Cassie to watch the front of the room, but Cassie didn't have the same train of thought. She stared at him, smiling to herself. My teeth clamped together.

Why should I care what way Cassie looked at him? I didn't even like him. Really, I didn't. Even if he didn't have wings, he could be more involved than he wanted me to know.

Right. It wasn't Cassie's fault. It was Cam's. Because of that crooked thing he does with his lip when he's concentrating too hard.

Great, now I was staring.

My head was nowhere near the Revolutionary War.

He glanced up at me once or twice, but I pretended to be focused on our assignment, though I had no clue what it was.

***

To most students, the final bell meant one thing: freedom. Today, the bell meant something better than freedom: my first day at work and a chance to be normal. I hiked up my getting-heavier-by-the-day backpack and joined the tail end of the traffic filing down the hall toward the stairs.

"Rayna." Cam's feathers tickled the hairs on my arms, sending deathly chills through the riddled holes in my sanity. I stared at my arm. The ghost of feathers as soft as down brushed my skin there. I rubbed the touch away.

Wings passed through things. That's what they did. But Cam's had *touched* me. How could that be? Was it because I could see them?

There was so, so much I didn't know.

I jerked away, stumbling several steps back.

"You left class so quickly. I really need to speak with you." He took my hand in his and led me away from the crowd filing down the stairs. His touch was warm and gentle. His fingers were as soft as I remembered.

I studied the scratched paint on the lockers beside us to gather my thoughts.

Cam's voice dropped when his hand did. "I need your help."

I lifted my chin and found my spine. "How do you know I can help you?"

"Luke Harper is in trouble."

"What do you mean he's in trouble? How?"

He tilted his head to the side as if to say, really? His gentle demeanor slipped away, replaced by Business Cam. "I can't say."

I slanted a look at the remainder of the student body, desperate to be free of this building. "This is ridiculous." I shook my head and crossed my arms. "I'm not buying it."

His lips quirked to the side. "What is it you think you need to *buy into*? You can see what I am. Doesn't that tell you anything?"

"I've seen your kind for years. Not one of you has made my life anything but more difficult."

He tilted his chin up a fraction of an inch. "You have." The statement fell somewhere between a question and a fact, but it sounded like news coming from his mouth.

"You want help from me? Then I need to know a few things first."

Walk away. Why didn't I just walk away?

"Fine." He brushed off his irritation with a flick of his wings. Patience was not in his wheelhouse. "Something may be watching him."

Yeah, you. Oh, and well, me. "You seemed to be watching him pretty closely after lunch." I never would have been this brave if not for the sheer number of witnesses still in the hall.

"The same way you were caught eavesdropping on his conversation with his girlfriend in the hall."

Touché.

"But I'm not ... well, I don't have ..." I waved a finger in the general direction of his wings.

His voice dipped again. "I thought after yesterday you would trust me."

"Well, you thought wrong." I balled my fists by my side to strengthen my resolve. "What is it you think you need my help with?"

He shook his head.

"Unless you can tell me something, I'm out of here." I turned on my heel.

"Wait." He leaned forward, his lips brushing the hair by my ears. "There are others," he whispered.

He held our closeness. I resisted turning back to him and spoke louder than he had. "Others?"

He hedged, turning away to watch the last few students push past us and trickle down the stairs, leaving the hallway empty, except for him and me.

I glanced up and down the hall in case I'd need an escape route. Cam was blocking the main stairwell. The back stairs would be my only option. A different type of chill worked its way down to the inside of my sinking stomach as I relived the still-warm blood soaking into my jeans the last time I took the back stairs. I wouldn't go that way again. Ever. I took a step back from him to gain an inch of personal space. Dragging one useful little detail out of him was like pulling teeth. And each word took all my nerve to spit out. "If you want to tell me something, now's your chance."

"Just … I need to know if you've seen any more of … my kind. Lately."

"No," I said, then curved around him, giving his wings a wide berth, and walked down the stairs, praying he wouldn't follow.

"I meant, tell me if you do."

I stopped on the landing between the third floor and the second, but I didn't turn around. "Are you expecting more?"

"Hopefully not."

Sweat built on the back of my neck. I continued down the stairs, taking them two at a time, unable to get away fast enough. I didn't know what more wings had to do with Luke, but nuh-uh. No way. I couldn't handle any more wings. One way or another, I was out of this mess.

Chapter Eighteen

S till reeling from my conversation with Cam, I took out my frustration on the school's front doors, throwing them open as hard as I could.

I reached the bottom of the stairs, and someone sprang out at me. "Hey."

I jumped and pushed him back a good four feet before I noticed it was Lee and not a gorgeous blond boy with wings. "Lee, don't do that! You nearly gave me a coronary."

He caught himself just before tipping back over the railing. "Geez, sorry, Ray. I was just tryin' to lighten up the mood around here."

"I'm sorry. It's fine," I said, but my thundering pulse didn't agree. "Just don't do it again, okay?"

"You almost cracked my head open with those super-spy skills, but it's no prob."

I was starting to wonder if he hadn't been entirely joking yesterday, that part of him really did think I'd been a spy in Arizona. We began a quicker march than usual to Roxy's Diner. Thanks to my detour with Cam, I was in danger of being late my first day on the job.

"Ya know, I never got a chance to ask you how things went with Cam yesterday."

A frown tugged at my lips, and I tightened my grip on the straps of my backpack.

"Yeah, about that. Don't try to set me up again. Ever."

His cheeks boasted the slightest rosy blush. "I take it you two didn't hit it off."

We turned the corner and trudged up the Powell Street hill.

"The two of us have nothing in common. I will never have anything in common with him." My tone was sharper than it needed to be, but I couldn't help it; frustration still pumped through me. I shook my head, dismissing Cam from my thoughts. Lee didn't deserve the wrath of Crazy Ray. I swore softly. "I'm sorry. Do you want to come to the diner, maybe we can hang out on my break?"

"No can do. Heading home today."

He used his Bad Robot impression to separate every syllable of his speech. Or Star Trek. I could never keep them straight. "I'll see you at Roxy's tomorrow morning for H.C., though."

His code for hot chocolate made me laugh the same way it always did, in little chuckles that rode up my throat. If anyone could get my mind off wings, it was Lee.

We climbed the rest of the hill in much-needed silence. When we reached Roxy's, I went inside and waved at him from the window, then checked in with Daphne.

She towed me through the kitchen and to the beginning of a long hallway. The off-white walls shone with grease or steam or something I wanted to know nothing about since I actually enjoyed the burgers here. "The first door on the left," Daphne pointed to a stainless-steel door with a pull handle, "is the walk-in freezer." Rows of metal shelves lined the wall beside the walk-in, storage space for all the non-refrigerated items. "First door on the right is for employee storage, with a small break room. There are lockers, but I haven't had time to clear one out for you. Next door on the right is my office. That's the tour."

Daphne ducked into her office to grab my uniform, which she promptly tossed to me. "Go ahead and get dressed, then I'll have Shelly go over the menu with you. Let me know if you have any questions."

I hugged the uniform to my chest and smiled. My first real job. My own space where I could create a more normal version of myself, away from the prying eyes of my family, counselors, and classmates. A place where I could be me.

I exited through the kitchen, rounded the counter, and changed in the ladies' room—which wasn't as easy as it sounds in a cramped stall. I shimmied into the bubble-gum pink uniform, complete with white collar and ruffled apron. The white nurse shoes and tan pantyhose fought for the title of Most Horrible part of the outfit. Until I saw the white, frilly cap.

Oh no. No, no, no.

Instead of putting it on, I returned to the counter where Shelly, the girl Daphne had assigned me to shadow for the day, stood, cap-less. "What's the deal with the cap?" I asked, maybe a little too panicky.

"You know, I swear the owner put those in with the uniforms so he could walk in one day and just laugh and laugh at us. You can wear a headband or tie a cute little scarf over a ponytail instead." She adjusted her black-and-white polka dot headband. "Your hair should be fine for today," she flipped the bottom of my ponytail, "but make sure you have one for tomorrow, otherwise Daph'll have kittens."

Shelly glanced at the back of a soupspoon to check her jet-black hair, sweeping aside a thick streak of orange as she blew a watermelon-scented bubble with her gum. She breathed on the spoon, then wiped it with her apron so she could get a better look. With a tart smile, she dropped the spoon inside a cup of tomato soup at the pickup counter and delivered it to an elderly man at table twelve.

On her way back, she reluctantly picked up a check from the next table over. I'd noticed them trying to get her attention since before Daphne took me in the back. She rolled her eyes and checked her phone. "There's just something about old people that really gives me the willies." She set the check and money beside the cash register and leaned on it with her elbow. "I think it's the wrinkles. But you wouldn't know anything about that. Your skin is major." She leaned in dangerously close, invading my personal space.

Great, I'd found the one girl in this city who was on more drugs than I was.

"Sorry, I have a thing for faces. With a little makeup you could really be a looker—I mean, that plain-Jane gig works for some girls, but there's a lot of competition out there. How old are you?"

"Uh, sixteen."

Her eyes lit up with a spark of yearning. "Ugh, to be young again. Let me just say, my high school experience was *top-notch*." The way her voice changed with each syllable, it sounded more like she was singing than talking. But there was something about Shelly that you couldn't ignore. She had too much life in her for one person—something I'd heard my mom say once. But it totally fit her.

She finally turned her attention to the check under her elbow, and I picked up a menu I almost knew by heart already. It took Shelly four minutes to make change for a bill that was $21.98, but in her defense, the girl never stopped talking. "The one thing you need to know about high school is to go for it. Whatever you have the opportunity to do, do it—and do it *a lot*." She rolled her eyes and smiled this enormous, scary smile.

A blush crept up my cheeks at her innuendo, and I had to look away.

"What? Oh my God, did I embarrass you?" She set the change on the counter again and took hold of my shoulders, turning me toward her. "It's Ray, right?"

I nodded, completely unsure how to interact with Shelly. She wore her hair like a fifties style pin-up, with thick, curled-under bangs and waves at the bottom. And those had to be tattoos snaking up both her legs beneath her stockings. She wore a lot of makeup over her eyes in blacks and grays, and a foundation that might have been a shade too light for her, all of which made her look older than she probably was. My guess was late twenties.

"I'm Shelly, and I'm not right—hell, the world's not right—get over it." She flashed the underside of her wrist where inked in black letters were the words "get over it." "A little icebreaker." She smiled, her deep red lipstick doing its job to play up her thin lips. "Just don't pay too much attention to me and don't stress the small stuff, and you'll do fine here."

She popped her gum once more, then released her grip on my arms. When she returned the change to her table, the man argued that he gave her forty dollars and got change for thirty.

She snatched the bill, then angrily riffled through the cash register. "See what I mean?" she whispered. "Freaky." She took out an extra ten and delivered it to the man, who muttered complaints to his lady friend all the way to the door.

"Thanks, come again!" she hollered after the door closed behind them. Then she turned to me again.

I braced myself.

"What was I saying? Oh, yeah! High school. Make the most of it. I used to be a sad, boring little kid. But the summer before ninth grade, *bam*! Hit by a car. I spent a week in the hospital, almost died. The rest of summer, physical therapy. But I survived and I vowed to live each day to its fullest, because, babycakes, you only live once. Tomorrow we could both be dead. Don't spend your life hiding behind long brown hair and a plain face. Have fun with it." She flipped my ponytail again.

My jaw had dropped somewhere in the middle of her story. This girl had something I'd always wondered about. Life. Spark. Originality.

A weird kinship bloomed between us. She'd been me, and I'd been, well I'd been crazy, so I was a little like her.

I sighed softly. If only I could afford to act like that.

Unlike me, Shelly wasn't under a microscope. But she was brave, not caring about what other people thought, just jumping in without worrying about consequences. One day I'd like to live like that, reinvent myself and discover who I really am.

I smiled at her as she picked up the menu I was looking at. "So, now that my lecture is done—geez, I sounded like my mother there for a sec—I guess I should like, teach you something about how to waitress."

Maybe Daphne wanted me to shadow her so I'd know exactly what *not* to do as a waitress. At least she was patient with me. She was patient when I dropped food. She was patient when I spilled water on one of the customers. And she was still patient when, less than an hour before closing, a man with dark wings breezed through the door and I dropped the coffee pot, sending shards of glass and scalding hot coffee rushing across the floor.

Chapter Nineteen

Coffee burned through my pantyhose, searing my skin. I swiped a handful of napkins from the dispenser and blotted my leg until the pain ceased.

From my vantage point, squatting behind the counter, I watched the man shake out his dark wings. Their rainbow sheen reminded me of an oil-slick.

"Geez, girl, are you okay?" Shelly dropped a wet rag on my foot. "Sorry, Ray." She nudged the dingy rag over with the toe of her shoe—her way of wiping up my mess—and leaned into the counter where he sat. "Hi, Kade." She rested her elbows on the Formica.

Kade?

Holy crap, holy crap, holy crap. This couldn't be real. My heart thundered like it was going to burst out of my chest. He—those black wings—couldn't be real. I swallowed, panic ticking in the back of my throat. Black wings, just like Allison's drawing. Just like Luke had been dreaming of. The same wings I had dreamt of last night.

One corner of his lip turned up in amusement. "How's it going, Shelly?" His rich, brown eyes slid to the left, taking me in. "Another tryout?"

"Aw!" She squealed and tapped his hand in a

playful scolding. "You're just awful. Ray's doin' great. I'll get a new pot of coffee started for you, hon."

She couldn't have seen what I saw; otherwise she'd be running straight for Morpheus's blue pill instead of flirting.

Great, a *Matrix* reference. I'd been spending way too much time with Lee.

From the far end of the counter, I heard Shelly scooping coffee and pouring water. The smell of stale bitterness wafted up from the floor, and the remaining droplets on my pantyhose turned cold. I avoided another look at him as I focused on scooping up the large pieces of glass.

"Careful you don't cut yourself." The thick smoke of his voice engulfed me.

I looked up to find him leaning over the counter. His folded wings cast an ominous black shadow over me. I darted up and hit my head on the overhang of the counter. Pain exploded behind my eyes, and white spots stormed my vision. Glass crunched under me as I slumped to the floor.

He chuckled and reached over the front of the counter to offer me his hand. "You're a jumpy one, aren't you?"

Only around creepy, unearthly guys.

I looked up at him.

Big mistake.

His dark hair was messily styled in the sexiest way. The natural bronze tone of his skin accompanied the strange darkness of those wings a little too well. Stubble traced a neat line along a too-perfect jaw. And those eyes—deeper than a bottomless pit. They seemed to breathe the very essence of night into my soul.

Studying him was stupid. Pointless. Dangerous.

My hand floated into his before I could stop it. His

hand was warm, his palm rough. A chill raced up my arm as I imagined his fingers wrapped around Tony's throat, holding a blade to Allison's wrists. And catching me in my nightmare. His face had been immersed in shadow, and his voice sounded completely different, but I would never forget those wings.

He pulled me to my feet.

"Thanks." I pulled my hand away as soon as I could think again.

I blinked the image of those cavernous depths away and went to grab a broom and dustpan from the back. The urge to run was stronger than it had ever been with any other winged men. But if I left, I would lose the job. And real or not, I was done letting wings ruin my life.

After tossing the remaining glass, I returned to my post behind the counter. I may have been trembling like a leaf, but I held my ground.

I watched everyone else in the diner to avoid looking at him—at his wings. Shelly tended to the three tables that were finishing up, the closest patron a lone man two tables back from the counter, the farthest a young couple snuggling in the same side of a booth in the corner.

This one couldn't know I could see him. That had caused nothing but problems with Cam. One slip-up and now he seemed to think we were friends, that I would help him out. He'd want to hear about this. Tension rode my shoulders, filling the space between them. I'd have to decide whether or not to tell him about Kade at school tomorrow. Then again, I had about as much trust in Cam as I had in loose-lipped Gina Garson.

A light gust drifted past me, blowing my ponytail back. I fought my panic and looked up to find those iridescent wings fully extended. The right side of his wing tip turned to smoke as it passed through a chair against the far wall. Moonlight poured in through the windows, and silver fire bounced off his wingspan, radiating through the diner with the shine of a disco ball.

Gooseflesh crept up my arms.

Why would he do that? When Cam had done the same thing in History class, he'd been testing me. I think. Because I was acting like, well, like a girl who could see wings.

His eyes searched my face, filled with an ominous curiosity. That could mean this one was testing me, too. But why? I'd been much more careful.

Aside from the people who thought I was crazy, Cam was the only one who knew—who believed—in my … ability to see them. It would be just my luck if he had shared that knowledge with Mr. Black Wings here.

This had never happened in Safford. Now, it seemed like everyone could see through me, straight to my secret.

Overwhelming fear stuck me to the floor. Determined to hold it together, I wiped all emotion from my face. I wouldn't expose my curse again. Cam had gotten lucky. Kade wouldn't. If he didn't already know.

Shelly returned with another check, passing straight through one of his extended wings. I practically snatched the check and credit card from her and ran it through the machine.

"Whoa there," she said.

"Sorry, it's just—you said I should do the next credit card transaction—so I can learn the system."

Each of the dark angel's feathers moved in its own rhythm, the ends waving like fingers.

I riveted my gaze to the machine.

"See, what'd I tell you, Kady? Ray's doing a great job."

Kady?

In the corner of my eye, I caught the glint of his smile. "She's a regular angel."

My eyes widened. My finger slipped, punched a wrong button, and the machine beeped a loud complaint at me. My breath came too loud, too fast. Instead of letting him crack me, I used the distraction of the credit card machine to conceal my fear. "Why is it beeping at me?" I pressed Enter again. The machine spit out some paper, almost like it was disgusted with me, and beeped again.

Shelly muscled in. "It's nothing; you just pushed the wrong code or something." She hit the red Cancel button, then swiped the card again.

"Sorry—"

"Stop saying sorry; it's fine." Shelly tore off the slip from the machine, the sound punctuating her words. "Be bold, Ray." She bumped her hip against mine and sauntered back to the couple's table.

All this time, I could feel his eyes on me.

The woman and her teenage son two booths in front of the lovers waved and exited the diner. The clock above the door told me Daphne was still on break. Too bad, 'cause now would be a great time for my own break.

Kade cleared his throat. I tried to think of something to do, anything to distract myself from the hypnotic ripples of his wings, and my stomach. I spotted another rag on the counter and flew to it, concentrating on making small circles over the celestially silver-speckled Formica.

I'd parted my lips to ask if he wanted anything else, when Kade's wings came down with the force of a hurricane. A millisecond later, the door opened, sending in a gust of wind. I blinked through the current, but got lost in a tangle of hair and lashes, the two jockeying for the more painful position in my eyes.

I swiped a hand across my eyes to clear my vision. A squeak told me the dark angel's weight had shifted in the counter's swivel seat. I looked up to find his hand coming toward me. One that could have murdered Allison and Tony. His fingers brushed the center of my cheek. I tripped over my own feet, stumbling back, and slammed into the back counter. I couldn't rub the chill on my arms away, or let him see the quaking of my knees behind the counter, without fear of being exposed.

His lips quirked the slightest bit. "Eyelash." He turned the angle of his hand to show me a black eyelash on his finger.

He knew I saw him. He had to.

The bell on the door chimed as it closed. The wind from the door could have replaced the force of his wings and saved my sorry ass from being completely exposed. Kade retracted his dark wings with a frown.

I swallowed and turned up a self-satisfied smile. After I was sure he saw it, I aimed it at the new customer. "Welcome to Roxy's. Sit anywhere you like." The guy plopped his messenger bag with a red Academy of Art University logo on the table by the door.

Shelly returned, almost brushing into the tip of a wing, with a fresh pot in one hand and a mug in the other. "How 'bout a slice of pie?" she asked Handsy Kade.

He didn't answer her, just continued to spear me with his stare.

Shelly exhaled loudly, looking from him to me. She propped a hand on her hip and cleared her throat, obviously not used to being ignored. The glare she leveled at me could freeze the latest flare up in the kitchen.

Yikes. "You know I only come for the coffee," he finally responded.

Shelly harrumphed. "Is that all? Just the coffee, not the sparkling conversation?"

Kade turned on the charm the second a coffee cup landed in front of him, flashing Shelly a winning smile. "The coffee and the company."

"Ray, would you mind?" Shelly asked, tilting her head toward the art student. "Daph should be off break soon. Wouldn't want her thinking you can't handle this."

Gladly.

Abandoning the dingy rag on the counter, I grabbed a menu from beside the register, relieved to have an excuse to put distance between us, and hurried toward the diner floor. Kade flicked his wings open again, effectively blocking my exit. I stopped, swallowing a gasp, just as he shot me a smug "gotcha" look.

Chapter Twenty

A sick feeling churned inside me. So far I'd done my best ignore-the-wings impression, while Kade did everything short of flying through the diner. But now he had me trapped. For whatever reason, I couldn't just pass through them like everything else. I'd learned that when Cam's had brushed my arm. I inched forward, looking smack dab into those terrifying black feathers.

"Problem?" He asked.

My heart thudded in my chest. There was no telling what he'd do if he found out I could see him. After all, Allison drew a man with wings—and therefore might have seen one—right before she died. What if Kade was that winged man? What if he killed people who could see him for what he was? What if Allison had the same ability as me and she was dead because he had learned her secret?

My anxiety flared, causing my hands to tremble, threatening to cripple my tenuous grip on reality.

He angled to the side to watch me closer, his wings leaving me the narrowest walkway. I leapt at the opportunity and edged through the small space. It probably looked odd to anyone who watched me edging along the wall, but at least I was out of there.

He knew now. He had to. I'd made it so obvious. I should have gone into the back instead. Insisted I had a headache or needed a break.

Something dragged across the counter. I jumped and spun around. Shelly shot me a confused look as she pulled Kade's mug closer to her.

Swallowing, I hurried to the art student's table. The lovey-dovey couple in the corner left before I was done scribbling down the student's order. Instead of returning to the counter, I shouted the medium-rare burger order to Shelly and cleared the couple's table.

To keep as far away from Kade as possible, I wiped down all the tables. Starting with the ones along the window, the farthest away from him. Still, I felt him watching me. I didn't turn around.

Back from break, Daphne delivered the last order of the night. The overwhelming scent of grease and stale coffee cloyed the air.

I took my time wiping the tables four, five, six times, doing my best not to startle at every sound.

When Shelly finally called out, "Closing time," I nearly collapsed with relief. "Rayna, time to get the eff outta here. I've got three parties to go to tonight, and I can't leave until you do."

Was it me, or did she sound a little colder than before? *She's the least of your issues*, I reminded myself while preparing to look over my shoulder. It took me three tries, but when I did, Kade was gone. His mug sat on the counter, cooling and untouched.

I hadn't even heard the bell chime when he left.

But at least, finally, something was going my way.

I tried to shake the feeling of being watched as I grabbed my backpack and hurried through the dining room and out the front door, assuming Shelly would lock up behind me. After all, I didn't have keys yet.

Dad's SUV waited at the curb. Right on time. I

climbed inside, swallowing the sour taste of fear in my mouth.

"How was your first day?"

Too close. Way too close. And scary beyond belief. I plunked down my heavy backpack and tentatively waved bye to Shelly. "Not bad."

"I like your uniform."

Annoyance flushed across my face. The thought of small talk made me itchy, like my skin was too tight. Spending the last hour of my shift avoiding Kade had left me exhausted and jumpy, and talking to my dad—the one person with the power to send me back to the SS Crazy—while I was too tired to censor myself was dangerous.

But he was trying. I knew he was trying. We were all still trying to figure out how to interact with each other after being apart for so long.

In the end, I tamped down my aggression and said, "Yeah, thanks. I wasn't enough of a freak, so I decided to dress like this." I tried to force out a laugh, but it sounded more like a sob, so I swallowed and shut my mouth.

He looked at me the way everyone had the last few days. God, I was sick of that look. I had to tell him something so he knew I wasn't losing it again. I considered divulging news of Tony DiMeeko's suicide, but thought better of it, considering how well that went last time. Instead, I went with the good old, "Sorry, Dad. It's been a long day."

He nodded and pulled away from the curb, fidgeting with the temperature knobs. "Ray, I'm concerned."

Not again. "Didn't we have enough of this last night? Can't we just have twenty-four hours of peace before we start this again?" I could feel the distance growing between me and Dad. I pulled down the unfeeling, stone face I'd relied on when he sent me away.

"It *has* been over twenty-four hours, but we don't have to talk if you don't want to."

Great.

"I do want to apologize for last night, for Laylah."

I peeked out from under the shade of stone. "Laylah can't apologize to me herself?" Tornadoes would swirl and carry me away to *Oz* before that was going to happen.

Dad sighed, but his shoulders bunched with tension. "She said some hurtful things, but she was only expressing herself—" He pressed more dashboard buttons, always fiddling with his toys. "—which is what they told us to do in therapy—the family therapy she and I went to whenever you were away."

Away. That was what he called it. Like it had been my choice to leave. I gripped the side of the door to keep from screaming.

"It was difficult for her when you went … in for treatment. She looked up to you—" Looked. Past tense. "—but it's been her and me for a long time." Because I had checked out for so long. "We're all readjusting. We're going through a sort of reformatting. It might not hurt if you two spent more time together, tried wiping the hard drive clean and starting again."

I rolled my eyes. It was just like Dad to turn to his computers when things got too personal. Like that would help him distance himself so he didn't have to deal with something emotional. "So now it's my fault?" I didn't want to play the antagonist, but that seemed to be the role he kept pushing me into. Even now I could feel the wedge growing between me and Team Dad-and-Laylah. "You know, Dad, that might actually happen if she didn't spend every waking hour with those damn Musketeers of hers." I wrapped my arms around my stomach and looked out the window. "I feel like she told them." And why shouldn't she tell them? I thought about Laylah's friends. Not that I really cared what they thought, but Laylah could have told them her messed-up older sister was certifiable. To stay away from her because she still belonged locked up. That living with me was a nightmare of psychiatric proportions, and no one should have to put up with that. "The way they look at me. It's like they know I'm crazy—was—was crazy. I'm—I'm totally not anymore. I don't see … anything."

God, I was such a bad liar. Dad and Laylah had to know I still wasn't quite right. Maybe they were just biding their time, waiting for me to snap so the SS Crazy would have to take me back. Blood roared behind my eyes, sneaking in a new ache. Sweat formed in unlikely places, slicking the back of my neck, the crooks of my knees, and the flats of my palms.

Please don't send me back there. Please don't send me back there. Please don't send me back there.

He patted my knee. "It's okay, Ray. I know you're in remission. Relax."

I did. Slightly. Wondering if he was humoring me or trying to convince himself, too.

"Your sister would never tell her friends. And they make Laylah as happy as a Seagate four-terabyte hard drive makes me. As long as that keeps up, those girls are welcome any day, any time. The same goes for Lee. Speaking of, we haven't seen much of him in the last few days. I miss talking graphics cards and beta games; he's the only one I know outside of work who can keep up. Is everything okay with you two?"

Our SUV rounded the corner. Our street was mostly quiet once the sun went down, the families around us all home from a long day. The car's headlights brightened the trees and small planters that lined the street as we passed, but left them in shadows as we crept forward. Darkness engulfed the park across the street.

We pulled up to the house. The porch light illuminated my potted flowers and plants crowding the front stairs. The car reached the steep down slope of the driveway, and we rolled toward our basement garage. Through the side mirror, I spotted the tree with the halo from the street lamp above. I swallowed, banishing the memory of the haunting nightmare out of my head.

Dad pushed the garage-door opener and flicked a questioning look at me.

Lee, he asked about Lee. "I think so." I didn't know it was a lie until the words rolled off my tongue. Lee and his mom had been close since his dad's death, but he didn't normally spend so much time with her right after school. He usually spent that time with me. Was he avoiding me? He wasn't acting any differently, but then I'd been distracted and hadn't been paying the closest attention to him, either.

Just one more thing I didn't want to think about right now.

Dad pulled into the garage and killed the engine. We got out of the car and trekked back up the driveway toward the front door. No one liked climbing the basement stairs. They were rickety and in desperate need of repair.

"He's been spending a lot of time at home," I added, hoping that would convince Dad to drop it.

Dad opened the door for us, and I swung my backpack over my shoulder. "I've got loads of homework to do, and I had a big bowl of soup at the diner, so I'm going to hit the books. Goodnight, Dad."

I headed straight through the living room, taking the stairs two at a time, not waiting for a reply. I spent the rest of the night in my room, but I didn't so much as crack a book; not a school book, anyway. Instead, I skipped the hot shower I'd promised myself, grabbed a pen, and scribbled in my crazy-book until well past midnight.

Chapter Twenty-One

The next morning, fatigue burned behind my eyes and weighed heavy in my limbs. I threw on dark jeans and a lavender floral top, brushed my teeth, and slid on flat, brown suede boots which would have looked great with my Aunt Nora original jacket. But that was sitting in an evidence bag somewhere. I settled for a black, fleece-lined hoodie.

I made my way down to Roxy's Diner, a place I was convinced I'd want to burn down in a week if Kade kept coming in, and waited for Lee.

He never showed.

If I had a cell phone I could've called him, but to me, cell phones were just another leash.

I waited twenty minutes, then finished the walk down the tourist-encrusted street alone, reaching the third floor before the warning bell rang.

I slid into my seat, feeling like Honors English and I hadn't exactly been friends lately. In an effort to enjoy part of my day before a set of wings ruined it, I buried my nose in my favorite summer-romance novel until the late bell rang. When I looked up from the book—which had almost every other page dog-eared— I noticed an empty seat beside me. Cam was either late or he wasn't showing up for first period. It had only been a few days since he'd arrived, but he didn't seem the type to skip.

Unless he was off looking for Luke.

Or another victim.

Or was that Kade's job?

I pushed those thoughts to the furthest part of my mind and pulled out our assigned book, *Fahrenheit 451.* I didn't know anything for sure. Cam didn't look like a lying murderer, but then, what does a lying murderer look like? Probably more like Kade. I flipped through my worn copy of the book with more force than necessary, ripping a few of the pages. Nothing was certain. I just had to keep my eye on those two and not drive myself crazy in the process.

I had the next two periods with Luke. He missed both of them.

By lunch, the smell of my veggie chips and sugar-free juice made my stomach lurch.

"You notice Gina Garson and Luke aren't here today?" Lee said between bites of his tuna-fish sandwich.

Had I said something out loud? I shifted in my seat. "Of course I didn't notice. Why would I notice?"

Lee stopped chewing. "A little touchy today?"

"Yeah, right. Wait, Gina Garson's gone too?" She'd seemed all right yesterday, but she'd been sick enough Tuesday to interrupt my pill-popping session. I hoped it wasn't serious.

"Yep. I heard she's …" His gaze shifted around the lunchroom and his voice dropped to a whisper, "… pregnant."

"Pregnant?" I repeated.

"Keep your voice down. Do you want the whole school to know?"

I resisted an eye roll; if Lee knew, that meant the whole school probably already knew.

He adjusted his black-rimmed square frames. "Is that why you're upset?" He rewrapped his sandwich and pulled out a chocolate bar. "You actually *like* that tool, don't you?"

"What?"

"You sprang to life the moment I said Luke's name. He's been trying to get at you since you got here. Didn't I tell you he was bad news?" Lee set his chocolate bar down on the table without opening it. I'd never seen him refuse candy before. Whatever the reason, this hate for Luke was bigger than I'd thought.

"What happened between you two?" I asked.

"Why would you spy on Luke and Gina yesterday? Who does that?"

Great, now *that* was all over school, too? I couldn't catch a freaking break!

"I—it was stupid. Nothing."

"He got all up in my face about it, like I knew what you were up to." His brows drew together. "If my teacher hadn't been there, I swear he would've tried to kick my ass."

I balked at his use of an actual, real-life curse word. My stalking had intensified whatever issues Luke had with Lee, but why threaten him for something I'd done? It made no sense. Maybe whatever Luke and Gina had been talking about was important enough to send him over the edge.

"So is that why you don't like Cam, 'cause you're already in-*like* with Luke?"

"Um? Not really. Lee—"

"I'm right, aren't I?" A worried peak formed a mountain above his brows. "Ray, you *didn't*. Not with that jerk."

"Didn't what? Lee ... I ..." What could I say? *No, Lee, I didn't hook up with Luke. I'm concerned for him because the suicides happening around here might not be suicides at all, but attacks by winged men. Oh, and by the way, I was in a mental hospital before I came here, and I very well might be going back there if I see another person with wings.*

I couldn't lie to my best friend—my only friend. But I couldn't exactly tell him the truth either, or I *would* be going back. I had no choice but to let him think whatever he wanted.

I dropped my head into my hands. Could this day get any worse?

"So you *did* hook up with him."

His accusation knotted my stomach, but I remained silent.

"Wow, okay. Thanks for tellin' me, Ray." His voice was low, betrayed. "Whatever. It's good to know what a great friend you are. And thanks for askin' where I was this morning. It shows how much you care."

My head shot up. "Oh crap." I had screwed up. Once again, someone else had a problem, and I was stuck thinking about myself, being the worst friend possible. Lee was one of my few tethers to reality. Lately, life felt like a hot air balloon ride, one where the ropes holding the basket were snapping. I'd already lost Laylah. Only Dad and Lee were left now.

"I was there this time—really. And I'm sorry I missed yesterday. I wanted to ask you why you didn't show today; I've just had a lot on my mind." I flinched at my words. Too much on my mind. Too distracted with things that didn't involve him.

He wiped the emotion from his face. "No problem." He stuffed his half-eaten sandwich and unopened chocolate bar into his crumpled lunch bag and stood. "I'll catch up with you tomorrow or something."

"But tomorrow's a faculty day, and I'm working all weekend—" He was already walking away.

The rest of the school day was a blur. My stomach

complained about its vast emptiness as I hiked up our hill alone. Lee hadn't been waiting outside for me after school. I half-expected to find him inside Roxy's, or at the bus stop playing with his phone, but he wasn't there, either.

I paused outside Roxy's, leaning against a streetlamp to collect myself. My eyes kept darting to the empty bus stop. I'd managed to alienate my only friend. Luke might be in some kind of trouble with the angels. And in five minutes, I'd have to slip on the world's ugliest outfit, smile, and pretend to be normal for the next five hours. Like I even knew what normal was anymore.

Two days ago, I was desperate for this job. For a piece of normal. Now I would have given anything to slog home and hole up under the blankets for the rest of the weekend. I was beginning to learn it didn't matter what I did; I couldn't escape the crazy. It was part of me; it was who I was. The best I could do was try to hold it together while everything unraveled around me. Because I wouldn't go back to the SS Crazy. I *wouldn't*. So I pulled myself together. I gulped in the crisp October air, swept my hair back into a ponytail, secured it with a black ribbon, and began my shift.

***

Friday's faculty day meant no school, but I still had to work the dinner shift. Nothing went right. Shelly had the night off, so it was up to me and Daphne, who ordered me around with the finesse of a slave driver. I messed up orders, spilled food, and broke plates. The worst part had to be when the senior citizens came in for the early-bird dinner special—a tasty-smelling pot roast—and one broke out his cell phone, calling all his friends to come check out the new bumbling, fumbling waitress at Roxy's.

The old buzzards filed in over the next hour, a select few snickering at me as they packed the place with blue hair, canes, and walkers with little green tennis balls on the ends. With only two waitresses, Daphne and I had our hands full—Daphne waiting on the customers, me cleaning up my own messes.

The rush eventually ended. My feet ached, my knees and ankles rebelled when I moved, and if I smelled another pot roast, I'd have to puke. The diner closed at midnight on Fridays, but my shift ended at ten. Daphne was in the back, "resting her corns." If I had a choice between seeing those corns and smelling the pot roast, hands down, I'd take the pot roast.

My last customer of the night, a pretty blonde, sat alone. Her fork clanked against her plate as I trekked toward her with as genuine a smile as I could scrape up.

"Anything else I can get you?" I asked, check in hand.

She shook her head and rubbed her flat stomach. I placed the check on the corner of the table.

The door's bell chimed. I glanced up and saw nothing but black feathers, tanned skin, and handsome boy. My heart twisted, and a shudder crawled under my skin. I suddenly missed the rush crowd desperately. I forced my chin up and cleared the fear from my throat. "Coffee?"

His dark eyes were shaded as he nodded and claimed the same squeaky stool he'd occupied on Wednesday night. He dipped one wing and glanced over his shoulder, grinning at my very interested-looking customer.

I snatched the coffee pot off its warming plate and slid a mug across the counter.

"You mind making a fresh pot?" he asked, full attention on me now. "The ladies always make me a fresh pot."

"I'm sure they do," I mumbled acridly as I stomped to the coffee station. It wouldn't surprise me if *the ladies* all fell at his feet, either.

I dumped five scoops of ground coffee into a new filter, added water to the line, and flipped the switch. I spun back around, telling myself I wouldn't see those hideous, intriguing black things. But I did. "Can I get you anything else while you're waiting?" I didn't even try to force another smile. I was tapped out. On edge. Being so close to him did strange things to me.

He shook his head, his gaze following me in a mesmerizing way.

I looked down, avoiding those dark pools of danger.

"Can I tell you something?" His voice flowed like the roughest velvet, softening my resolve.

My temper flared at my reaction to his voice. I slapped my hand down on the counter and glared at him. "No, you can't, but I'm going to tell *you* something." My self-control was dissolving, things slipping from my lips I never intended to think—let alone say—with him in earshot. The weight of a horrible week pressed down on me harder than I could handle. The appearance of Cam, Allison's suicide, Cam discovering I could see him, Tony's suicide, an introduction to the first set of black wings I'd ever seen, the arguments with Dad and Laylah …

I closed my eyes in an effort to calm myself down, but it didn't work. Kade was pushing all the wrong buttons. Anger steamrolled my fear, and I let loose on him. "I know what you are. Those abominations you carry behind you? I *see* them."

Chapter Twenty-Two

W hat had I done? I backed away, fighting to keep my horror from showing. His face, on the other hand, was suddenly as expressive as stone. A ripple ran over his wings, and I got the sudden impression he was feeling *something*. Maybe he didn't bother to hide his wing movement because most people can't see them. But I could, and they were way more expressive than his face could possibly be. I couldn't be one hundred percent sure what that ripple meant, but I'd damn sure be paying closer attention to them from now on.

I tried my best to keep my voice even as I added, "And don't think, even for a second, that I'm afraid of you."

He stilled. "Actually, I was going to tell you the coffee pot's overflowing. You added too much water."

I'd expected him to be shocked, angry, threatening to rip my head off my shoulders. If this was a trick to get me off my guard, he had another thing coming. I'd learned quickly—after the first time I'd been attacked by a fellow patient—to never turn your back on someone who just might be crazier than you. But when the sound of a small waterfall caught my attention, I did turn. Hot coffee rained from the back counter into a fast-growing pool of brown bitterness.

"Shit!"

I threw a rag into the slop and ran into the kitchen for a mop. I searched frantically for the bucket and Pine-Sol Daphne had used to mop up my last mess less than an hour ago. When I finally found them tucked away in the opposite corner, I returned to the ever-growing spill. The mop sloshed around in the liquid before it absorbed a single drop, and the coffee still streamed. I switched the machine off and unplugged it so I could wipe up the rest of the mess.

When another of my wonderful messes was cleaned, I looked up again. He was gone. I pressed my hand to my chest and almost sunk below the counter until I remembered my other customer.

I steadied myself, measuring each step as I walked to the blonde's empty table, needing something easy and normal to calm my nerves. A fifty-cent tip. Par for my day. I stuffed it into my pocket and collected her plate. The pie was only half-eaten. I returned to the counter and dropped the plate off in the dirty dish bin.

"What's this?" Daphne emerged from the back, wearing the same look she'd had every time I'd failed at my tasks the last two days.

"Trouble with the coffeepot."

"The only trouble with the coffeepot is that you don't know how to use it. I'll rinse the mop; why don't you go take out the garbage."

Taking out the garbage, a job that was impossible to screw up. I cinched the bag shut with a plastic strip tie and dragged it through the kitchen, past the office, and out the back door into the chilly fall night. The dumpster was only a few yards from the door. I took a step toward it, but stopped when I spotted a set of familiar black wings folded around a blonde.

I squinted through the darkness, spotting that unmistakably messy-sexy hair beside bright platinum blonde. I heard noises. Were they ...?

Yep. They were making out next to the trash bin. How, well, trashy.

The iridescent wings shimmered, growing brighter with every passing second. If Cam's wings glowed like the sun, Kade's shone like a starry night. The girl drew in a long, jagged breath. Kade tilted his face to the sky, lips parted, as if waiting to catch raindrops on his tongue. He sucked in a mouthful of air like he was drowning. Starlight danced and swirled along his wings.

Without it, I'd have never seen the strange, crimson smoke that curled between Kade and the woman. The blonde's head rolled to her shoulder, and more smoke poured from her mouth. He lowered his head to hers, drinking in the smoke like he was stealing something from her. Something important. Something necessary.

The bag of garbage clunked to the ground. My hands were shaking so badly I was surprised I'd managed to hang on to it that long. He turned to me then, his eyes consumed with black. Under the glow of his wings, the red smoke deepened as it disappeared into him.

My feet screamed at me to run. And run I did, back into the kitchen, through the dining room, and straight out the front door.

"Kay, wait!" I heard him shout, even as I sprinted up the street. "Kay!" he screamed again. I ran faster.

A tiny part of my brain noticed he'd screwed up my name. Kay, not Ray. At least he didn't know my name.

I darted across the street. Headlights blared, casting my long shadow across the asphalt. A horn honked. To my right, a car barreled toward me. Tires screeched. I jumped out of the way, barely escaping being flattened on the dark street.

With my heart threatening to explode in my chest, I kept going. I took a few different turns in case Kade was on my heels. Right, left, up another block, then left again.

I sprinted faster. My legs were weak, but I pressed them on as if my life depended on it. Because I was pretty sure it did. Shadows seemed to be following me. Dark corners breathed with life. Glowing eyes peeked out from everywhere.

A streetlight illuminated the reflective white street sign at the top of the block. Sacramento Street. I was still several blocks from home, but at least I'd be on the right street. I made a left, looking over my shoulder as I rounded the corner. No one was there. That meant nothing. He could be anywhere.

My legs shook from fatigue, and my lungs burned with a fire I couldn't sate. Tears blurred the world in front of me. I pushed forward, glancing behind me every few seconds to make sure he wasn't behind me. Hunting. Coming to steal from me whatever he'd stolen from that girl. Or maybe just to kill me. But there was nothing but shadows, buildings, and streetlights.

When I turned to glance behind me again, I slammed into something. Pain shot through my shoulder. My breath whooshed out, leaving my lungs empty. Strong arms wrapped around me. Arms that kept me from tumbling back onto the concrete. Or escaping.

Adrenaline kicked in. I fought through tear-clouded vision and oxygen-deprived lungs. My kicking and struggling did little good against the tight grip that wouldn't loosen. Every beat of my heart slammed against my ribcage. I tried to beat my fists against him, but they were clamped between us. Fire crept up my lungs, searing them before I could scream.

A deep, worried voice broke through my panic. "Rayna!"

Rayna, not Kay. It wasn't Kade.

I melted in relief for half a second. Then I remembered that Kay was my mother's name.

Chapter Twenty-Three

Her name was Kayleigh, and only Dad ever called her Kay. I couldn't help remembering how Dad's eyes always softened every time she asked him for something, her head tilted to the side, and he'd say, "All right, Kay." When Mom wasn't on one of her long, working vacations, she'd stay home with Laylah and me, turn up the music, and we'd all hold hands and dance. Even when Dad would take Laylah and me out, or bring us home from school, Mom would be waiting on the couch with snacks, always so happy to see us. Mom was the glue that held us all together, the light in Dad's laughter, the master of the kitchen, the Band-aid queen, and hair-fixer. Mom was Kay, the love of Dad's life and the best mother two girls could have ever asked for.

I blinked away tears, shoving memories of my mom back to a safe corner of my mind, and made out a blurry head of blond hair—*blond, not black*. I'd given up my fight, but tension still locked my knees. Digging my nails into my palms tore the soft skin, dripping warm blood down my wrists.

"Rayna, are you all right? What happened?" Slate eyes searched my face, my throat, my arms. Cam stopped at the blood on my wrists. As quickly as his arms wrapped around me, they retreated. "Are you hurt?" He took my elbows in his hands gently, allowing my fists to uncurl. "Who did this?" His fingers clenched tighter to me. "Rayna, what happened to you?" The power in his voice, his concern, focused me.

I backed away. He reluctantly released me, his grip tensing before slacking.

Panic intensified inside me. My breathing stopped short. I turned in every direction, trying to get my bearings, looking for a counterweight to keep me from tumbling over the edge.

We were in a park. The same park he'd walked me to on Tuesday. Over the tips of his wings, I could see the white church across the street.

But ... Mom. Kade. Black wings. Red. My vision tunneled. My eyes welled. The air I breathed wasn't enough. And cold. It was so cold. A shiver racked my body. My teeth chattered together.

Cam stared at me, concern obvious on his face. "Is everything okay?" When I didn't respond, he grabbed my shoulders and shook me. "Rayna."

I pushed away from him and swiped at the hair that had fallen over my shoulder. He let me go. My knees threatened to buckle, and my head spun.

Cam's arm curled behind my back, guiding me to the nearest bench. His warm, frustrated breath rushed by my ear. He sat me on the bench and kneeled in front of me. "Can you tell me what happened?"

I swallowed and shook my head. There was no way to explain what I'd seen in the alley. What Kade had done to that poor girl ... or why he'd called me Kay. I glanced back down the street, searching all the places the amber streetlights failed to touch. When I looked again, the sight of Cam's wings sent a torrent of chills up one side of my spine and down the other.

"Was someone chasing you?" His eyes narrowed

and searched mine. If he was looking for sanity, he wouldn't find it there, not with me.

I looked away, choosing instead to watch the shadows in the park. During the day, the park was lively, beautiful. At night ... another shiver skipped across my shoulders, and I dragged my gaze back to Cam's. "I don't know." I cleared my desert-dry throat and continued. "I was at work ... worst day ever ... took out the trash ... he was there, like a ... vampire, stealing ... blood-red smoke."

Silence cloaked the air.

I wasn't making any sense. He thought I was crazy. *I* thought I was crazy. It was a far too familiar feeling.

"Red smoke?" He whispered across the night. "Where?" Urgency spiked in his voice. "Where did you see this?"

My heart fought against the adrenaline. "What was it?"

His expression took on a hard edge. His gaze burrowed into mine. Like he believed me. "Where, Rayna?"

"What—what was it?"

His tongue peeked out from between the dryness of his lips to moisten them. "He ..." His brows drew together and he shook his head. After a long, long time, Cam finally dropped his head down toward his chest and sighed. "He has to be a Dark One. An angel who chose to stray from the path of light and was cast out of Heaven and away from the light of God."

I reeled from the information, but pressed forward. "A—and what ... I saw him doing?"

"A punishment handed down from on high. Or, rather, from on low." He lifted his chin. A fight warred within his eyes. "I wish there was an easier way to tell you."

I could barely breathe. "Tell me ...?"

"Everything you need to know." He blinked and shook his head, then pushed on. "The Fallen Ones are destined to roam the earth, feeding on that which they once defended. Souls."

I gasped. Souls? Human souls? My thoughts swam in circles before they tipped over the edge. They really were angels. I couldn't move, just sat there staring into the night, shock numbing everything around me. It was all too much, and my brain needed a vacation—one for which it was already packed. The world seemed to get further away. I'd spent years in this state of mind, and it seemed all too easy to give in to the familiar tug of insanity.

Cam's fingertips brushed the backs of my hands. When I didn't pull away, his grip firmed around my fingers, warm and soothing as his thumbs drew lazy, calming circles in the sensitive skin between my thumb and forefinger, bringing me gently back from the brink of madness. A flutter tensed in my stomach.

Finally, I found I could meet Cam's gaze, I could bring air into my lungs without fear, and I could ask the one question I didn't want to know the answer to. "Are you really sent from God?"

Cam closed his eyes in a pained gesture, like I'd punched him in the stomach. "There is a hierarchy, a chain of command that ... I'm ... not allowed to divulge the specifics of."

"But you just did."

He stood from his kneeling position and threw his hands up in the air. "That was information you *needed*." He huffed and eased onto the bench beside me. "I'm not supposed to interfere in human affairs. But there are a few things you have to know." He took my hands in his again, stroking my knuckles with the sides of his thumbs.

Wind rustled through the dying tree leaves, and a

chill crept across my skin. I drew my elbows in closer to ward off the cold.

"I can't reveal too much. We've never asked for a human's assistance before, but you're special. I've been instructed to answer all your questions, within reason."

I pulled my hands free from his, not liking the sudden shift in the conversation. "Special how?"

"You can see us. Angels, I mean. And apparently Dark Ones as well." He swallowed, his thumbs now circling over his own clenched fists. "I … truly didn't think it was possible. A human has never been able to see us before. When I caught you staring at my wings, I didn't know what to do. I reported you to my superiors that afternoon—I had to. I couldn't hide something like this. I know you have no reason to trust me, but I'm asking you to do just that. You've seen what their kind does. How they survive. All my kind want is peace. They've been responsible for so much bloodshed. Including, we believe, the deaths of your two classmates."

The weight of a bus slammed into my chest. My head spun. "Good angels, bad angels. Tony and Allison's suicides." My chest rose and fell, inflating and deflating faster than should be possible. Lightness filled my head, threatening to lift it off my shoulders, then slam it into the ground.

"Rayna, stay with me."

I dug my hands through my hair, wishing I could dig in the ground instead, needing soil beneath my nails and bright petals to help me see clearly.

"I know this is a lot to take in." He kneeled in front of me, pulling me back from the edge with his hands. A strange, bluish-white light beamed from his eyes as he looked at me, into me. The spinning stopped.

He blinked, and the light disappeared. I felt calmer

somehow. I only had a second to wonder what he'd done before he continued. "Your world is in peril." He rushed his words, probably trying to get them out before I lost it completely. "That's why we've been sent down. Evil is here. The Fallen have been in search of souls to add to their army for centuries. Lost souls. What better way to send a soul to Hell than by making its last act on Earth a sin? Now, though, the situation here is different. We've heard rumors that these souls, your classmates, are being used to build something specific. We think it could be a weapon."

"What kind of weapon?" Cold fingers encircled my heart. I couldn't shake the image of demonic ... angels using Allison and Tony, sucking up every soul they could like the proton packs in *Ghostbusters*. A smaller twinkle of sadness reminded me of the first time Lee and I watched his favorite ghost movie together.

Cam pried my hands from my hair and waited for me to blink. "We don't know for sure." I lowered my head, ready to retreat. "Stay with me." His voice was smooth, calm. He cupped my face, tilting my head up to look at him. "I'm here. I know it's shocking. Ask me anything. It may help."

Demons. Demons were real. Bad angels. A weapon. No. *No.* None of it was real. Couldn't be. Not real. *Not. Real.* I whispered those words to myself, over and over, as I rocked on the bench, back and forth. Back and forth. *Not real. Not real. Not ...*

"Rayna," he drew out my name in a whisper. "I need you with me." The solid steel of his irises strengthened me. His eyes reminded me of a tropical, silver-blue hibiscus called Feelin' Blue. Especially when they lit up in that unnaturally bright way again. The light flooded into me, calming me.

I straightened up. His fingers fell from my face and wound around my hands again. This time I moved my fingertips along his hand, my heart pounding with each stroke.

"How did you do that?"

A small smile brightened his face. "I told you: people are at ease with me."

"They *are* at ease, or you use that thing with your eyes to *put them* at ease, like some kind of angel ... magic?"

"You can *see* when I do that?"

I nodded, releasing his hands again. He rested them on the knees of my pink uniform.

"We shouldn't be having this conversation. I shouldn't be interfering."

Now that Cam's liquid calm had been injected into my veins, I took advantage of his willingness to answer questions, and tried an easy one first. "So these ... Fallen," I tested the word on my tongue. Didn't like it. "They're responsible for the suicides?"

Cam nodded. "I don't know how, but we think they're forcing your classmates' hands."

I left the bench, testing the stability of my legs. They were good enough to pace on. "How do I know this isn't a trick?" *How do I know I'm not completely off the deep end?*

"I can't answer that for you." He hesitated. "Does it feel real?"

I scratched my palms. They burned. I remembered the cuts I'd made. Red coated the inside of my hands and wrists. I checked Cam's and found dried blood on them too. "My blood—I'm sorry." With my clean forearm, I tried wiping it away furiously. The friction of our skin burning like fire.

He stopped me. "It's nothing to worry about. Maybe if you tried to focus ..."

Like I wasn't trying already. "You're sure Tony and Allison's deaths were ... murders?" It made no sense.

He took his time answering. "Unfortunately."

"How many of *them* are there?"

"Here? There could be one, or twenty. There's no way to know. We really have to—"

"There was a picture. Allison saw—drew—the dark silhouette of a man with wings. Tony drew the same thing in his notebook, and Luke told me he's been seeing it in his dreams. Is that why they're after him?"

Cam stood. He turned his back on me and ran a hand through his hair. "Rayna, I … you can't just expect me to—" He huffed and turned back around. "I was sent for Luke specifically, to guard his life. He's strong, which is why they want him. I have no idea about the drawings."

"You were sent? Like, a guardian angel?"

"Something like that." He pressed his hands down in the air. "Listen, after I spoke to my superiors about you being able to see me, they ordered me to find out if you could see the Dark Ones. My kind can't. Their wings are as invisible to us as ours are to them."

"I can't do this."

"You can help save lives."

"You'd say just about anything to get me on board, wouldn't you?"

He closed his eyes. When he opened them again, the gray that swept over me was softer than silk. His stony expression was gone, leaving only kindness. "No. The last thing I want to do is mislead you."

A shiver crept up my arms. "A liar would say that, too."

His jaw clenched beneath a half-day's worth of blond stubble. "I can't make you trust me. You must make your own choice."

"But you can make me *feel* something."

"That's an artificial calm. It won't hurt you."

He couldn't really expect me to trust him. Them.

Angels. Especially when every appearance of their wings had sent me back to that place, stripped me of my freedom, and basically brought me back to square one with my therapy. Therapy I'd never needed, if they were real. And now he wanted me to seek them out. Purposely. How crazy did he think I was?

What if Cam wasn't an angel at all, but some sicko who got off on messing with the clinically ill?

I knew nothing about him.

I needed to test him, to know if I could really trust the things I'd been seeing. But if he was messing with me, he'd just lie. I stepped closer. He didn't move, but watched me warily. Before I was aware of what I was doing, I touched his arm. His breathing stalled. I tentatively removed my hand. Emptiness welled inside me. I tested a theory, pressing my fingertips to his chest. There was nothing. Cam didn't have a heartbeat.

Yeah, that certainly helps the fight for sanity.

Then again, those lips didn't help, either. Especially now, when they were so close I could touch them with my own. If I'd wanted to. Did I want to? I'd never done anything like that before. What would angel lips taste like? Sunshine? Marshmallows? Or something altogether different? Maybe buttered-popcorn jelly beans.

Could he be influencing me? Distracting me? Christ, he doesn't even have a heartbeat!

I almost pulled away, but I had to know. I rose to the toes of my horrid nurse shoes and skimmed my hands toward his shoulders. He tensed.

"What are you doing?" His voice was a rough whisper.

I shook my head, reaching farther over his shoulder. Soft feathers and numbness brushed my fingers.

Cam stumbled back, shuddering.

He'd given me answers. Now it was up to me to believe them.

When he spoke, his voice was thick, affected. "Can you tell me where you saw The Fallen?"

"Roxy's Diner, where I work."

The night shaded his face as he looked down at me. "Can you tell me anything about him?"

I nodded, fighting back flashes of soul-sucking and sparkling black wings. "Tall, dark hair, dark eyes. His name's Kade."

"Kasade." His voice adopted a rough edge.

"Kass-aid? What, do you know him or something?"

His fists balled by his side, the action creating an odd pressure inside my head. "Yeah, I know him."

"Did he kill Allison and Tony?"

The disdain in his face bloomed, intensifying the pounding behind my eyes. "Maybe."

I swallowed and pressed a hand against my right eye. "Well you obviously know who he is and what he looks like. Why don't you just take him out or whatever? Why do you need me?"

"There could be more than just him. And if there are, you could be instrumental in helping us save lives. More than just Luke's."

I shuffled two steps back, fighting to get a handle on the pain.

Cam looked up at me and blinked. He was different again, softer. In a moment, my headache faded.

"Did you just … give me a headache?"

"I'm sorry. I guess I have to watch my feelings around you. You're more sensitive to them than others. Which is how I think you ended up here."

"What do you mean?"

"I was thinking about you just before you showed up."

"Nuh-uh. No way. I was running from that

monster." I checked over my right shoulder, then the left, unable to believe I'd let my guard down enough to forget that he might have followed me here.

"It's okay if you don't believe me. Eventually, you will."

"Right." I nodded. "Wait, why were you thinking about me?"

A small smile broke across his face, but was gone in a blink. "It's late. Can I walk you home? His fingers pressed against the middle of my back and gently led me forward.

Great. I was caught in the middle of an angel war and *both* sides scared the crap out of me. *Figures.*

"Yeah, okay."

Cam wanted my help and unwavering trust while he gave me next to nothing, except a headache. But with Kade out there, I was grateful for the escort. I angled toward home, no longer afraid to show Cam where I lived. If he wanted me dead, he'd already had two chances, and I was still alive.

"So does this mean you're real? Really real?"

Cam's hand was still on my back. He didn't say anything, but he didn't need to. I couldn't get any more proof than I already had.

Chapter Twenty-Four

T he moment I came through the front door, I discovered how late it really was.

Dad sat in the dining-room chair facing the foyer, arms crossed over his chest. "Where have you been? I was there at ten to pick you up. Your boss said you ran out before your shift was over. I drove around for half an hour looking for you." His fingers drummed over his arm, a sure sign he was barely keeping his voice under control.

I rubbed the back of my neck, suppressing the utter joy inside me. I'd been forbidden from seeing the men with wings—angels—had lost so much of my life denying them, but now … now I knew they were real. Or my symptoms were intensifying. But Cam … his questions, his answers, our entire conversation, I couldn't have made that up.

Tears pricked my eyes and my nose stung. I wasn't crazy. Not for seeing them. Three years in-and-out of the SS Crazy. Pills. Therapy. None of it had been necessary.

I would never take another med again.

My mouth slid opened, and I took my first full breath in years. Hope for true sanity bloomed in my chest.

I hadn't allowed myself to think about it on my way home, and I sure as hell couldn't relish it now. They'd all still see it as crazy because they couldn't know the truth. I also wasn't prepared to pull an excuse out of the air. But I should have been. "Dad, could we please talk about this in the morning? I had a weird day and—"

He uncrossed his arms and leaned forward in his chair. "Have you been crying?" His voice softened. He left his seat and hugged me. I tried to stand still and let him. "Do you need to talk to someone?" The way he said *someone* told me he meant a professional.

Not Dr. G. I shook my head, but he only squeezed me tighter. His leniency should have been an incredible gift, but Dad usually only softened this way because he was afraid of pushing too hard, worried I'd break. He must have thought I was losing it again. Running out of the diner before my shift ended probably made me look pretty crazy.

The fragile way he stroked my hair made me realize just how close I was to being sent back. Tears blurred my eyes for the twentieth time tonight, and the wetness streaked down my face.

"Don't cry, Ray, please. We can talk about this tomorrow, after I get you a cell phone."

"Cell phone? I don't want one." Of all the things to obsess over, I chose the damn cell phone. Guess it was easier to fight than mental hospital stuff.

"I know you don't, but you are getting one, and you *will* answer when I call. I need to know where you are. At all times." The dad-voice intensified.

Exactly why I didn't want one. "Sorry, Dad. Not happening."

He stepped back, breaking the hug. "You don't have a choice, young lady." He returned to his seat, tapping his foot on the floor. "Unless you quit your job, then maybe we can put off the cell phone."

After what I saw there today, quitting didn't sound like such a bad idea. The thought of having to return to Roxy's Diner and see that ... that soul stealer, to face him with the terror dripping from my palms, made me feel ill.

Dad frowned, emphasizing lines around his mouth I'd never noticed before. His long face showed how tired he was, how ready to give up. Would things be different if Mom was still here? *Of course they would.* I pushed the thought away.

"I'll take the cell phone. And keep my job."

I trudged up the stairs to my room, washed my face, and climbed into bed. Anxiety pounded through me every time I closed my eyes. There would be no sleep this night.

***

Saturday came and went without a trace of Kade, though I checked around every corner and held my breath whenever the bell over the diner door chimed— especially after nightfall.

Sunday broke my lucky streak. Daphne rested her corns in the back, and Shelly called in sick—something about her partying too hard and never making it home. Between two or three in the afternoon, the sky darkened with the promise of rain. It was then the soul stealer strolled through the diner door.

Of all the diners in all the world ... he has to stroll into mine. Mom's favorite movie had been *Casablanca*.

I glanced over my last few customers and stepped back, only stopping when I bumped into the back counter. The new cell phone Dad had forced into my pocket this morning dug into my hip. I took a deep, steadying breath, squared my shoulders, and grabbed the coffee pot.

"Coffee today?"

I remembered the way he'd sucked the soul out of the blonde in the back alley. "'Cause we're not sating any other needs here tonight." Maybe it was stupid, but somehow, I wanted him to know what I'd seen. And that I wasn't scared of him. Because I wasn't. I was terrified.

His smile was all pleasantness. It was the only part of his face I allowed my gaze to drift over. "Coffee's fine."

I poured the lunch-batch tar into a mug. My hands shook as I set it in front of him, and a little sloshed over the rim. He ignored the spill, wrapping his large hands around the mug and tapping the rim with an impatient finger.

"So, wild night Friday."

I fired him the dirtiest look I could manage. It was a mistake, as it put those rich, dark orbs in my direct line of view. One corner of his desperately in-need-of-a-shave lip twisted up. The charcoal cable-knit sweater he wore over a black t-shirt was thick enough to battle the light mist outside, but he made a show of turning up the collar. His darkly stained wings flared, swallowing the whole length of the counter.

The chill that crept beneath my pink dress had nothing to do with the temperature inside the diner. Again, I hardened my expression and dropped my gaze.

"How do you do it?" The smoky bass in his voice rode my spine like a rollercoaster.

I returned the coffee pot to its holder—before I dropped it again—and leaned back against the counter. I rested my elbows back on either side of me, hoping for an air of casualness I didn't feel. "Do what?"

His smile stretched in an almost genuine way. "See me." He tipped his chin up, gesturing to his wings. He folded them back behind his back.

I tried to shrug, but ended up with a jerky, half-movement. "Magic."

He sipped his coffee. "Sarcasm. Didn't know you had it in you."

I had enough fear in me to run screaming from him—or pass out behind the counter—but the SS Crazy had taught me more than just a love of gardening. It had taught me how to mask what I was feeling. Most of the time. Guess being on the inside was finally starting to pay off. Then again, I'd never had a true, life-or-death motivation before. "How do *you* do it?"

He glanced up. His brows lifted, creasing his forehead. "Do what?"

"Take innocent lives." I didn't know that the blonde was dead, but it seemed a safe bet after what Cam had told me in the park Friday night.

The laugh that rolled from his throat wasn't the malicious one I expected. "What are you talking about? I love humans, as much as my maker does. I wouldn't kill them. You all ... *fascinate* me." He didn't even have the good sense to lower his voice.

I shuddered. "Can't say I believe you after what I saw."

He smiled again, this time baring perfect teeth. "Can't say I blame you." His voice was darker. "Now, can I get some more coffee?"

Only if I can spit in it first. My gaze dodged his, looking toward the kitchen. I hoped Daphne would return soon.

I grabbed the pot. "I think you're a murderer." My voice came out low, keeping his secret from the eleven other patrons in the diner. I placed my hand on the counter to steady myself as I poured.

His hand snapped around my wrist. I jerked back, spilling a perfectly yucky cup of coffee.

Kade abandoned his seat. Both his hands encircled

my arms, steadying me, looking for all the world like he was comforting the poor, clumsy waitress.

I gathered a handful of pink skirt in my free hand to keep from shouting and drawing more unwanted attention. I shot invisible lasers at him and imagined slamming the coffee pot in his face just to keep it together. To take my mind off his hands around me, I closed my eyes. I couldn't let anyone see the crazy. No way I'd ever go back, and I damn sure wasn't about to let Kade be the one to put me there.

"You're right," he whispered, his mouth too close to my ear. I shot a frantic look around the diner, but except for a few curious glances, no one seemed ready to intervene. "But I don't kill humans. That girl is just fine." His dark gaze bore through me, drifted across my skin. I scratched the scabs in my right palm and they burst free. Pain throbbed in my nerve endings. Warm liquid filled my palm and absorbed into my skirt. He released me.

I stumbled back, slipping on the spilled coffee. Kade watched as my back slammed into the back counter and I went down. The coffee pot shattered against the tile floor, littering me with tiny fragments of glass and a hot rush of coffee. I called out, but let the shout die down to a gasp when the closest table of customers popped up from their seats.

Kade dipped down and pulled me up by my hands before I could scurry away across the glass. "You okay?" A slight grin rode the curve of his lip.

Once on my feet, I inched back from him, careful not to slip.

All eyes were on me. It felt like the cafeteria at school all over again. I squeezed my eyes shut. *Regroup.*

I opened my eyes again and forced a chuckle. With Kade securely in the corner of my eye, I took a bow, first to the right, then the left. A few of the customers applauded, and the two who had stood up returned to their seats, looking embarrassed for me. With my teeth gritted and a half-smile still on my lips, I hissed at Kade, "Get back."

To my surprise, he did, returning to his seat at the counter. I retreated into the back for the mop and nearly lost it. I'd pressed myself against the wall beside the kitchen's swinging doors for a few seconds too long when I noticed Jose, my favorite cook, watching me. Braving another fake smile, I pulled the mop bucket out, accidentally doubling the normal amount of solution, and turned on the hot water. Suds formed a dome over the top of the bucket too quickly, so I switched off the water.

Daphne's office door remained closed. At least one person had missed my spectacular fail. But what on earth was I going to do with Kade? Jose flipped the two burgers on the flat top and added cheese to one. He shook out the excess oil from the fry basket. I wrapped two paper towels around my right hand to stay the bleeding, then wheeled the mop and bucket out to the diner floor.

I mopped, replaced the broken coffee pot with an extra from the back, and served table fifteen their burgers when Jose put them out. I used the time to collect myself. At first all I could think about was running. Then I thought about Allison. Tony. Luke. If Cam was right, whoever was taking the lives of my classmates wasn't done. Still, it wasn't my fight. Just because I could see their wings didn't mean I was somehow going to save the world. The thought of that was not only ridiculous, but absurd. I was only a girl; a tired, confused girl who could barely keep herself out of a mental hospital.

I looked down at the mop bucket. The water was

red. I jerked back, blinked. The mucky water in the bucket was a dirty brown. Not blood. Not Allison's spilled across the bathroom floor.

My mind worked, wondering if Kade had cut Allison's wrists so many days ago. If he came to Tony DiMeeko's house and fashioned him a noose. If he would soon track down Luke.

No. If I got involved, I would be so far beyond screwed. One way or another, it would be the nail in my coffin. Either I would be sent back, or I'd end up dead, too.

I had to stay out of this. I had to. Absolutely had to.

Unless …

I shook my head and wrung the mop out, refusing another look at Kade as I rolled the entire contraption into the back to dump the bucket and rinse the mop in clean water.

I could tell Cam that I saw the Fallen again. No one would know, so long as I stayed out of it beyond that. It would be between him and me. If I was feeling brave, I could question Kade while he was here, among so many other people. I could use his own trick against him. Then I could report back to Cam.

But I'd have to catch him off guard.

I tucked the mop and bucket away in the kitchen corner beside the swinging doors. Nothing would catch him more off guard than if I stitched myself together and interrogated him right now.

I pushed through the doors and returned to the counter. Before Kade could find another way to rattle me, or I could talk myself out of this, I said, "Cam told me you and your kind are responsible for the suicides at Stratford Independence High School." My heart pounded between each word.

His lip curled up in a sneer at Cam's name, much the same reaction Cam had had when I'd mentioned

Kade's name to him. Flat black filled the whites of his eyes, swallowing the once rich brown of his irises. "Aren't you full of surprises?"

"So it *is* true."

"Camael's partly right. But I'm staying out of *their* mess. I've got enough problems without adding all the shit I'm sure is following your precious *Cam* around these days."

Holy crap. Cam was right. The dark-winged angels were responsible. Maybe, if I kept him talking, I could find out who was behind Allison and Tony's murders. I'd spent enough time making friends with unstable people, and Kade didn't seem too different from them—both required the need to watch my back.

Kade leaned forward on the counter. "I'm not here for all that. I'm here for you."

"For me?" I glanced around the diner, glad for the patrons still at their tables.

He smirked, his fingers tapping a staccato on his empty coffee mug. "Yep. *All* for you."

"Heh." I breathed out a nervous laugh. He had to be pushing my buttons on purpose, messing with me to see how far he could push me before I snapped. The joke was on him, because I'd snapped a long time ago.

I couldn't believe a word he said, I reminded myself. Except for my mother's name. That, I had to know about. "The other night. You called me Kay."

Something flickered across his face, gone before I could categorize it. Hurt, maybe. Yikes. This was getting weirder by the second. "Yeah, and?" he snipped.

"Kay was my mother's name." I watched his Adam's apple bob as he swallowed. "Did you ... know my mother?"

Stop it! He didn't know Mom. He couldn't have. She was too good to have anything to do with him.

"Oh, I knew her all right."

His answer crashed into me. I reached back for the counter, suddenly afraid my legs would give out.

He's lying.

I took my best shot at nonchalance. And failed. "Yeah. Sure you did."

His dark eyes narrowed at me, and his lips pressed together. Silence filled the space between us, stretching out like the tall shadows I had imagined following me last night.

"That's what I thought," I spat.

"You want me to prove I knew her? You were too young to know her half as well as I did. She wasn't the saint you remember."

His words were venom, pushing into my veins.

I didn't even notice the two larger groups leaving the diner until the bell chimed. The third table, burger with cheese and burger without, waved a credit card in the air.

Without feeling my feet moving, I printed out their bill and returned with their card, running it through the machine, never once looking at Kade.

"I'll never believe that. You've got the wrong person." I snapped in a low voice, tearing the credit card slip from the machine. I snatched a pen from beside the register and brought a handful of peppermint candies to table fifteen.

Please stick around, I begged silently, not wanting to be left alone with Kade and his lies.

Kade stood and called across the diner, "Oh, and, Ray?"

Table fifteen stood and walked around me to leave. Only one table left.

"Keep your voice down." I could hear the desperation in my own, the trembling beneath my words.

"She was Kayleigh Ardenell when we met."

Ardenell was my mother's maiden name.

Everything in me would have crawled at his feet to know more about my mother. No one talked about her at home. It was like her name was forbidden. Her death never made sense to law enforcement, family members, anyone—no one drowns in Arizona off the side of the highway in the middle of summer. If there was a sliver of a chance he knew anything at all—about her life, or her death—I had to jump.

"Fine." I fought off a tremor. "If you think you knew her, then tell me more."

"Really? You're not what I expected at all." He tapped his finger over the counter, as if deciding whether or not to say more. Strange, considering the way he'd tried to push it in my face before. "Why should I tell you anything?"

He was offering up something I never thought I could have, something I'd never get anywhere else: information about Mom. He had to know what he was doing in baiting me. On the other hand, this topic had stirred him up, too. For the first time, he was something less than pulled together.

"I have no idea," I said. "Maybe because, deep down somewhere, you have a shred of decency in you."

"Don't kid yourself about that." He smirked, and I clenched my teeth. I should have known better. "But maybe this time I'll throw you a bone. Let's start at the beginning." He shifted in his stool, settling in, and leaned his forearms on the counter. "My kind— Warriors, different from Cam, who's a Protector—were created to fight the demons who merged with humans. We were made more like men, to *think* like men, and to *out*think them. Our urges were stronger than any of our brothers before us. But did anyone up high care when we started faltering? Falling? Did they bend any of the rules for us? No. They didn't give two shits that most of us never returned. Those who did weren't allowed out again."

There was a certain sense of familiarity in his story. I knew what it was like to be shunned by those you thought loved you, banished away and forgotten.

"How …" I swallowed, bringing my voice as soft as I could get it. "How does an angel Fall?"

"When they break the rules and submit to … certain human emotions." His voice was gasoline, soaking into my pink uniform.

"What emotions?" I pressed.

"Silly romantic ones. I'm sure I don't have to specify." He took one last sip of his coffee. Another smirk quirked his lips. "What you'll really want to know is, I Fell for her."

Chapter Twenty-Five

His words struck me like lightning. I drew back, my breath faltering. Waves of shock rolled up my stomach. *This is all to get a rise out of you. Don't believe one word.*

"You *mean* …" I couldn't finish. My memories— of *my* mother, I couldn't let him tarnish them. They were all I had left. The nights she read to us, the dinners we helped with, Sunday mornings when she'd make fruit pancakes from whatever she had in the greenhouse and would shape them like our favorite cartoon characters. None of those moments could change. I refused to believe my mother would read us stories and then sneak off into the night with him. That while we cleaned up dinner, she was looking out the window wondering *what if.* Or that, on her way to gather fruit from the greenhouse, she stopped for a quick affair …

Something inside me withered.

No. Kade had said he'd known Mom by her maiden name. She never would have cheated on Dad. Never.

I buried my fingertips into the napkin in my right hand. The pain eased the panic enough to allow for a clear moment to think. As intact as I wanted to keep her memory, I realized I knew very little about who my mother really was. Dad refused to talk about her; he put his feelings in the grave the day we lowered her in.

I swallowed the instinct to plead for him to tell me everything about her and asked something marginally less intimate. "Could my mother see you—as you are?"

"No." His answer was short, clipped. "As far as I know, you're the first cursed with that particular gift."

Nope, didn't like that answer. "You called me Kay. Why? She's dead." I channeled my anger, flinging it at him in the hopes the dagger in my heart would somehow find purchase in his chest as well.

He lowered his gaze to his empty cup. "When you found me feeding, and I saw you standing under that yellow light above the back door—" he looked up, and the darkness in his eyes melted me, though I wished it hadn't. "—you looked like her. *Exactly* like her."

Lies, lies! I looked nothing like Mom.

He was like all the others, avoiding her death, skipping over it like it was a chapter he didn't agree with in a book. I *would* get more from him later. No matter what it took.

He thought I looked like her. No telling what he'd do if he saw Laylah. The thought left me cold.

Another person I'd have to protect. He'd never get anywhere near my sister.

"You have her eyes."

Slivers of ice cut into my bones, rendering them useless. If it weren't for my hold beneath the counter, I might have puddled onto the lemon-scented floor. My mother's eyes. If only he was right, if only I could look into the mirror and see even the smallest piece of her. But I couldn't.

"Ray-na." The terrifying sing-song way he said my name helped pull me back together.

I hadn't prepared for such a personal battle, and he was undoing me. I'd thought to erect protective walls in front of me, not behind. And now there was a metaphorical knife in my back. *Pull yourself together. Change the subject and calm down.* This time, I obeyed. "More coffee?" I turned toward the new, empty carafe, fighting to keep the ire from seeping into my voice. "I'll make a fresh pot."

"Sounds good."

His movements softened, became less sharp. The hard line of his jaw didn't seem so much like steel. And he'd finally stopped that incessant tapping on his coffee mug.

I could do this.

I threw in a few scoops of coffee and filled the water—up to the proper line this time. The bell over the door chimed. The sound threw me back into the real world. I grabbed three menus from beside the cash register and sat the new customers at a table by the window, as far away from Kade as possible.

As I took their drink orders, I watched Kade from behind. His wings were still, but not statue-still. Like Cam's, they rose and fell with each breath. But while Cam's wings would be glimmering even in the diffused light of the dreary afternoon, Kade's glossy black wings looked nothing like when he drained the blonde Friday night. Then, the sparkles had overpowered even the moon. I'd never forget the sight, beautifully haunting in the most terrifying way, much like he was.

Yep, definitely losing it.

I returned to the counter and filled three cups halfway up with ice, then pushed them, one at a time, under the red Coke lever. Sprinkles of fizzled soda splashed over the clear cup's rim and onto the bloody napkin still in my hand.

Gross.

I peeled the napkin off my palm and slapped the biggest Band-aid I could find beneath the cash register onto it. I looked up to find Kade watching me. "Coffee's almost done."

Yeah, like he couldn't see that for himself. I needed something to keep him here, to keep the information coming, and sadly enough, that bitter mud seemed to be his weakness. I bit into the side of my cheek, torn.

Mom's old adage of "you'll catch more flies with honey than with vinegar" inspired me to try a different tactic. As much as it chapped my ass to be nice to him, I had to know more. About Mom. About the suicides. "You want anything to eat, slice of pie or something? I hear the Lemon Meringue's heavenly." I cringed at my choice of words.

His face filled with light. His gruff laughter tickled the hair on the back of my neck. "Just coffee."

The light tone of his reaction disarmed me. Instead of thinking about his shift in attitude, I held one finger up and delivered the Cokes, too eager to return to Kade and our round of Twenty Questions to hurry the table's order.

This time, I tried to keep my questions less accusing, more conversational—as conversational as discussing a demon angel and his practices could be. "So you don't eat." It was a guess, but since he didn't correct me, I pushed forward and poured him a cup of his precious coffee. "And your," I lowered my voice and glanced at the far table filled with tourists, still browsing their menus, " ... wings. They don't cast light, the way Cam's do."

At the mention of Cam's name, his feathers ruffled and his fingers stiffened. "That name again." He drew up a terrifying smile. "If I didn't know better, I'd tell you to be careful, or he'll be the next to Fall."

Kade's words stopped me.

Until Friday night, I was afraid of Cam. Until Friday night, I thought I was dropping back into insanity every time I saw him and those beautiful, terrifying wings. But Friday night was different. I'd felt ... something. Something I'd never felt before.

I looked at Kade then. His black wings marked him as different. I imagined an earthbound existence would turn Cam into something different, someone different.

No. That would never happen to Cam. He was too controlled, too focused.

I thought about Kade's accusation and wondered again what my mother had done to him. I clenched my fists below the counter at the thought. Before today, before Kade's arrival, I wanted so badly to be like my mother, to have her soft patience, her free-spirited laughter, her warm, fear-shattering hugs. I had none of those things. And now I didn't know if I wanted them. Kade had made me question the last happy memories I had left.

"Hmm. I'm not far off, am I?" He leaned in, wings tipping back. "Can't say I blame him." His near-black gaze drank me in, head-to-waist, stopping at the counter. I dug my heels in to avoid squirming. He was goading me, getting off on flipping my switches. And I'd let him.

The tease in his gaze was almost gone. I parted my lips to say ... something. Anything. But I had nothing. All I knew was no one had ever looked at me that way before. Not even Cam.

Kade sat back, breaking the moment apart like he'd swung a sledgehammer through it. He swallowed hard and reached for his full coffee cup, pulling it between us like armor. "Never thought I'd live to see Perfect Cam be tempted, but it happens to the best of us." It sounded too bitter to be a lie. "You mentioned S.I., that independent place down the street. Your school?"

My lips twisted at his candor, but I decided against answering.

"Thought as much. So, suicides, huh? A few of them, I'm guessing."

Keep him talking. "Friends of yours?" I asked, accusingly.

"Rayna, sweetheart." His voice lacked concern. "I'm ostracized by my own kind. But it definitely wasn't one of your friends with the *golden wings*." The throaty way he growled the last two words rolled up my shoulders. He pretended not to notice. "Camael isn't protecting you, you know. If he was, you wouldn't know anything about us. What'd he tell you about me, anyway?" His forearms claimed the countertop as he leaned farther forward. An ominous, Cheshire grin brought my attention back to his teeth. "Wait, let me guess. I'm evil, right? Dangerous." He lowered his voice to a whisper, "Sinful."

Heat warmed my cheeks. I didn't need to hear any of those things from Cam to know they were true—at least to an extent. I mean, look at him.

Kade sipped his coffee, not a line of worry marring his face. "I'm not the one your angel needs to worry about." His gaze drifted away. "Too bad, too. I could use a good fight. It's been too long. But, whatever's turning your students suicidal sounds like more of a threat than even me. How many so far?"

"Two."

He shrugged. "That doesn't sound so bad. But if your boyfriend's already there, then you really do have a problem."

"He's not my boyfriend, I never said he was there, and two deaths is two too many."

He shot me a do-I-look-stupid face. "It's been a while, but I do remember how these things work." Thought shone through his eyes as he tapped a finger on the counter. "I may have an idea who it could be."

I waited. He glanced inside his mug, which I

noticed was, once again, empty. "Care to share?" I prompted.

"What's in it for me?"

"My undying gratitude." It came out sharper than I intended.

"Not enough."

My breath wavered. "What then?" He already had my fear. I was practically drenched in it. I smoothed the ends of my ponytail and worried the corner of my lower lip between my teeth.

A quiet change stirred in his face, softening around his eyes. "You're so much like her."

His comment burrowed into me in a way it shouldn't have. I tightened the ribbon that held my hair back, then tightened my resolve. "That's not an answer."

He swirled his empty cup. "I'm not sure what I want from you yet."

That makes two of us, because I had no idea what exactly I wanted from him either, besides answers. "There are lives at stake. I won't stand here and play your cat-and-mouse games while we wait for others to die. Just tell me what you know."

He watched me a moment more, than gave a curt nod. "Decisive. I like that. My guess is Az has found himself a new sandbox, one you happen to be playing in. If I'm right, you'd better get the hell out of there."

Before I could ask who this Az was, the impatient tourists in the corner waved for their waitress. I looked around for Daphne. Oh, right. *I* was their waitress. I shot Kade a don't-think-this-is-over glare and hurried to my customers. Jose was half-asleep when I put their order in, but perked right up with one look at the ticket.

Through the kitchen, I heard Daphne call my name. I knew if I left Kade alone for too long, he'd slink away, so I pretended not to hear her and turned back toward him instead.

Two seconds later, Daphne emerged from the kitchen carrying a zippered black case and sporting a mascara smudge on the inside corner of her eye. "Rayna, I have to make a drop to the bank," she said. "I have my cell if you need me, but I'll be back before five so you can get out of here on time." She sashayed out of the diner looking happier than I'd ever seen her before. What could have her in such a good mood?

The kitchen bell dinged. I hesitated, eyes on Kade. "If you ever want coffee from here again, don't go anywhere." It was an empty threat since Daphne and Shelly would serve him, and we both knew it. As an added incentive, I refilled his cup and spared him a smile, though I was sure it looked nothing like Mom's ever had.

I picked up two salads and a minestrone soup and delivered them to the tourists. Another couple came in when I was inches from returning to the counter. I grabbed two menus, sat them, and took their drink orders.

"One strawberry milkshake and one Tornado Breeze."

I cursed to myself. Of course they would want a handmade milkshake and the diner's special sundae, each of which took nearly five minutes of constant attention—and noise—to make. I shot Kade another glare and turned my back on him to begin the painstaking process of creating dairy magic.

The burgers were waiting at the pick-up counter when I finished, and another set of customers had walked in. By the time I had a second to devote to Kade, my shift was less than five minutes from being over. All of my late afternoon customers were eating. I peeked into the kitchen and reminded Jose to take his break. It was long overdue, and I needed the privacy.

Two days ago I was begging *not* to be alone with Kade. Strange how quickly things change.

"So, who's Az?"

"A Fallen."

"Like you."

Kade sneered. "He and I have nothing in common. You have to understand, when we're first cast out, it's difficult being cut off from the kind of family we're used to. Az was quick to align himself with the wrong crowd."

The bell jingled again. Perfect. The other night I couldn't get him to shut up, and now I couldn't keep him talking. I looked up, frustrated. Cam's white wings caught the gray light, spreading it across every inch of the diner. My irritation dissolved. Kade must have seen something in my expression, because his wings ticked back and froze against his stiffened spine.

Cam's soft features took on an edge of fury. His wings snapped open with the force and sound of a gunshot. The span reached almost from one wall to the other.

Uh oh. This was not going to be good.

Chapter Twenty-Six

K ade slid from his seat and turned to face Cam. "Speak of the devil."

I thought about correcting him, telling Cam we'd been talking about Az, not him, but the seriousness in both their faces didn't leave much room for my input.

Kade shot a dark glare at the couple sharing a sundae, his eyes swirling black. Cam tipped his wings down to level a glare at the three tourists, that white-blue light emanating from his eyes.

My stomach clenched, a reminder of Friday night. Kade with that woman in the alley. His eyes consumed with black. Cam, using that light on me.

Both sets of customers grabbed their things and scurried out without paying for their checks.

"Hey!" I called after them, but they were long gone.

If they could scare people away with just their eyes, what else were these two capable of?

Kade's dark wings shot to the sides, their width rivaling Cam's. The gust sent me stumbling back into the counter. My black ribbon blew free from my hair. The sound reminded me of rain beating against a plastic tarp. In the seconds it took me to sweep my hair from my face, they'd closed all but a foot of the distance between them.

Wings filled the expanse of the diner, turning to white smoke where they touched the counter, a table, or chairs. Kade's back was to me, his black wings blocking my view of Cam, but I could still see Cam's white wings extended, their light radiating onto Kade.

"What are you doing here?" Cam's voice breached the tangle of wings.

"I could ask you the same thing."

"You need to leave the humans alone."

Kade scoffed. "You mean *your* human?"

Something fluttered in my chest. Silence squeezed the diner, choking it with two hands.

"I mean all humans. If I find out you had any hand in the recent deaths—"

"Kids aren't my cup of tea. And I don't like you threatening me, brother."

Brother?

"Don't call me that," Cam bit out. "Our ties were severed the day you Fell."

Kade's feathers curled in a little at the ends. "Anything else before you go?" he asked.

"You terrified her," Cam said, and I knew he was talking about Kade's Friday night soul-kabob.

"Not terrified," I corrected, even though it was a blatant lie, but neither of them seemed to hear me.

"Sorry, Rayna," Kade said. He didn't sound sorry.

Cam must not have thought so either, because his wings curled back, like he was rolling his shoulders. Preparing for a fight. In answer, Kade's wings bit the air at the farthest ends of the diner and curled toward Cam. If they destroyed Roxy's, I would be so fired.

"Kade thinks this Az guy is responsible for the suicides," I said.

Cam's wings relaxed.

"Jealous I can tell her things you can't?" Kade gloated.

I narrowed my eyes at Kade's back. Now his willingness to answer my questions made a little more sense.

"Not hardly. Those of us still in Heaven's good graces work to remain above human emotion."

I thought back to Friday night. The concern in Cam's eyes and his words, the way they lit this calming tunnel of fire beneath me that had nothing to do with that strange light. The conversation, his actions ... it had made me think he cared. Not just about what I saw or what I knew, but about me, my feelings, if I was okay. But if he was so above feelings, as he'd just said, I had to wonder if that was all an act to get me to trust him.

"What about Azriel? It's been years since I've heard that name."

"Why would I tell you a damn thing?"

This peacocking had gone on long enough, especially if what Cam had said about them not being able to see each other's wings was true. I pressed forward, but a thick set of black feathers was in my way. With more courage than I thought I had, I grabbed a handful of wing. Kade sneered at me, but he didn't forfeit an inch. I expected them to feel oily because of their sheen, but they were as soft and delicate as Cam's.

My fingers lingered for a second too long. Kade's sneer faded. His eyes pierced me, and this time it wasn't in warning. I'd never seen that kind of look on anyone's face before. Disarmed by his stare, I unclamped my fingers and pushed past him before I could decipher the meaning behind that look.

"That's enough!" I pressed a hand to each of their chests, fighting to put some distance between them. Heat and electricity crackled through my fingertips. Both sets of eyes seared holes through me. If it didn't scare the hell out of me, I might have been in Heaven between these two. I blinked the treacherous thought away and peered up at each of them.

A moment after my gaze touched Cam's, his face softened in apology. Kade moved against my hand, no doubt taunting Cam.

I trusted Cam to keep himself in check more than I trusted Kade to, well, do anything I wanted him to. Kade wouldn't meet my gaze, although those rich, chocolate eyes swirled with black. That couldn't be good.

"Kade."

He ignored me, still challenging Cam with those dark eyes.

"Kade!" I wrapped my fist in his cable-knit sweater. My fingertips sunk into the luxuriously soft fibers. He closed his eyes. When they opened again, those strange, black depths were on me. His lips twisted up in a smirk. He was seconds from snapping. I could feel it in the tension ratcheting up in his muscles. There was no telling what would happen if Cam's strength and Kade's collided.

"Please." I kept my voice as soothing as I could manage with my heart jumping up into my throat. I slowly released my grip on Kade's sweater and stepped from between them.

Kade's shoulders loosened, and he huffed at me. "My guess is Az is taking her classmates. I can help. If you ask nice."

"And why would you do that?" Cam asked.

I frowned at Cam. Though I didn't know how much I trusted Kade, we needed him.

"Well you shouldn't interfere in a human's life you're not protecting. Those still are the rules, right?" Kade glanced at me, allowing his gaze to travel the length of my body. "So think real hard, lover boy. Do you want my help or do you want them all to die?"

All of us? "The whole school's in danger?" I asked.

Cam fisted Kade's sweater, and his wings projected even brighter light.

"Cam, no." I placed a hand on his shirt this time.

He shrugged me off and pushed me aside.

Another flick of wings sent my hair into my face again. I fought it back in time to see Cam punch Kade in the face.

The tiniest drop of red dripped from the corner of Kade's lip, the readiness to strike written all over his face. His fist sailed toward Cam. Before I could think better of it, I dove between them.

Kade pulled back just in time to avoid hitting me. I squeaked in relief.

Cam backed up two steps, bumping into a table and shattering something. The new distance between them satisfied me. It didn't hurt that their wings were tucked away and the air I breathed didn't taste of distain.

The broken remains of a mug sparkled on the floor, reflecting the gold from Cam's wings. I knelt to sweep the debris into my hand. Pain sliced into my index finger, and I dropped the shards, scattering the pieces again.

"Ow!" One of the larger pieces clanked against a metal chair leg.

Kade stalked toward me. Cam moved to step between us, but Kade quickened his pace to slide past him. I matched each of Kade's steps with a backward one of my own. Three steps later, I fell into a chair. Kade knelt before me and held out his hand.

No way. I shook my head, cradling my hand to my chest. The blood welling reminded me I was vulnerable. Human. After what I saw Friday night in the back alley, I knew Kade was far from either of those things. He brushed ceramic dust and splinters from my hand, and brought my finger to his mouth. I wanted to struggle, to pull back, but something in his rich brown eyes stopped me. Brown, not black.

Then his tongue rolled around my finger, and my heart stopped.

Leaving my blood in Kade's hands—or mouth—bittered the taste on my tongue. Part of me worried he'd be able to suck my soul this way. If I continued to stare into his eyes, there was no telling where I'd end up. Mental images of the morgue, or worse, the alley behind the diner, flashed before me. Another part of me—a smaller, stupider part—didn't want this to end.

I glanced up to Cam. His fiery glower pierced Kade's back.

Regaining the feeling in my legs, I snatched my finger from him, making sure to keep clear of his teeth, and rose to my feet, determined not to let my knees betray me.

Cam rammed Kade into the wall, and pinned his forearm against Kade's neck.

"Don't worry," Kade choked out. "Blood has nothing to do with the soul transfer. And the small slivers of souls I have to take in order to survive don't drive me into a bloodlust the way it does some of the others."

I tapped Cam's shoulder, hoping he'd release Kade and not disembowel him. "Can we please put a lid on the conflict? My boss will be back any minute." I glanced over at the clock to find my shift had ended seven minutes ago. Through the front window, I spotted Daphne crossing the street. "Or like now." Behind me the two of them scuffled, separating. I pulled the front door open, latching it into place to allow fresh air in. Otherwise, Daphne might wonder why it reeked of testosterone in here.

Dad's SUV was parked at the curb. Thank God. I'd had enough.

"Daphne, I have to go. I'm going to be late for my classmate's wake," I shouted from the front door. Without a glance back at either angel, I added, "I don't care which one of you does it, but someone's paying for those abandoned bills."

I hopped up into Dad's SUV, counting my minimal tips to keep from remembering the way Cam had lost control and hit Kade, the hidden relationship between Kade and my mother, and the idea that there was still a Fallen out there looking to take my classmates' souls.

Chapter Twenty-Seven

Allison's wake sucked. The funeral parlor had been a wash of black clothes and tear-stained faces. Most of the floral arrangements were predictable, scent-less white Calla Lilies. It reminded me in every way of Mom's funeral. Allison's friends whispered about me being the one to find her body, and Dad kept patting my knee, annoying the hell out of me. I'd caught a glimpse of Cam's wings near the back of the room, but he was gone by the time I was able to break away and look for him.

That night, I fell asleep with my pen in my hand, furiously scribbling in my secret notebook everything that had happened at the diner.

The next morning, I bolted out of bed, raced through the shower, and swept the books off my bed and into my backpack. I rolled up my angel notebook and stashed it in a boot tucked under my bed. Wet hair dripped down the back of my sweatshirt as I raced down the Powell Street hill to meet Lee at Roxy's before school. I'd called him on my way out the door, but he hadn't picked up. He hadn't picked up the dozen times I'd called him over the weekend, either. I left him another message, along with my cell number. Just in case he'd lost the other six messages I'd left with it.

I pushed through the door of Roxy's and claimed our booth. Daphne took an order from a couple in their forties and nodded to me. The other waitress, a girl I hadn't worked with yet, stepped from behind the counter and headed my way with a pencil and pad in hand.

"Need a menu?" she asked.

I shook my head and ordered two hot chocolates, one with extra whipped cream. Lee was a sucker for whipped cream.

Someone slid into the seat across from me.

I zipped my bag closed. "Lee, I—" Only when I looked up, it wasn't Lee sitting across from me, drumming blunt fingers against the tabletop like I was already boring him. Someone much darker sat in his place.

"Lee, huh?" Kade's voice slid across the table, burrowing beneath my skin. "You must be pretty popular with the boys at school, what with them starting to drop like flies and you seeing angels and all."

"Wow," I said flatly. "You're just full of tact. Only one boy is dead. And for your information, I don't go around announcing my ..."—insanity, madness, curse—"... *issues* to people. Now if you don't mind, I'm expecting someone."

The waitress returned, sliding the hot chocolates across the table. "You two enjoy," she said with a wink at Kade.

Hmm. Guess all it took was a pretty face to put her in a good mood.

Before I could stop him, Kade grabbed Lee's extra-whip H.C. and raised an eyebrow at me. "Sweetheart," he pushed the drink away and flashed the waitress a wry smile. "No self-respecting man drinks this crap. Could I get a cup of coffee, please?"

Her smile shot to life, awakening her slim face with beauty. "No problem. Be right back."

I turned to look out the window, watching the corner Lee usually rounded.

"If your Lee was smart, he'd stay away from a girl as crazy as you."

His thoughtless comment bored through me. "Why don't you take that cup of coffee to your usual stool and leave me the hell alone? I'm sure you'd prefer that, anyway. You have to be used to it by now. Being alone, I mean." It was a low blow, but I had no doubt that his sole reason for sitting with me was to ruin my day. Or to collect on the agreement I'd foolishly made in exchange for information.

"Ouch," He pressed a hand against his chest in a gesture of mock pain. "Teenage angst cuts the deepest." The dryness in his voice was palpable. "But I'm not the one being stood up."

I reached for my bag and slid out of the booth. It was after the time I usually met Lee anyway, and I was going to be late for school.

"Rayna, don't go. I was just having some fun with you. Teasing. Isn't that what humans do?"

"I doubt that. And you're not human." I kept my voice tight and low while remaining on my feet. "Tell me more about Az."

"Sit down and have breakfast with me."

"I thought you didn't eat."

"I don't, but you should. You're too skinny."

I looked down at my stomach, my belt cinched to the point I'd had to pierce an extra hole into it, and remembered the blonde he'd soul-sucked in the back alley. "I thought you liked skinny girls."

"No, I like thin women. Now sit down and order something."

Eat breakfast and try to get information out of

Kade, or sit awkwardly next to Cam in first period trying to figure out what the hell I felt for him?

"Would this be the payment for our agreement yesterday?"

"No, this would be breakfast."

I hauled my bag to my shoulder and moved for the door.

"With information," he added.

I stopped. He was playing with me, like I was a shiny new toy, but it didn't matter. What he had, I needed. It was as simple as that.

Irked, I scooted my bag over and plunked down in the booth. "I eat, you talk."

***

I made it to school at the tail end of lunch. Lee wasn't at our usual table. I glanced around for another familiar face. Luke sat with Gina Garson and a few of his buddies. The billowy top Gina was wearing didn't do anything to help with the rumors. At least Az hadn't gotten to Luke yet.

The lunch bell rang, and I fumbled my way through the rest of the day. Cam and I didn't have a chance to talk during History thanks to a pop quiz that spanned the entire period.

After school, I hung around outside for a few extra minutes, waiting, hoping Lee would show up. He didn't.

Worry bit at me like a pesky mosquito. Lee was the only person in this world I could trust—with everything but the angel thing; no one would believe that. And to repay his kindness, I'd gone and twisted myself up with Cam and Kade, leaving him high and dry. What a spectacular friend I was turning out to be. No wonder he'd missed school; he was probably avoiding me.

Although, missing school just because he was pissed at me didn't sound like something he'd do. Lee could be mad at me at school, and he could avoid me at school. He knew that I'd never push him into talking to me if he needed a few days to blow off steam.

Now I was beginning to think Lee wasn't just angry at me, but so fed up with my craziness that he didn't want to be my friend anymore. I should have seen something like this coming. Sure, we'd had fun together before the angels showed up, but I'd been a walled-off nut-job since then.

Maybe he'd even caught a glance at my secret-notebook ramblings. Or seen the drawing. Wind blew dirt and small yellow leaves up from the ground, swirling them around. I swallowed and headed back inside, needing a moment to think without the chatter of students waiting to board the yellow school busses.

I turned the corner to bypass the stairs and slammed into someone. Not just someone. Cam.

Annoyance furrowed his features. He steadied me and held me at arm's length, his anger dissolving when he realized I was his collision partner. "I've been looking for you." A few boys in gym clothes trickled down the stairs. Cam took the sleeve of my sweater and towed me toward the first floor hallway, which was empty.

He dropped my sleeve. That annoyed look returned to his face. "I can't believe after what happened Friday you'd actually go back to work at the diner. I didn't think I'd have to tell you to stay away from there. What were you thinking?" The growing worry inside me must have shown in my face. "What's wrong?"

"I don't know. Lee wasn't in school today. He hasn't been answering my calls or meeting me for breakfast. I don't know. I think he's … this is stupid, I know."

"Do you think he's in trouble?"

"Trouble? Like … like the *Az* kind of trouble?" I stared at him, desperate to know if that's where he was going. In the window behind him, darker clouds rolled over the fog.

A group of girls passed us, and he lowered his voice. "I don't know. It's a possibility, I suppose."

I ran a hand through my hair, taking in the casual way he'd just told me my best friend could be in serious angel trouble. "He hasn't been himself lately. Not since all this angel stuff started. Not since Allison's death. He's never ignored me this way before." I shook my head. "Now I'm really worried." I yanked my cell phone from my back pocket and called Lee again. I bit my lower lip harder with each ring. "He didn't answer. Should I be worried? I mean, what guarantee do you have that Luke's going to be the next victim?"

"There are never any guarantees in these situations, but if they sent me here to watch Luke, then there's a reason."

"I have to go check on him."

"You can't go alone. If Azriel, or whoever is taking lives here, finds out you can see us."

He didn't need to finish that sentence. Suffice it to say, if that happened, I was in deep crap.

"Then come with me."

Cam glanced down at his watch. "Now? I can't. I finally found an in with Luke. He's probably waiting for me outside right now."

The more I thought about the possibility of a soul-sucking, suicide-inducing angel anywhere near Lee, the faster my fear rose.

"Lee's my best friend—my only friend. And something isn't right." My voice lifted high above the remaining students.

Cam led me farther back into the hall, away from the front door and main stairwell. "It's going to be okay."

"You can't guarantee that, you said it yourself." I slapped his hand away. "These people, every single one of us except for Luke, we mean nothing to you. You'll go on whether you save us or not when you're called away to your next mission. But Lee means something to me!"

Cam fired back at me so fast I didn't have time to brace myself for it. "Don't ever say that. They mean *everything* to me." My heart beat faster against my ribcage. The tension in my fists slackened.

They mean everything to him, not *you*.

I swallowed back the rejection I hadn't expected to feel. Determined to go before I said—or did—something I'd regret, I stepped around him, ignoring the brush of his wings against my shoulder.

"Rayna," Cam called out calmly, but I didn't hear him come after me. Good. That would make things easier.

Before I reached the stairs, my phone vibrated against my thigh. I pulled it from my pocket and pushed the green button to answer before thinking to check the caller ID.

"Hello?"

"Ms. Evans, Detective Rhodes."

I stopped.

"Ms. Evans, are you there?"

"Uh, yeah. Sorry. I thought you'd be my dad." I worked hard to keep a tremble from my voice.

"He and I just spoke. He was kind enough to pass along your cell number." In the background, I could hear him tapping on computer keys. "The reason I'm calling is to give you an update on Allison Woodward's case. Your art teacher corroborated your story from last

Tuesday." A man's voice called for the detective. "Ms. Evans, can you hold on?"

"Sure, I guess."

At first the detective's words were too muffled to make out, but the longer he kept me on hold, the clearer his conversation became. I turned the volume on my phone up all the way. Eventually, I could make out entire sentences.

"The medical examiner placed the time of death within the time Allison Woodward left class and when the nine-one-one call was made."

I swallowed and listened harder.

"Now here's where the discrepancy comes in. According to the medical examiner, the twenty to twenty-five minutes Allison was unaccounted for and the cuts on her wrists don't line up. Jim said she shouldn't have bled out before the paramedics arrived."

I reeled, placing my hand on the locker door beside me. Cam circled in front of me, though I had no idea how long he'd been there. He was too distracting to look at, so I turned, leaning my backpack against the row of lockers instead.

"Under normal circumstances..." His voice died off for half a second before I could hear him again. "Should have taken closer to forty minutes to bleed out from those particular cuts."

The other man asked something I couldn't make out.

"No. Negative for drugs and alcohol. Jim said there's no medical explanation that he can find. I know, and he's the expert. When you're done writing that up, get me a burger, will ya?"

"Miss Evans? You still there?" His voice blared in my ear. I jerked the phone away and lowered the volume.

"Hello?" I tried to pretend I hadn't just heard his

very his-ears-only conversation, or that I forgot I was on the phone at all. I probably failed at both.

"Sorry about that. I was just calling to let you know we've been looking into the Allison Woodward case, and due to the nature of her death, we're labeling it an official homicide investigation. Just thought I'd let you know, since we may need to call you in to ask you some more questions. Thanks for your time." His end of the line clicked as he hung up on me.

Chapter Twenty-Eight

C am caught me as I sank to the floor. He didn't ask what was wrong; instead he helped me shed my backpack and sat on the ground beside me while I processed Detective Rhode's conversation.

"The police think Allison's death wasn't a suicide. They're opening an investigation." A nuclear blast went off in my stomach. "I found her, so I'm probably near the top of the suspect list." *Plus I just left a mental hospital three months ago, so rocket me up to suspect number one.*

This couldn't be happening. I wanted to stand, to pace, but I stayed where I was, hiding my shaking hands behind my back. What was going to happen when the evidence led the police to a Fallen angel? Nothing, because that wouldn't happen. More likely, I'd become the scapegoat.

"I—" I started. "I don't know what to do."

Cam pulled me into a hug. "It's okay. We'll figure something out." His fresh-cut grass scent was softer today, but oh so present.

The warmth from his arms calmed me. Either that or he'd used some of that angel mojo again. Could he do that without looking into my eyes?

Only moments ago, shock fired in every cell of my

body, but not now. Now all I felt was his arms around me. His chest pressed against me, calming the storm inside. I squeezed my eyes closed to keep this moment from passing by, from fading away. Butterflies wiggled around in my stomach. Cam was the vacuum that took the bad away, the one person whose embrace felt right.

I held my breath and slid my arms around him, avoiding his wings. His trademark earthy scent made me feel like I was home again. Safe. Slowly, I splayed my hand out across the soft fabric of his shirt and wound the material around my fingers. Shivers forged from desire unblocked the butterflies, and they swarmed me.

He rubbed the back of my neck, his fingertips brushing through the ends of my ponytail.

He drew me closer and pressed his cheek against my temple. The world stopped. Even the air stilled. The muscles in his jaw clenched against the side of my head, but the resistance dissipated a moment later. Soft lips pressed against my temple.

His lips retreated, but his closeness didn't, until he trailed another kiss to my cheek. My entire body burned with expectation. I drew closer, needing to feel more of him.

I sighed, my breath shaking. He pulled back. I could hear my own heartbeat echo through the hall.

He edged closer. There had never been another being on this earth like Cam, of that I was sure. But he wasn't mine to keep. He belonged up there. I belonged, well, I wasn't sure where I belonged—maybe the loony bin—but my place sure as hell wasn't with the angels.

When his lips pressed against mine, I couldn't have stopped them if I wanted to—and I didn't.

His lips tasted of pure, raw sunshine. The sunshine I'd been missing ever since leaving Arizona. I reveled in it, pulled myself tighter to him. His hand moved up to cup my cheek, and my head soared in the clouds. Yet I could still feel him, every inch of him, ethereal wings and all.

"Ray?" Luke's voice shattered the moment.

Cam and I parted, separating like oil and water. The sudden absence of his touch left me hollow.

Luke shook his head in disbelief and thundered down the hall toward the front door.

"What was that?" I asked Cam.

Cam ignored me and ran to the stairs, where he shouted, "Luke, wait!" With his hand still around the corner, he turned back to me. "He likes you, Ray. You must know that." Cam closed his eyes. For an instant, regret showed all over his face. "This is a nightmare. I have to go. I have to keep him safe."

My cheeks were on fire as Cam darted after him, abandoning me for his assignment. He'd called our first kiss—my first kiss—a nightmare.

I lowered my head in my hands and groaned. Why would Cam …?

My chest ached like it was being ripped in two. He'd left me. Luke was more important. Luke was his job. I sank back against the lockers.

A mistake.

His words repeated over and over in my head. My chin trembled. I pressed my lips together to keep them from doing the same. Cam was gone. He'd never wanted me.

And why would he? Why would anyone want to be stuck with someone so flawed, so … crazy?

I tucked my elbows in to my sides and tried to forget this had ever happened. To force myself to think about something else.

Lee. I needed to forget about myself and help Lee.

Twenty minutes later, I was still doing a sloppy job of convincing myself the kiss hadn't mattered, that it didn't rip me apart when Cam abandoned me, and that I didn't desperately want to do it again. Yep, I told myself those three things over and over again. All the way to Lee's house, and during the five minutes I spent banging my knuckles raw at his front door. He obviously wasn't home. I cursed loud enough to draw the attention of his nosy neighbors. If Lee was here he would have corrected my foul language with some obscure *Doctor Who* reference.

Instead of crying in defeat, I caught the first bus to the Korean Consulate—technically it was the temporary location since the main office on Van Ness was still being remodeled. I'd be sure to tell Lee I'd found it all by myself when this was all over.

Fifteen minutes later, I got off the bus and walked to Clay Street. The area was filled with upscale apartment buildings and older, well-maintained homes. The gardens in front of the yellow mansion of the temporary Korean Consulate were purple and blue and yellow. Breathtaking. I strived for my window box and the few pots on the front steps to look half as vibrant, but this late in the season, it became difficult to keep the chill from claiming the petals.

From what Lee had told me about his mom, she was old-school Korean. Stern and *very* traditional. Offending her with my craziness wasn't in the plan, but with any luck Lee would be there to act as the buffer.

I swallowed back a lump and pressed the bell. The gate's buzzer sounded. I jerked it and the dark door open and made my way inside, where I checked the building directory. Then I made my way up the stairs to office 203.

"Mrs. Kyon?" I rapped softly on her door.

"What can I do for you, young lady?" She stood up from her cushy office chair and gestured to the seat across from her walnut desk. As soon as I took it, she straightened her navy suit jacket and settled back into her chair. Her dark hair was short, as was her stature, but she in no way looked fragile. The firm set of her mouth took care of that. And there was no Lee in sight, but she did have a beautifully trimmed Bonsai behind her.

Focus. I gathered my nerve, but had no idea what to say. "Mrs. Kyon, I'm Rayna Evans, a friend of Leland's. Is he here, by any chance?"

She looked puzzled. I hesitated, wondering if I was overreacting. Maybe Lee was cutting school to avoid me and I was about to get him in trouble, which would make him doubly pissed. But what if I was right to worry, and he was in danger. No, I'd come this far. I was doing this.

"He didn't make it to school today, and he hasn't been answering my calls. I'm so sorry to bother you at work, but I was wondering if you could tell me ..."

Her puzzled look deepened into tight frown lines. "Rayna?" She sounded like she'd never heard the name before. Oh, God. His mom had never heard of me. Maybe this whole time I'd been making up how close we were. Maybe he wasn't in trouble at all, but ignoring me. It was a mistake to come here, to assume ...

"You mean Ray?"

I nodded, so relieved I could almost throw up. "Yes, ma'am."

She made a disapproving sound through her nose. "I always thought Ray was a boy."

This is going well.

A long silence dragged out. "But *you* are Ray. And you've come to ask me how Leland is feeling?"

I nodded, feeling foolish and a little crazy under her scrutiny. "I was worried and—"

She leveled me with a considering look, then

nodded. "I won't pretend I like the idea of my son's best friend being female, but you are good to come ask about him." The toughness fled her face. "Unfortunately, he has a bad case of the flu."

"The flu?" I asked, disbelief raising my voice an octave too high. "That's all?"

"He's been in bed for days."

"Oh, of course, I mean, he's sick. I just meant … I was concerned is all." I tapped my nails together. Too sick to answer the door? "Would you please tell him I stopped by today, the house and here?"

She tipped her chin down. "I will."

My cell phone rang before I could so much as thank her. I excused myself and stepped out into the hallway. This time Dad's name came up on the caller ID, the only number programmed into its memory.

"Rayna Jane Evans, I need you home. Now!"

I winced, taking the stairs two at a time. "Sorry I didn't call, Dad. But Lee's not feeling well, and I thought—"

"I don't care. Where are you? I'll pick you up myself."

Crap. I checked the time on my phone. It was only a couple of minutes after four. He was really milking this cell phone thing. "No, Dad, it's fine. I'm fine. I'm with Lee's mom now, but I'm getting ready to—"

"Where are you, Ray? I don't care what you're doing. Tell me where you are." How his voice could get any harsher, I didn't know, but it left my insides cold.

I sighed, defeated, knowing full well what the consequences would be if I disobeyed and ran off to visit Lee anyway, maybe suck up with some chicken soup. I wouldn't be helping anyone if I violated Dad's rules. He'd send me back to therapy, where Dr. G. would see right through me. Only one slip away. And if

I went back, I wouldn't be able to help anybody. Not Lee. Not Luke. And certainly not myself.

Sweat laced my palms. It would take me at least thirty minutes to get home. "Dad? Dad, my phone's making a weird noise." I moved the receiver against my shirt to create static, then slid it shut. I clicked the power button before he could return the "dropped" call.

That's the thing about those trusty cell phones. Batteries ran out all the time.

The bus ride lasted forever, and my stomach churned all the way. It only intensified when I climbed the front stairs. Dad sat at the dining room table, facing away from the front door. His phone rested beside him, on top of a small book.

"Sorry, Dad. I kept trying to get the phone working again, but—"

Tension knotted his shoulders, and his fingers drummed the table impatiently. He looked over his shoulder at me. His eyes were tired, but there was something off about them, too. Something weary, yet upset. He stood up and pushed his phone off the small, curved book. He lumbered toward me, anger slowly spreading to contort his face. "What is this, Ray?" He held the book up.

There, in his hand, was my angel notebook, and all of my crazy secrets.

Chapter Twenty-Nine

"What the hell is this, Ray?"

I reached for the entryway table, but my knees gave out, and I sank to the floor, shaking. I couldn't think. Couldn't move. I knew I wasn't breathing.

"I thought you were done with this. I thought you were better." He paced, tears leaking from his red-rimmed eyes.

"Where did you get that?" My voice was less than a whisper.

"I went through your room. I'm your father, I have every right." He swiped at his eyes, banishing the tears. "Tell me you have an explanation. Tell me *something*, Ray."

For a brief, desperate moment, I thought about telling him everything. About Cam. Kade. Az. About the suicides that weren't suicides. Telling him angels—and *demons*—were real. Telling him that I wasn't crazy and never had been. After all, he was willing to listen. *Begging* me to save myself.

Another tear leaked from the corner of his eye, and I felt the moisture pooling behind my own. I wanted to tell him—tell someone—so badly it hurt. My gaze snagged on the notebook he held loosely at his side.

He'd read it. He already knew what I would say, and he didn't believe me. No one would.

I wound my arms around my stomach and sobbed. Even if he would believe me, I loved them too much to put them in the middle of this.

"What do you have to say for yourself?"

I closed my eyes and gathered every drop of courage, all the strength I had left inside me, and looked up at him through waves of tears. "Nothing." It came out broken, torn. A lie of the greatest proportion. I had everything to say, and nothing I'd allow him to hear.

A memory pressed forward, one that released my mother's sweet voice. She held me in her arms and made me promise I'd always tell the truth. "A liar," she said, "is the worst kind of person, one who earns neither strength nor trust."

Her words scratched so deep I tucked my legs into my chest to help protect against the emotional blow, and then they were gone, my mother's embrace turning as cold as Dad's stare.

"I saw the cuts on your hands last night, and found full vials of your medication in your closet. After talking it over with Ms. Morehouse and Dr. Graham, we've agreed. You're going back." Now *his* words echoed in my head. "Laylah and I can't help you if you refuse to help yourself." I'd never heard such bitterness in his voice before; it was like the edge of a dull blade running up the length of me, from belly to throat. "I've already called the clinic. They're sending a car for you."

All I could do was cry and shake.

Time didn't pass in any consistent way as the world spun out of control. Darkness settled on our disquieted home. Soon, the doorbell rang.

I grabbed the leg of the entryway table to stay the

tidal waves of fear hammering into me and to keep from drowning in remorse.

Dad opened the door and pulled me to my feet, but my knees gave out. I sank halfway to the ground before Dad straightened me up, holding me there. Two large men dressed in white waited on the front stairs. Dad handed me off like a pig to the slaughterhouse.

The men in white. They'd come for me many times before, but somehow, after almost four months of freedom, this time was worse. My nightmare come true.

They carried me out the front door to their waiting van.

I ran the last time they came for me. It had taken them thirty minutes to catch me. In the end, it had only added more time to my required therapy.

My Converse sneakers hit the stairs one clunk at a time as they towed me closer to the van with the SS Crazy's yellow sunflower logo on the side. I flailed, suddenly regretting my decision to go quietly.

I changed my mind. Running was totally an option.

I thrashed and broke from one man's grasp, then looked up the street while I fought the other. A beautiful man stood on the sidewalk across the street, no more than fifty feet away, confusion twisting his face.

"Cam," I shouted. "Cam, help me!"

He looked so striking under the cover of night. So beautiful.

I jumped off the curb and ran into the street. The first orderly reclaimed his grip, crushing my arm under his own.

"Please, Cam." I wondered what he was doing here, but instantly decided it didn't matter, as long as he was here. As long as he saved me.

His lips parted and his brows knotted. He stepped

forward, then stopped, as if he was rooted to the sidewalk. And then he turned. Walked away. As if he hadn't heard me. Hadn't seen me at all.

Shit. Fire churned in my stomach, and the last of my hope dripped off my skin and seeped into the cracks of the sidewalk. A car honked, swerving around us. The men pulled me back from the street.

Dad handed the man I'd kicked a small suitcase and had the nerve to wave goodbye to me from the curb. Of course he wouldn't come with us. We'd been through this dozens of times before. We all knew the drill.

The men shoved me into the van and forced a happy little injection into my arm. "To calm you down. Don't fight it," one of them said.

The world spun, and my eyes grew heavy. Cam floated away, along with the rest of the world.

Chapter Thirty

W hen I regained consciousness, I was in that old, familiar place. The colorless peeling paint, the stale scent of despair. I waded over to the window, pressing both palms to the cold glass. The Sunflower Serenity Mental Health Clinic sat low on the Sierra Nevada Mountains, looking down on the small Northern California town of Sonora. In the quiet hours, I watched the sun rise over the mountain range, completely numb.

All the months I'd spent on the outside—honing my self-esteem, learning who I truly was, finding ways to open myself up to Lee, Cam, and, to some extent, even Kade—they were all lost. That knowledge was completely pointless here.

People dressed all in white escorted me to therapy, where I played their little game, denying the existence of angels. They gave me six pills a day. They watched me in the shower, at meal time, and during free time. But they didn't let me outside to tend the garden, the one thing that might have helped. They were in control of everything I did, but they couldn't control what was inside me. I knew Cam and Kade were real, no matter what Dr. G said. And he had a lot to say in our morning meeting, including not sounding hopeful about releasing me after the seventy-two hour hold. He always used his "one day at a time" tactic, but I knew that wasn't good.

A day later, I had my first visitor. I thought it might be Cam, finally coming to help, but the delusion faded in the tick of a second. He wouldn't break the rules. After the way he'd left me, I wouldn't want to see him, anyway.

With the weight of this place on my shoulders, I stumbled my way down the long, celery-green corridor that led to the visiting area, dragging my fingers along the tightly woven links of iron soldered over the windows, masking off and distorting the outside world.

The man behind the glass at the end of the hallway asked me my name. I slurred it on my first try, but eventually got it out. I chipped at the loose paint on the door while I waited, revealing layer after layer of the same, muted tone. Colors were bland in this place. They wouldn't want to counteract their precious drugs by using a vivid color to stimulate us.

A buzzer chimed in three erratic tones, and the door slid back. The movement happened too fast for my drugged eyes, and I leaned through the doorway to steady myself. Stupid antipsychotics. They must have had to up my med doses to stabilize me, but they came with one hell of a kick.

Dad rushed to my side and helped me to an empty table. "Are you okay, Ray?"

"No. No thanks to you." I couldn't help the bitterness that laced my tone. He had no clue what was going on out there, and now, neither did I.

If I'd had more time, I might have gotten Cam and Kade to work together. They could have stopped Az. Had there been more deaths? What had happened to Luke?

But it didn't make a glimmer of difference because

I was stuck in here and couldn't do a damn thing behind the foot-thick walls and reinforced glass.

"I don't deserve that." Dad shook his head and spoke in whispered tones, half to himself, half to his crazy daughter, as if that was the only way us crazies could hear. "You needed help, and you lied to us."

It was the same crap he'd spewed every time he left me to these wolves. I recognized the rhetoric as Dr. G's and wondered if Dad had prepared to visit me by first talking to him. I narrowed my eyes, the anger in me spreading like so much poison.

He sighed. "You need more time. Maybe this was a bad idea."

"Maybe it was," I agreed, the words running into one. "Where's Laylah?"

"I pulled her from school to come up here, but she's in the car."

"Then tell her to get her butt moving." My voice sounded loopy, even to me.

"She doesn't want to see you, Ray."

My heart fractured.

"I tried to talk her into coming up ..." Dad reached for my hands. I slid them off the table, and they flopped lifelessly beside me. "But she's devastated."

No. I twisted around and waved at the man behind the glass, the motion sending blurry aftershocks into my vision. The man in charge of the door sent a woman in bland blue scrubs out. "I need a pen and paper," I told her, clenching my teeth to keep my jaw from flopping around. The nurse eyed me suspiciously, probably wondering if I'd jab it into Dad's neck. Or my own. I turned back to Dad. "If I write her a letter, will you take it to her?"

"Of course I will." He looked like he was holding back tears.

The nurse nodded and retreated back to the other

side of the glass. She returned with a single piece of paper and a blunt-tipped pencil. I should have been offended that she didn't trust me with the stronger tip of a pen. Instead, I touched the pencil tip to the paper and wrote:

Laylah,

I'm sorry things happened this way. I'm sorry you sold me out. You have no idea what was going on, and now you never will. Remember, no matter what you think of me right now, I'm still your big sister. I'm the one who took care of you when Dad couldn't, after Mom died. Don't forget those cold nights when I used to let you crawl into my bed, when you used to be a real sister to me.

-Ray

I folded the note and handed it to Dad. "Have her read this before you go."

He nodded solemnly. We said nothing else to each other before he left.

I waited for Laylah, watching the quivering clock in the room, surrounded by its own, cozy little wire fence. I knew my sister couldn't pass up a fight. Ten minutes passed. I told myself what I wrote wasn't enough. *I* wasn't enough. She wasn't coming.

My sister was so done with me she couldn't even be bothered to fight with me anymore. We hadn't given each other much of a chance after this last release, but we were family. The one constant in my life, and I'd let it all slip away.

I stood up, bracing against the table, waiting for the colored spots that circled when I moved too fast to pass.

Another buzzer sounded, and Laylah's voice rang out. "What the hell was that letter about?" She stood by the door. "Don't blame me because you're crazy!"

The pencil nurse slid in again, speed walking over

to chastise Laylah. "Young lady, if you're going to be here, you can't yell. And we don't use the *C* word."

"That's fine. I'm done." She turned back to the door. "Let me out!"

Crap on a stale cracker. "Laylah, don't go." I swallowed the numbness the pills created in my throat. "I needed you to get over yourself and come up here." I blinked twice to make sure she was really there. "So I wrote something I knew would piss you off. Lately, yelling at me is the only way you'll …" I almost lost the thought, but lassoed it back just in time. "… talk to me." She stood there with her back to me, her blonde hair somehow shining in this dark, awful place. But she hadn't left yet. I still had a chance. "Yes, I screwed everything up. I made life hell for you again. And I'm so, so sorry."

She turned around and looked at me. She moved fast, plunking down across from me.

I gave into the vertigo and giddiness and lowered myself down onto the bench at the table. "I'm so sorry," I said again, feeling the pain of every syllable.

"Me, too." She rolled her eyes. "I guess." Her throat bobbed as she swallowed. Wetness welled in the inner corners of her eyes. At twelve, she seemed so grown up. If you wore earplugs.

I took a deep breath, trying to concentrate through the haze of drugs. "Laylah, I have to tell you something. The men I see, they're angels, and they're real. I can touch them, talk to them." *Kiss them.* I swallowed and gauged her reaction.

She frowned the way some of the inmates here did when pills stuck in their throats. Understandable. I'd just asked her to swallow a rather large pill. "Yeah," she dragged the word across the floor and back again like she didn't believe me. "Let them help you this time. It would be nice to have a normal sister." She stood and flipped her hair in a way that reminded me of her little Musketeer friends. "I'm so out of here." She turned to leave.

Desperate, I reached for her, but with the nurse staring at me, I didn't dare grab her. "Laylah."

She sighed and turned back to me. "What?"

Cam wouldn't do anything to jeopardize his damn code of not being able to interfere in a life he's not charged to protect, but Kade had no code. "I need you to get a message to someone." She didn't move. "Please, Laylah."

Thankfully, Laylah didn't head for the door. She leveled a curious glare at me. "Is it a boy?"

"What? Yeah, it's a boy." The meds were doing a number on me, but for the life of me I couldn't figure out why that mattered.

"A boyfriend?"

"Boyfriend? No. No boy—"

She crossed her arms and quirked a brow.

"Yeah, okay, I guess you can call him that." *But please don't.*

"Seriously?" She took a step closer to the table I sat at. "How did you pull that one off?"

"Just, can you go talk to him? Tomorrow if possible?"

"I guess. Where do I find him?"

"Roxy's Diner, the place I worked. Look for a guy with dark"—*not wings*—"hair and eyes. Handsome, tan, tall. He looks maybe twenty, sits at the counter, and only drinks coffee. His name is Kade. I need you to tell him where I am. Tell him—" I paused. What did you tell a Fallen angel when you needed him to break you out of a mental hospital? "Tell him I'm going to owe him another favor."

"How am I supposed to know who he is? Dark hair tells me nothing."

Mom. She looked so much like Mom. "One look at you and he'll know exactly who you are." It was getting harder and harder to string words together. My tongue swelled, as if there was cotton in my mouth.

"Fine. Creepy, but fine. And for the record, I'm only doing this 'cause I have to see the loser who would date you." She swallowed then, pushing her thumbs together. "Just get better this time. And don't do anything stupid."

She did care. Tears flooded my eyes again, and relief settled in my chest as I watched her leave. "Don't worry. I'll be safe. No matter what you hear."

My sister rolled her eyes and shook her head as the bars closed behind her.

I had no idea if Kade would come. The more I thought about it, the sillier it sounded. I mean, how could he? He was a Fallen angel, not a magician. Not even wings would help him breach these walls.

Still, that evening at dinner, when the nurses handed me my pills, I spilled them out into my hand and pretended to swallow them. My chances of escape might have been slim, but I had to hold onto that hope. And if it *did* happen, I had to be ready. I couldn't let the drugs slow me down any longer. Nurse Tina checked my mouth, nodded, and marked me off the list. I hid the pills in my bra and flushed them when I had the chance.

Chapter Thirty-One

Withdrawals gave me an earsplitting headache that night, and I had trouble getting to sleep. When I did, I dreamt of a black-winged angel flying toward me, the bluish light behind him mirroring Allison's painting. He'd called my name again and again, in the same, deep voice I remembered from my previous nightmare. At first I thought maybe it was Kade, but that voice was nothing like anything I'd heard in real life before.

I woke in a cold sweat. At first, I thought it was the nightmare that had pulled me from my sleep, but then I heard the noise outside my door. I slipped out of bed, pausing to grab the nightstand when the throbbing in my head protested the movement. I managed to creep across the room to peer out the door's window, smaller than a sheet of notebook paper. Nurses surrounded the doorway across the hall. I waited, and soon enough they cleared to allow a gurney to be rolled from the cell. A lump the size of a small body lay on top, covered by a sheet.

I stared at that gurney as it was wheeled down the hall, followed by a mournful parade of nurses. My head pounded behind my eyes. I started to turn back to bed, but a swirl of color caught my eye. I looked past the few remaining nurses. Inside that room, blue and black swirls swept across the wall. The tips of the black reminded me of something. Something familiar, and frightening, though I couldn't remember why. The pounding in my head was too thick. Too consuming.

I forced my hand to turn the doorknob and open the door. "What happened?" My voice rasped like it belonged to an old woman who had smoked for half her life.

One of the nurses broke from the pack and rushed toward me. "Get back to bed, Rayna."

"What happened?" I tried to peak at the gurney one last time before it turned the shadowed corner.

She hustled me into my room.

"Tell me what happened!"

She sat me down on the bed and readied the blankets so she could tuck me in, like that would ensure I'd stay there.

But I needed to know. It was important. Those black swirls … "Tell me or I'll scream. It'll wake everyone up. Then you'll have to tell us all."

Her lips puckered together in disdain, but the fight had left her eyes, and I knew I'd won. The victory was short-lived. "It's Caroline. She somehow got a hold of some cleaning supplies. No one heard her."

For a long moment, the words didn't make any sense, lost to the thickness inside my head. But then they broke through, and I pieced it together. She'd poisoned herself.

The nurse dropped my blankets. "We were too late. She … took her life. Now, *please* go back to bed." A wet sheen caught in her eyes as she left to join the others in the hallway, closing my door behind her.

I backed away from the door.

The black and blue on Caroline's wall. It had

looked eerily familiar. I inched forward again, needing to get a better look. I peeked out my door's window again. The majority of the nurses followed the gurney, but two remained in the hallway by Caroline's door. I turned my doorknob slowly, to make sure no one noticed. When it wouldn't turn any farther, I yanked the door back and bolted across the hall, knocking the two nurses down. I stopped short at the doorway. I didn't need to go any farther to know it was true.

Spanning the length of Caroline's wall was a mural of a faceless, dark-winged angel. The same picture Allison and Tony had drawn.

No, no, NO!

Az had followed me.

He must have.

The hospital was three hours from San Francisco. Why else would he target this place? Poor Caroline. My fault. This was all my fault. I might have sunk to my knees. I don't remember, except when the nurses came, they had to reach down to grab my arms in order to drag me back to my room. They laid me in bed and posted a nurse outside my door.

I didn't sleep any more that night. Couldn't. Guilt and worry ate away at me. The possibility that Az would come for me next felt too real. Too close.

On my way to breakfast the next morning, I peered around corners, looked closer at each of my fellow patients, even watched the nurses more carefully. Az was near, he was coming for me. He could be anywhere. Any*one*. And everyone seemed to be watching me differently today. Everyone.

What were Az's angel powers? Could he influence people like Cam, or intimidate the way Kade had once at the diner? Or could his gifts be something worse? He could be in the very air I breathed. When I sat down for Arts and Crafts time, I watched everyone and held my breath until my lungs burned. The nurses paid attention then, so I stopped that.

Az had been here last night, and I hadn't seen him. What if he was still here? He could be anyone. Allison hadn't drawn his face, I didn't think. I hadn't seen his face in either of my dreams. A schizophrenic with a lazy eye had followed me down the hall yesterday. I saw him watching me sometimes, whispering to friends I couldn't see. What if he was the angel? I sat in the corner with my back between a wall and a window so I could watch the large activity room and no one would be able to sneak behind me.

Despite the awful withdrawals, I continued stashing my meds instead of swallowing them. What if the pills were keeping me from seeing wings? From seeing Az? I couldn't defend myself against what I couldn't see. He was here. Somewhere. My life now depended on being able to see the angels.

At lunch, I circled the cafeteria, waving my hands behind the other inmates—patients. Patients. That earned me some odd looks. But it didn't matter. I walked the room in a wide circle, brushing against backs, pretending to stumble, pretending to zombie walk.

I hadn't felt any feathers brush my fingers. I hadn't found him yet, but I would. I pressed the side of my face to the glass. If I angled in just the right way … there! Below my window I could see the best part of the garden. I was still there when they came to get me for dinner.

After dinner, a nurse in pink scrubs delivered my meds. The colorful lanyard clipped to her elastic waistband twisted as she stood there. I looked up to find her eyeing me suspiciously. I tucked my knees tighter to my chest and curled my toes under my orange plastic chair. She thrust the pills closer to my face. I didn't budge. We stared at each other. If she wanted a contest, I'd give her one.

I wouldn't be the first to break, I wouldn't be the first to break, I wouldn't—

Damn. I blinked.

Okay, do over. I wouldn't be the first to break, I—

"Are you going to take your meds, or are we going to have a problem?" she asked.

I tentatively stretched my hand out. There was something strange about this nurse. I could feel it. Az could be anywhere. He could be pretending to be a nurse, instead of a patient. He could be *this* nurse.

A loud crash caught her attention, and she turned. Across the room, another patient slammed her plastic tray against the table again and again and again.

I squinted, trying desperately to see wings. Wings, wings, c'mon wings. But I saw nothing. I waved my hands behind her. Again, nothing. Maybe the meds had dulled my sense of touch, too. While she was still distracted, I stood on my chair and pressed both my hands into her back, moving them around, tapping them in different places. Again I felt nothing.

"What are you doing?" She turned around so fast I almost fell off my chair. "Dear, don't play with me. Time for your pills."

I shook my head, the world suddenly turning.

The nurse forced the pills into my mouth, covered my lips, and pinched my nose until I swallowed. I kicked and struggled, falling off my chair, and the woman, who was at least twice my size, followed me to the floor.

The instant she released me, I darted to the bathroom, slammed the stall door closed, and stuck my finger down my throat.

The nurse banged at the door. When my stomach was empty, I leaned against the stall door with all my weight. The door's catch snapped against my weight, springing back into the nurse's face. She fell to the floor with her hand over her nose and called in help. Another nurse entered with a syringe.

When the needle pierced my skin, I thought of Kade. How he'd never come for me. The liquid fire shot through my thigh, and within seconds heaviness took my muscles and my joints turned to jelly.

I'd never get to tell Cam the kiss we shared meant more to me than even I understood—despite how mad I still was at him. And now we'd never share another. I'd be stuck in here forever. Or until Az came for me.

The nurses lifted me onto a gurney, and wheeled me to my room.

The larger nurse shook her head. "I don't know what goes through your minds when you girls fight us so hard."

"This is your fault." I slurred my words together like I was drunk. One of those pills had to be a sleeping pill or an elephant tranquilizer, because usually the shots weren't this good on their own. "You, all of you, made me believe the angels weren't real. They are!" I swallowed the ridiculous excess of saliva pooling in my mouth. "They're everywhere!" The drugs shot waves through my vision. The only way to make them stop was to close my eyes. "Everywhere," I said again. I thought I heard her leave, the door clicking softly behind her, but couldn't peek through a single eyelash to check.

Sleep came fast, and the drugs trapped me in my nightmares.

Chapter Thirty-Two

A loud snap woke me. Still drowsy, I tried to sit up, but heaviness weighted down my body. I struggled, tried to kick, but my legs were afflicted by the same strange … the shot and possibly a sleeping pill. My heart thundered. That could only mean I was at the Sunflower Serenity … the crazy house.

Tears formed in my eyes. My eyelids were heavy. When I finally wrestled them halfway open, the first thing I saw was darkness. Not darkness, but a starry night. The stars shone and whirled. Wait. Not a starry night. A set of black wings.

He's come for me.

I tried to scream, but my mouth was too dry to make a noise. Nails of fear scraped down my throat and into my chest. I fought grogginess. My wide eyes focused on the Dark One, watched as he stood over me. This was it. He was going to kill me. My breath froze in my lungs. I struck him with my right hand. The sound and feel of the hit resonated through the spaghetti of my muscles. He caught my wrist easily, although he needn't have bothered; I didn't have the strength to hit him again.

I screamed. This time it sounded clearer, but my brain was fringed and hazy from the drugs.

His hand clamped over my mouth.

No, no no! I struggled harder.

He was going to suffocate me. Make it look like I killed myself. What would Dad think? Or Laylah? I squeezed my eyes closed and fought against his hands, one over my mouth, one pinning my wrist to my chest.

My heart thundered in my ears. Nothing I did mattered. I was going to die, become part of some twisted Fallen angel's super weapon. What would that mean for me after this life? Would I suffer? Burn in hell? Or would I just disappear?

And I realized something. If Az killed me, then I wouldn't be committing suicide, so I wouldn't go to hell. If he killed me outright, his plan was spoiled.

Not that that would stop him.

I tried one last time to scream and spit and bite at the hand.

"Rayna, would you shut up?" The dark angel hissed in my ear.

I stopped struggling. Blinked and tried to focus on his face. He slowly lifted his hand off my mouth, like he didn't trust me not to scream again. Or try to bite him. Yeah, I'm pretty sure that happened.

"Kade?" I couldn't believe it. Wait... "Is this a dream?"

"Is that anyway to talk to your boyfriend?" He turned up a half smile.

Boyfriend?

Laylah. She always had a knack for finding new and interesting ways to humiliate me.

He pulled me to my feet. I nearly flopped onto my face, but he swept me up and steadied me against him. The world spun, tangled, waved like heat off the Arizona asphalt. Strong arms wound around my waist, pulling me closer. He brushed a sweaty tangle of hair from my eyes. "They really have you doped up."

Blood roared in my ears, like tiny, evil lions. I tilted my head up to look at him, but he was so far away. And spinning. "Is it really you?"

He said something like, "You're not dead yet, so what do you think?" But I couldn't think. Couldn't really hear. Couldn't … anything.

He tried to tow me forward a few steps, then I was near the floor again. Stupid floor. He swooped in and stood me beside him, wrapping his arm around my back. We shuffled toward the door. Kade leaned me against the wall while he opened the door and glanced down the hall. "It's clear."

I took one step toward him and flopped to the floor. Muted pain throbbed in the right side of my face.

"Ow," I said into the ground through the side of my mouth.

"Screw this." Kade lifted me off the ground and carried me in his arms.

He moved quickly, bolting down the hall with me in his arms, like I weighed no more than a kitten.

"How did you find me?" I asked. "How did you get in?"

He shushed me, pressed his back to the wall, then peered down the next hallway.

I ignored his shushing and whispered, "You're acting all spy movie. It's funny." I started humming the *Mission Impossible* theme song between hushed giggles.

Kade bit back a smile, making his lips do this adorable, squiggly-line thing. Then he shook his head. "This might go smoother with you quiet."

I brought my hand up to cover my laughter and smacked myself in the face. Which wasn't very funny at all. But Kade laughed that time.

We collected ourselves, and after what felt like a long time, he ran to the first open door, halfway down the next hall.

The smell of food wafted through the air. Burnt chicken. My stomach growled so loud I swore it would get us caught. Kade looked down at me, fighting another smile.

Footsteps clacked down the hall. He wrapped one of his wings around us. Those cool, black feathers contoured to my skin. I stiffened. Then I submitted to the silky soft feathers. I splayed my hand across his wing, waving it back and forth. "So soft." I pressed my cheek against them, rubbing it up and down.

He watched me and shook his head. "You're so gone."

The footsteps in the hall quieted, eventually disappearing. His wings flicked and in an instant were tucked behind his back. "Can you walk?" When he whispered, his voice was missing that deep bass I'd come to not completely hate.

"I can try."

He lowered me down. My feet felt foreign. My ankles wobbled. But I balanced myself against the wall. His hand snaked around my waist, and he yanked me close to him. Together, we peeked around the corner.

An older nurse waddled behind the nurses' station carrying an overflowing plate of food. Another door closed. We were on the move again, sneaking our way down the hallway. The muscles in my legs twitched like grasshoppers cueing up a song, but Kade more than shouldered my weight.

We crawled past the nurses' station, one at a time, to avoid being seen. When we made it far enough, he stood and helped me up. Everything blurred, then doubled. Tripled. I grabbed for the middle Kade. My muscles shook, refusing to cooperate. "Bad muscles. Bad." I looked up at him and poked my bottom lip out. He covered my mouth with his hand. Another smile lit up his face.

Hmm. It was a good face.

Another fit of giggles tackled my self-control.

Louder voices echoed from the nurses' station. I swallowed a bubble of air and slapped a hand over his mouth. The lights flicked on above us. We both tensed and looked at each other. My breath stopped.

"Hey!" A nurse shouted from down the hall.

We ran. I didn't look back, just kept pushing my rubbery legs forward. I almost lost my footing, but Kade's grip kept me upright. We rounded a corner, and he pulled me into a stairwell. The door clicked closed behind us. Our fingers slid apart. I inched toward the side of the stairs that led down to the main level. No guards. I inched down two stairs before an alarm blared. The stairwell lit up with painfully bright florescent lights.

Kade grabbed my wrist and yanked me the other way. I stumbled again, up the stairs. My lungs burned. My head ached. I couldn't keep up and tripped over my own feet. He pulled me close, locking his arm around my waist, and towed me the rest of the way.

Warm. So warm.

But there were so many stairs. So many floors. A set of double doors appeared when we rounded the final corner. At the top was a metal door.

I rested my hands above my knees and hunched over. I fought to find a breath that wouldn't sear my insides.

"C'mon," he said, pulling me by the wrist again. We broke through a door that should have been locked and burst onto the roof.

The freezing air grabbed and pulled the life out of me. Darkness claimed the world up here, except for the spotlights atop the high, barbed gates surrounding the hospital's grounds.

"What do we do? We're trapped!" I looked to him

for an answer, but he seemed lost in thought. "Kade?" My voice wavered. We were so close. I couldn't go back now.

I stretched as close to the edge as I dared. Vertigo twisted the drop. I curled my toes, dislodging some of the loose rocks beneath them. The trees below looked like cotton balls, the paths like rope. I wondered how many floors up we were. If I jumped, would I feel it?

I'd do anything not to go back in. Anything.

Kade stepped onto the ledge. He turned his back to the drop off and reached a hand out to me. The alarms continued to squeal through the otherwise quiet fall night. It was now or never.

I took one step toward him, my hand disappearing in his. He wasted no time, jerking me forward, wrapping me up in his arms. "Do you trust me?" he asked, the stubble on his chin catching in my hair.

Did I? I looked over the side of the building again. Straight down, too many stories.

His wings stretched out, the stars in them aligning with those in the sky. I gazed at him in wonder. A shiver tapped my spine. Those dark, mysterious wings. Against my better wishes, my scrambled brain connected Kade's wings to the killer's. I tensed in his arms.

I'd been looking for Az everywhere inside: as a patient, as a nurse, but he could be here with me now. I could be pressed against his chest with his arms around me.

If Kade really was Az somehow, then this was it for me. They'd find my body splattered on the pavement. No one would remember him. They'd think I committed suicide.

I swallowed, forcing the hard lump down my throat. Either I trusted him or I'd get caught, be dragged, kicking and screaming, back to my room and psych cocktails. Of course, if I did give myself over to him completely, there was that pesky little possible side effect of death to deal with. I closed my eyes and shook my head, trying to convince myself to trust him. Because I had about three seconds to do just that.

Kade hesitated. His warm breath tickled my eyelashes. "Something's wrong."

I glanced up at him. "Wrong? What's wrong?"

"Someone's near."

I tried to push off him and look around, but he squashed my face to his chest with one hand.

"We have to go. Don't make a sound."

Before I could take my next breath, he tipped us over the edge. I bit back a scream as we plummeted to our deaths.

I waited for the end. It was too cold to take in anything but sharp breaths. And my body was still so numb that when we did finally hit the ground, I might not even feel it. The thought became a comfort all on its own.

But death didn't come.

It no longer felt like we were falling. Wind still ripped passed me, but from the wrong direction. "It's okay, Rayna. You can look now."

Hiking my shoulders up to my ears, I tilted my head to the side and opened one eye. And screamed. Different shades of black and blue flew by beneath us as his dark wings flapped. Tiny reflections of stars danced off them. Above me, I could see only sky.

"Wh—who was on the roof with us?" I asked, my jaw chattering.

"Huh? Oh, no one. I ... was mistaken." His breath warmed the top of my head, but as quickly as it came it was gone. "It's okay now. You're out."

He was lying, I could tell, but I wasn't really in a position to question it. With the wind rushing beneath us and my adrenaline pumping, I'd just as soon let it go. It didn't matter. We were away from there now. Far away. "Where are we going?" There was no way I could just go home now. Not after escaping the mental hospital. Would I ever be able to go home again?

"For a skinny girl, you're sort of heavy. We'll never make it all the way back to San Francisco this way." He dipped his wings. Our flight path wobbled, like turbulence in an airplane. I clenched tighter to him, surprised my nails didn't draw blood. Kade laughed, a sound so full of life I almost enjoyed hearing it. If only it wasn't directed at me.

I kicked him before I could think better of it.

"Careful, or I'll really drop you," he added.

The icy air blasting us from every angle helped clear some of the fuzziness in my head. I turned my face back into his chest.

He'd come all that way. Why? Because I'd asked him to, or because he wanted me to owe him that favor? I swallowed. Whatever his reasons for breaking me out, I'd bet they weren't simple. Kade was a mystery wrapped in a dangerous package. And feathers. Can't forget the black feathers. They fit in there somewhere, too. He wasn't on my side; he just wanted something from me.

"Seriously though, I have to land. You're freezing, and," he paused thoughtfully, making me look up at him. "It takes a lot out of me to fly." Something in his face changed, hardened. Apparently, there was more to flying than he wanted me to know. I considered annoying him until he told me what it was, but I wasn't entirely sure he wouldn't just drop me. "We'll stop in Sonora."

I maneuvered just far enough away from his chest for my voice not to muffle. "Anything to get back on the ground."

At least the constant stream of cold air seemed to counteract the medication. Or maybe that was the adrenaline talking. My hair whipped into my face every time I braved a glance, so I pressed my forehead back to his chest.

Eventually, our angle changed. I felt us glide, so smoothly and evenly I could hardly tell we were flying anymore. He dropped his arms away. I freaked and clung to him.

"You can let go now. We're on the ground."

I opened my eyes to find myself standing on his shoes. I pried my arms from around him and stumbled back until I hit brick. Dizziness swirled around in my head. A streetlamp cast a faded amber glow down the darkened alley he'd set us down in. The color pulsed in my vision. The sour scent of garbage turned my already sensitive stomach.

"Wow, that was … something," I said after thick moments of silence spent trying to get a handle on the meds.

"Don't complain. Statistically, it's the safest way to travel." He stowed the twinkling wings behind him, as out of sight as they could be.

Somehow I doubted that. But he still … he came. He actually came. And as much as I hated to admit it, I owed him big for it. I opened my mouth to thank him, but something else came out instead. "What happens now?"

A dark grin shadowed his face. "Now, we party."

Chapter Thirty-Three

"What? No. I need to get home ... ish." I couldn't let myself believe San Francisco had nothing left for me. After all, Dad, Laylah, and Lee were there. It was almost funny how love for the city snuck up on me, considering I'd always clung to Safford as home before.

"You don't have a choice." He sounded like he truly believed this.

Small glitters of green glass littered the alley floor. Not good with the combination of shaking knees and still-potent drugs. "Actually," I stepped, barefoot, down the alley, my back to the wall. The crumbling brick and mortar gripped my pj bottoms, twisting and bunching them, but it was better than slicing open my foot. No way was I asking Kade to carry me again. "I can take the bus."

"Yeah. The mental-patient scrubs wouldn't give you away or anything. They'd have you back within the hour. You could always call your dad to pick you up."

I hated him for being right.

"Relax. I took a look around town before I came to get you. Some girl invited me to her party. We can lay low there until morning. That would be best for both of us, safer. Then we'll find a way back." Glass crunched under his feet, and when I peered up into his face, I could see traces of dark circles forming beneath his eyes. Or my vision was still wacky. He turned toward the mouth of the alley before I could get a better look.

I didn't push him, even though it really would have made more sense to skip town now. Again, I had to trust him. And again, I hated it.

"Fine, but do you really expect me to go to a party drugged up and dressed like an escaped mental patient?"

He looked over his shoulder. A smile stretched across his lips. "Ah, now that's the best part." He strode toward me, glass crunching beneath his feet. He straightened my clothes, and tugged his fingers through the tangles in my hair. "Where else but a Halloween party could an escaped mental patient and a Fallen angel find refuge from the authorities?"

A sound of disbelief left my lips. "You're unbelievable." I thought about that. "And *way* too good at this stuff."

He slid his arm over my shoulders and lifted me over the glass, setting me down at the mouth of the alley. "You have no idea."

We walked—well, he walked, I stumbled—less than two blocks before I heard shouts and the unmistakable bump of music. A block and a half later we arrived at what would have been an ordinary, two-story house, if the entire thing hadn't been lit red from the inside. Partiers spewed from every door, and a few poured out of the second story window to lounge on the roof over the garage. Of course Kade would not only get invited to a party in the short amount of time he was in town, but to the most intense party I'd ever seen—not that I'd been to any, only watched them in movies with Lee.

Everyone had dressed for the occasion. Outside, seven or eight guys joked and pushed each other. Two were dressed as women; the others had oozing sores that dripped fake blood over their faces and shirts. Two girls holding red plastic cups stepped through the front door, one dressed as a slutty wench, the other as a sluttier Dorothy from *The Wizard of Oz*. Which just seemed wrong. The second girl carried a stuffed Toto and barked—*barked!*—at Kade as we passed them. He grinned back at them, allowing his gaze to linger a moment too long on the sashaying hem of Dorothy's skirt. I rolled my eyes. And I was the one in the mental hospital.

Kade pushed through the front door, keeping me close. The hot rush of all those sweaty bodies packed together pumped my blood faster. Party goers quivered and jumped in my vision. Too many people. Too many faces. My breathing got shallow. Each time the bass pumped, my chest constricted. Tighter. Tighter. Sweat trickled down my palm. I squeezed Kade's hand to steady myself.

He slowed, his other hand seared into my back as he pressed us forward. It took three and a half songs to traverse to the other end of the living room, where it seemed even more crowded, thanks to the bar.

"You want a drink?" Kade asked.

I pinched the bridge of my nose in an effort to stop the pounding inside my head. It didn't help. "Can't. Drugged, remember?" I shouted as close to his ear as I could get.

Kade checked out the bar, the line winding halfway back to the door, and took another look at the mess I had to be. I must've looked pitiful, because he turned his back on the bar. "You wanna find somewhere quieter?"

I nodded, hoping the tears would wait another few

moments to fall. I would've rather cried alone, but as we moved deeper into the house, we discovered the line for the bathroom trailed twelve people strong, and I lost hope that we'd find so much as an empty closet to hole up in.

Kade towed me up the stairs behind him. My legs felt ready to collapse. He slowed, matching my pace. Up here was better. Less crowded, and not as loud. My chest relaxed a bit. Too bad the meds were still keeping my muscles and vision on lock down.

We checked each of the bedrooms, all of which were occupied by couples in various stages of undress. Kade seemed to find amusement in the embarrassed flush of my cheeks. He examined me every time we closed one of the doors, and each time, his grin was different. Wider. Mortification dulled the hypersensitivity invading my senses.

After we'd been through all five bedrooms, he grabbed a throw blanket off the back of a chair occupied by another couple and opened the window at the top of the stairs. He stepped out onto the first-floor roof and reached through to help me out. The roof laid flat enough for even my shaky feet. We weren't alone up here, and the vibrations from the music still buzzed through my bones, but the outside felt gentler somehow.

I stopped a few feet from the edge and sat down. The gritty shingles scratched my feet and poked through my thin asylum pj's, but it felt so good to finally relax. Kade slid down beside me and wrapped the throw around my shoulders.

I let out a small sigh and struggled to hold my head up. As impossible as it was, I was out. *Free.*

"You feeling all right?" he asked. A skanky chick in an angel costume stumbled out the window with a "woo!" He flicked an irritated glare in her direction.

"Much better. Thank you. For, um, everything." I gave up trying to fight the heaviness of my body and slouched against him. "Do you want some blanket? Do you guys even get cold?" I asked, already trying to figure out how to drape the small amount of fabric over those giant wings.

He accepted the blanket, making sure I was covered first before scooting closer and sliding his arm around my back. "You don't have to thank me, you just have to owe me. And yeah, we feel cold and hot, just not as extremely as you do."

The silence washed over us—as much as it could with the music still blasting inside—but it was more the stillness I enjoyed. Well, that, and the not being drugged in a mental hospital.

"Care to tell me why you were there?" His voice was soft and cautious, in a way I'd never thought possible.

"Because I see angels."

He stared at me for a beat, and then burst out laughing.

I sank deeper into his hold, taking in the dark surroundings and the twinkles in the clear sky. It reminded me of my first real home. I missed our little town in Arizona so much. Mom would always have dinner ready when Dad came home, and Laylah and I would take turns helping her with the dishes while Dad ate and worked more. The nights were like this. I used to look out the window after Mom tucked us in, wondering what a big city looked like.

"You all right?" His voice was like a hum in the background of the music.

It was the second time he'd asked that since we got up here. I could have worried about what I looked like, what he was thinking about, how I could change whatever I was doing to make myself more normal.

Instead, I mumbled, "Mmm-hmm," and let my eyes drift closed, giving them exactly what they wanted.

I felt his head turn against my cheek, the soft brush of his breath on my hair. He was watching me, but for once, I was too tired to care.

Chapter Thirty-Four

Cam and I lay on the grass, looking over the sandbox in my favorite park, the one Laylah and I grew up ten blocks from. His wings caught the sunlight and exploded it all around him, almost as if they were the sun itself.

"I'm so sorry for watching while those men took you to that awful place, Rayna. I would have given anything to take you away with me." He sat up, laying his hand behind me. Blades of the damp grass squeaked as he twined his fingers around them. "Anything."

I suppressed a sigh. No way he was getting off that easy. Words, no matter how pretty, would not melt me.

"And I'm sorry for getting you involved in this mess with the angels and the Fallen, for all the pain this has caused you." Behind him, a small field of orange flowers bloomed. Poppies. They were so much like Cam, thriving in full sunlight, just like his wings. "But in a small way, I'm not sorry. Getting to know you has been the best part of my existence."

Between the haze around me and the perfection of his words, I knew I was in a dream. And a good one at that.

"In that case, of course I forgive you." I settled

closer to him, determined to make this dream as worthwhile as possible.

Our arms brushed, and he rolled over on his side to smile that flawless smile. He slid closer, pulling me to him. I nestled my head onto his chest. He was so close. So warm. But he smelled nothing like grass and earth; instead, I smelled soap and leather. His fingers tentatively brushed up my back. When they went back down, my entire body shivered. Desire hooked its clutches into me in a way I'd never experienced.

In an effort to be closer to him, I hooked my leg over his. When had dream-me become so bold? His other hand rested on my knee, and his breath breezed softly against my cheek. Spearmint. His breath smelled like my favorite gum. He rested his forehead against my temple. Home. It was like being home.

His lips barely brushed the line of my jaw while his hand began a slow ascent up the outside of my thigh. He whispered my name. It almost broke me.

I clutched for the front of his shirt, but suddenly, he wasn't wearing one. All the better. I hooked my fingers around the back of his neck. The muscles there were thick and corded. "Cam," I whispered back and angled him toward my lips.

He froze, then pulled back.

The action knocked me out of the dream. I opened my eyes to find Kade staring back at me, our bodies intertwined exactly the way they had been in my dream. The dream. With Cam. Not Kade. Cam. I jerked back so fast I nearly gave myself whiplash. "What the hell are you doing?"

Kade tensed, every one of the muscles in his bare chest contracting. He stood, and the glare he leveled in my direction cut me in two. "What was *I* doing? *You* were all over *me*, princess."

Ugh. No way was I practically molesting Kade in

real life while dreaming about Cam. But it was entirely possible. I was sleeping the sleep of the dead—and doped up still. Anything could have been possible. Not that I would admit that to him. I crossed my arms over my chest. "Don't *ever* do that again. This is *not* cuddly-McCuddle time."

I sat up and inched back, putting more distance between us, and looked around. We weren't on the roof anymore. The blinds were pulled, keeping the shadows close, but I could see enough to tell we were in a bedroom. From the black paint and half-naked pictures of girls pinned up all over the walls, I'd guess we were still in the same house, in one of the previously occupied bedrooms. *Ew.* I lurched off the bed.

Kade looked away, like he couldn't stand the sight of me anymore, and cracked his knuckles.

Where was his shirt? I swallowed, beads of nerves gathering along the back of my neck. I'd just slept with him. I mean we didn't *sleep together* sleep together, but we'd shared a bed. And almost did more.

The definition in his abs had me thankful the bed separated us. I'd never seen such a perfect body up close before. A tingly feeling rose in my stomach. Which was one part exciting. And ninety-nine parts terrifying.

A smooth, pink scar on the left side of his chest marred the perfection of his body. The sight of it caused an ache in my own chest. A scar that large had to have been very painful to acquire. I traced fingertips over my own heart. He'd never looked more human to me than he did now, hurt or angry at me for what I'd accidentally done, for damaging us somehow.

No, no, no. Whatever I was thinking, or feeling, wasn't allowed. Kade was fine. I was fine.

"Next time you want to play make-believe, leave me the hell out of it." He turned to peek out the window, nearly breaking the blinds when he poked a finger through them and yanked down.

His wings connected at his shoulder blades. I inched closer to get a better look. A black pattern, almost like a star, spanned the skin around them. Instinctively, I circled the bed and brought my hand up. The wings drew me in. I had to be closer. If I could just touch them, maybe his reasons for breaking me out would make more sense. Maybe, somehow, everything would make more sense: my sight, his existence, Heaven and Earth, the world. My hand hovered inches from where the wings attached to his skin.

He spun around, his hand catching my wrist with a snap. I gasped, my heart lurching in my chest. The movement was faster than anything I'd seen before.

"Don't touch unless you intend to finish what you started." His voice was as cold as Antarctica.

He released my hand, and I took a step back, slamming my leg against the corner of the nightstand. "Sorry. I was curious."

"Yeah, well, curiosity killed the cat," he said, voice full of intensity.

I swallowed and sidestepped him, trying not to let the first ripples of fear show. "Yeah, well, you would know more about killing than I would."

He looked away, peering back out the window.

I glared at him, thankful, for once, for his attitude, a reminder of how I normally felt about him. I clung to that distaste for everything I was worth.

He cleared his throat, his shoulders still tense. "It's late. We should hurry. It'll be rush hour soon. We'll be lucky if we make it to the city before sundown."

He slipped into his shirt. It slid down over his wings before they shimmered through it.

I followed Kade out of the room at a distance. We maneuvered through a maze of garbage and bodies.

There were several people still in the house. The lucky ones had crashed on chairs and couches; the others lay passed out on the floor or in the bathrooms. The pungent reek of alcohol wafted up from dozens of empty red plastic cups and seeped from the unconscious guests' pores.

"We're not flying again, are we?" I whispered.

"No. Too dangerous during the day." He tugged a hand through the back of his hair.

If I didn't know better, I would have thought it was a lie. But no. I was fresh from a mental hospital, being paranoid. Of course we couldn't fly around during the day where everyone could see us.

I followed him through the living room and the front door. The crisp mountain air was so much cleaner and sharper than the city. Clouds partially obscured the sun that still burned too bright for eyes that hadn't been outside in days. I blinked against the daylight and shielded my eyes. Trees lined the sidewalk, coating the cold ground beneath my feet with leaves.

"First, we need to get you out of those clothes."

I dropped my hand and narrowed my eyes at him.

He cut a glare at me. "You are still dressed like an escapee, remember?"

I looked down at the drawstring pants. And I still had no damn shoes.

He started walking, and I had to hurry to catch up with him. When we reached the main road, he turned me toward him, looked me up and down, then bolted across the street. "Be right back," he called from the other side. The forced smirk on his face turned my stomach with worry. He slipped into the vintage clothing store across the street.

I crossed my arms nervously in front of me as car after car passed, some taking a second look at the crazy girl on the street. "Could she have been the one from the mental hospital I heard about on the news?" I could almost hear them say. I darted a look around, ready for the white coats to tackle me. *Get a hold of yourself.* I covered the side of my face and leaned against a tree so the numbers printed down the right side of my scrubs couldn't be seen as clearly by the passing cars.

Hyperventilation hovered in my lungs until Kade came out of the store and dashed across the street with a black plastic bag in hand. "We're going back to the party."

I opened my mouth to argue, but decided against it. I mean, I wasn't about to change in the alley.

Once we got there, he pulled me back into the same bedroom. He tossed the bag onto the bed, the plastic rustling as he opened it. "Put it on; I'll wait outside." He headed for the door.

An onslaught of crystals and red satin exploded from the bag. "Wait. What *is* this?" I asked, afraid to touch the fluffy, bedazzled mess.

"It's the day before Halloween. I got you something ... fun." I could see the distain ringing his dark eyes before he left, closing the door behind him. *Ass.*

I paced for a few moments, making sure the red satin poodle with a crystal collar wasn't going to jump out and attack me, before I removed the outfit from the bag. Crystals dripped from the bust of the corseted top, which, to its credit, had more fabric than the separate skirt. The ultra-mini bottom, basically just a huge puff of tulle with an elastic waistband, wouldn't leave much to the imagination. I left the clip-on devil tail and a red sequined horned headband in the bottom of the bag. This costume was *so* not anything I'd ever wear.

I shook my head and searched the room for something—anything—else, but it looked like a clothes bomb had gone off in here, and everything smelled like pot and B.O. Unless I was comfortable running around in late October in dirty, too-large boxer shorts, then I didn't have much choice.

I undressed and pulled up the skirt, then wrapped the corset top around me, but couldn't reach the laces. I groaned, covering up my chest as best I could before quietly calling out for Kade.

The doorknob turned, but the door didn't even open enough to creak. "Does it fit, little devil?"

Little devil? Keeping my back to him, I peered over my shoulder. "You're an ass. And I need help."

He grunted and swooped in, tugging the laces of the corset so hard my boobs almost jerked out of the dress. I readjusted the top before another unnecessarily hard tug stole my breath, and took back my previous assessment: "ass" was too kind a word.

My back must have been bare between the laces because I could feel every brush of his fingers causing chaos over my skin. The satin ribbon skimmed the back of my thigh, reminding me how much leg was showing. And of course there was a wide gap between the top and the skirt, revealing a good deal of midsection. I'd be more covered up in a bikini. Another swift tug.

His fingers worked fast, like he'd done it a thousand times before. The final tug knocked the breath right out of me. "That, right there, that sound. That's how you know it's tight enough." For the first time since we woke up, he no longer sounded like he hated me.

"Good to know." I sucked in air and found it a little too hard to breathe. I pulled my skirt up a bit to cover more of my midsection, but quickly changed my mind when I looked in the full-length mirror in the far corner of the room. "But could we make it a little looser?" I looked over my shoulder at him.

He shrugged. "We could if you want your tits to

pop out." Oh, so he was still angry then. Good to know.

"Tight it is, then." I tested my movements. The corset cinched in my waist, accenting my curves.

I glanced at Kade, who was staring at me, expression unreadable. "You're mighty good with a corset," I said, testing the waters.

"This isn't my first time at the ball." He avoided looking at me. "You look good in tiny clothes, by the way."

I shot him a glower and decided I was much too dignified to respond to that. He was right, though. I looked hot. The crystals clustered heavily on top and thinned at the bottom all the way around the blood-red fabric. The color seemed to brighten the shade of my hair and my too-pale skin, and I'd never seen my eyes so green. But there should still be twice this much fabric.

I moved away from the mirror. "What now?"

"Now, we borrow a car."

"You mean *steal*."

"You want to get home, right?"

I sighed. "Fine."

"It'll take me a few minutes to hotwire something. Meet me out front." He opened the bedroom door and walked outside.

I rolled my eyes and went back to the living room, where I fished in the nearest person's pocket. No keys, but he had a cell phone. I palmed that and spotted the bulge of what I hoped were keys in the pocket of a guy passed out on the couch. I inched my hand in and pulled out a set of keys.

Score.

By the front door, three sets of shoes sat unattended. I looked down at my bare feet and decided to try the Chucks first. Too big. I tried the flat ballet slippers next, but could only wriggle about three quarters of my foot in. I sighed at what was left. Super-high black heels studded along the back with silver spikes. They were a little loose, but they had to be better than bare feet. I tested my balance, having never worn heels over two inches before.

I wobbled outside to find Kade half inside a black car, fiddling with the wires under the steering wheel. I stood over him, blocking out his light. When he looked over, I jangled the keys.

He wriggled out from the car and stood, brushing himself off. "Maybe there's hope for you yet." He tried to snatch them from my hand.

I jerked them back. "We're borrowing. This is only until we get into the city. Then you'll call the police and leave an anonymous tip about a stolen car."

He grunted, but didn't argue. I handed over the keys. When he clicked the button, the car in the driveway's headlights popped on. It was a two-door, lowered, purple Acura with a spoiler and shiny rims.

Wonderful.

Kade started the car. It vroomed to life when he pulled up to me and threw the door open. I sighed and climbed in. Getting caught in a stolen car would not be awesome, but I couldn't hide in the party house forever.

Three hours was a long drive, and I'd never been a patient road-tripper, so I unlocked the cell phone I took off the first partier and punched in Lee's number. I couldn't wait any longer to talk to my best friend. I had no idea what to tell him. Maybe I could dance around some of his questions. The phone rang and rang. His voicemail came on. "Lee, it's Ray. Call me at this number when you get this. Sorry I've been … away. Hope you're doing well, and—well, just call me."

Kade darted sidelong glances at me every few seconds. I squirmed, not wanting to give any thought to this new shift happening between Kade and me. It was scary and uncomfortable, and this was going to be a long ride.

I pulled up the web browser app on the smartphone, checked my e-mail, then I checked Lee's social network pages. The last post on each one of them was a picture. A black-winged angel with a dark-blue background.

Chapter Thirty-Five

I sat back in the leather seat, bouncing my heel out of my borrowed stilettos. Lee was drawing the same angel Allison and Tony had before their deaths. Tucking my elbows in tight to my sides, I focused on my breathing.

"Ray? Ray, you okay?" Kade watched the road, keeping one hand on the wheel, and felt around for my hand, eventually settling for my arm.

"I think my friend's in trouble."

He didn't answer, just removed his hand to shift, pushing the car faster. The stolen car handled well on the tight mountain turns, but we were so screwed if party-boy woke up and reported it. The bright purple paint would give us up instantly.

"Kade, I need to know everything about Az. Anything that might help me save Lee."

"I haven't seen my brother in decades."

Brother. He'd called Cam brother, too, the day they were both at the diner. I frowned. He glanced over at me, but I checked the phone again, still staring at Lee's drawing.

"Not the same way as humans. Brother in the sense we have the same maker, grew up together, and fought together."

"Oh." I sent Lee a text and waited for a response. "So do you all know each other?"

"Of course not. There aren't many of us left these days, but newer wings are still made, and, though it isn't common, angels still Fall. One side can't see the other's wings. Good thing too, otherwise we'd all be annihilated by now."

Complete angel annihilation wouldn't be so bad for me.

"Look, I don't know how or why you're involved in all this, but—"

I cut him off. "Whatever you're going to say, don't. I've made my peace with it." Sort of. "I just need to know about Az."

"Gotcha. Cliff's Notes version. When an angel Falls, those still in good standing are forbidden to interact with the Fallen, unless their paths cross while an angel is on a mission. Then it usually breaks down to last man standing. Az Fell decades before I did, so there's no way to know how powerful he's become."

"How did he Fall?"

"Harm. He turned cold, calculated, and he took a human life."

I imagined someone with white wings as beautiful and pure as Cam's being splattered with human blood. "At the diner, you said succumbing to human emotion was the way your kind Falls."

"I said a lot of things."

I drew my gaze over to Kade. He'd been lying to me. Probably this entire time. What else had he been lying about? This morning maybe, when I woke up in his arms. Last night, when he said there was someone on the SS Crazy's roof with us to scare me, to get instant payback for the way I dragged him up the California coast to break me out. And before, about Mom. He had to be lying about that too. I'd struggled with myself, pushing harder than I thought I could stand to put the slightest inkling of trust in him, and he'd played me. I didn't want to look at him, didn't want to be in the same car with him.

"You have to understand where I'm coming from. Kay, she … things ended badly. I was angry for a long time. You were …"

"The perfect revenge," I filled in, realizing it was true. Tears pricked my eyes. All this time I was merely a play thing, a toy in a tiger's cage. A way for him to hurt Mom from beyond the grave. Just another way I lived in Mom's shadow. First I'd become the burden after her death, the crazy daughter who couldn't handle her passing without seeing wings. Then when I realized Laylah was growing into Mom, inheriting her long hair and heart-shaped face, looking like her in a way I never would. Now I was a Fallen angel's crumpled do-over. I held tighter to myself, pressing my arms across my stomach until the corset's boning dug into my flesh.

Kade jerked the wheel, correcting the car's path. He glanced from the road back to me several times.

"This isn't the right time. You had a bad night. The drugs and—"

I wiped my cheeks with the back of my hand. "I'm fine." But I so wasn't. My emotions were stitched haphazardly together, and the thread that held them was blowing loose in the breeze. "Let's just stay on Az. What can he do?"

He said nothing for a long time. Of that, I was grateful. It gave me time to collect myself.

"Az is one angry S.O.B. He'll be able to influence them."

"The way you and Cam did at the diner, to my customers?" Up until now I'd avoided saying Cam's name, for both our sakes, but after what he'd revealed, I didn't care anymore.

I watched him roll his shoulders back. I would have smiled, if I could.

"The Fallens' influence is different. It comes from a darker place. Usually that makes it stronger than what the others can do. As far as what else Az can do, I have no idea. Our kind gets stronger with every life taken."

"So he could have unmatched power." The thought prickled my skin.

"He could have the ability to compel someone to do almost anything, or, if he's really pushing himself, he could even amplify whatever emotions are lingering inside the human, however small. Both are dangerous."

"But what about the drawings?"

Kade glanced at me while switching lanes to get around a van with luggage piled high inside. "What drawings?"

I pulled up the web browser again and showed it to him. "Two of my classmates drew this not long before they supposedly killed themselves. And now Lee's been drawing it." I closed the browser, unable to look at it again, my stomach turning. "And Caroline. Two nights ago, the girl across from me drank cleaning supplies. When I looked in her room, that picture was on her wall."

Kade's eyes cut to me. "At the mental institution?"

Technically it was a mental health clinic, but I couldn't argue with that association; hell, even I'd called it that before. "Yeah."

"I ... felt something on the roof last night. Just before we jumped." So Az really had been there. Maybe Kade hadn't been lying about everything. "I thought—it must have been a fluke, but I think he was there, watching us. I could feel him."

"*Feel* him?"

Kade ignored my question. "We have a problem. Your friend, your classmates, your family, they could all be in trouble." He studied me for so long I almost had to warn him he was still driving. When he finally looked back at the road, he clamped his jaw together and shifted again, weaving through the cars in front of us.

I tried calling Lee again. Voicemail.

"Why was he there? And why would he be after Lee? Why *my* family? So the deaths were following me around?" I grabbed his sleeve. "Has anyone else died?"

"I've been keeping an eye on the news. No other deaths at your school."

But what about my family? The longer he sat in silence, the deeper his warning sank in. Lee, Dad, and Laylah. Weight gathered on my chest. I squeezed my eyes closed, determined to fight the panic attack. Would Az swoop in and force the hand of everyone I cared about?

I tried a different approach since Kade didn't want to answer my previous questions. "How likely do you think it is that he'll go after my family?" I asked the last question almost too quietly.

He flicked me a glance, and his expression softened before he looked back to the road. "I didn't mean to worry you. Just thought you should know the worst-case scenario. The probability isn't high. If he's after your friend and he waited three weeks to take him, my money's on him having a plan."

I opened my mouth to demand he tell me everything when he reached over and squeezed my hand. When he looked at me, his eyes were completely black. "Get some rest."

Against my wishes, I sank into the buttery leather seat, feeling its comfort surround me. He'd used his influence on me. That bastard. I glanced over my shoulder at him, cursing him under my breath. Freaking wonderful. But I couldn't fight my heavy eyelids any longer, and I found myself relaxing—truly relaxing, my carefully crafted walls melting away for the first time in days—and slipping into sleep. With my next deep breath, images came flooding in.

A black-winged creature soared toward me, blocking out the deep-blue sky. The creature stopped, hovering several yards in front of me. I knew he was a Fallen One, yet he looked nothing like Kade. His jaw was too broad for his face, his forehead too narrow. The splash of pale skin and hollow cheeks made him look even more sinister. Blackness coated his eyes, gleaming like a vacuum of hope.

I stepped back, and the fog surrounding him billowed forward.

"I've been watching you, human. I know you can see us for who we are." I recognized his voice as the one from my nightmares.

"What do you want?" I shouted.

"Your gift, seer."

My gift? What was he talking about? I was no one, nothing. Still, this was a dream. I could control this. I feigned bravery, pulling my shoulders back and raising my chin. "You can't have it." He blurred toward me, stopping a foot from me. His icy breath blew against my face. I squeezed my eyes closed and balled my fists to keep my knees from shaking. "You can't have any more souls, either. Go back to where you came from."

More wind blew me back as laughter, deeper than his voice, billowed. "And you think you can stop me? Silly girl. You can't even help yourself."

His fingers raked my skin. Shards of pain sliced the inside of my forearm. The ache expanded, tearing into the palm of my opposite hand. I looked down. One of his hands rested in my palm, the other draped across my forearm, where the pain emanated from.

The light behind him intensified. "Come with me.

Once you sacrifice your pitiful soul to us, we'll rule this world together—"

Rule the world? I jerked back from him, feeling colder for the experience, the frost of winter on every inch of my exposed skin—which was a lot in this flimsy outfit. "You and I have nothing together!"

"I will have you, one way or another." His black eyes bore into me. "There are easier ways than this to break you. You'll see. Very soon." He flapped his wings and rose high into the air. The force from his take-off knocked me over. His dark, ominous shadow floated like a raincloud over my vision.

Me. He wanted *me*.

Tires screeched. I slammed against my seatbelt, and the pain broke the dream's spell.

"Rayna!"

I sucked in sharp breaths until the wooziness subsided. The world outside the car was dark and unmoving. We were parked, not on the highway, but on a city street.

Kade's face beside me was pale, his deep brown eyes rounded. "Rayna, it's okay," he soothed, his gaze jumping from my hands to my face and back again, watching warily, like he was afraid to startle me.

I didn't understand, until I followed the direction of his gaze, to the large shard of glass I clenched in my hand and the three long gashes that ran down the inside of my forearm. Blood oozed from the cuts. My hands shook, and I dropped the shard into my lap.

Kade moved quickly, snatching it up and throwing it out his half-open window. "What were you thinking?" His voice boomed and quaked at the same time. He tore the sleeve from his shirt, grabbed my hand, and wrapped it in the soft cotton, cinching it tighter than I would have liked. He ripped his second sleeve into strips and tied them together for my forearm.

Tiny glass particles lay over me like a glittery blanket. None of the pieces looked one-twentieth as large as the one I'd sliced myself with.

"How ... how did I—the glass ... did I do this?"

"Please don't tell me you really are crazy," he mumbled while my blood soaked through his black t-shirt.

I pushed his hands away, accidentally slamming them into the steering wheel. Pain throbbed in my hands, up my arms. Still, I shoved him away again. "I'm not crazy!" My voice echoed through the broken window and out into the street. Broken window? When did it break, and how did I get a hold of the glass?

"Ray—"

I shook. Every part of me shook. "I'm not! I never was."

"Okay, okay. I didn't mean it. I'm sorry." Kade reached for my arm, slowing halfway to make sure I wasn't going to hit him again. I thought about it, I did. It would have been so satisfying after he'd called me crazy, but my arm hurt so much. He held it above and below my cuts. "Shit. This isn't good."

My head felt light, like the injection was still in my system. "I—I saw him."

He looked up from my arm. "Who did you see?"

"He demanded my gift. Called me a seer."

"Who?" His fingers tensed.

I glanced down at my arms. "His touch burned, like ice."

He squeezed harder and shook, his voice turning hostile. "Rayna, who?"

"The one killing them!"

"What did he look like?"

"Pale, gaunt, huge jaw, completely black eyes." The tension in his fingers made me exhale in pain. "Could you ...?"

"That's Az." Disgust wrinkled his nose. "And you actually *saw* him?"

"He … came to me, in my dream."

He released me. "This is my fault. If I hadn't influenced you to sleep, he wouldn't have found you. My head wasn't in the right place. I shouldn't have done it." He shook his head and started the car. "We have to get you out of here."

"No! I need to see Lee. Take me to North Beach."

His gaze shifted, its intensity sharp. "Az marked you." He cupped beneath my arm, and moved the blood-soaked cloth aside. Blood welled in the deep gashes, flooding over to drip down my arms. "Three scratches. Three is demonic." His breath quickened.

"Demonic?"

"This is bad news. It means Az has been stepping up, moving through the ranks in the circles of hell." He tightened the makeshift bandage and ran a hand over his forehead. "Do you have any idea why he's interested in you?"

My vision spotted, and a cold sweat flooded my body. I bit my lip and steeled myself. "He knows I can see him. He wants me to sacrifice myself so we can work together for … something. I don't know."

"Az is a piece of work. When he goes after something—and as long as I've known him, he's always been after something—I doubt sucking an entire soul would ever be good enough for him. He'll play with his prey. Feed on their fear. But he must want something else from you. We have to get you somewhere safe." His voice took on a false bravado as he switched off the engine. He opened the door and walked around the car. After he pulled me from the car, he dusted the window glass off me, and towed me down the sidewalk.

The towering heels that were half-a-size too big

made me stumble. I pulled him back. "He's in my dreams! Where the hell do you think we can go where he can't find me?"

"We can try," he growled.

I wrapped my arms around myself, that familiar numbing of insanity creeping up on me.

"It sounded like you were having nightmares," he said. "I figured even nightmares would be better than what you had to look forward to here, so I let you sleep. You punched your fist right through the window."

I touched the gashes through the strips of Kade's shirt. My fist, palm, and entire forearm pulsed. "How could I even do that? I thought car windows were made to break in small pieces, in case of accidents."

"They are."

I checked my hand again, remembering the sheer size of the shard I was holding when I awoke. "Then how did I get a hold of such a big piece?" The mist in the air intensified into larger drops of water, each coming stronger, faster than the ones before.

"I don't know, Ray. I just—I don't know. This is serious, but I don't think he wants you dead." I watched as he searched the face of each person who passed us.

I swallowed, trying not to let it all overwhelm me. "He said there were easier ways to get to me. That he was going to do it soon." He wanted my ability to see angels and the Fallen. Kade had said Az could go after my loved ones. The drawing. The blood drained from my face. "He's going after Lee."

Chapter Thirty-Six

Retracing our steps, we piled back into the car. I directed Kade to Lee's address from the back seat, to avoid the shattered glass on the passenger side. The night's mist intensified into rain as we drove, the drops splashing into my face from the broken window.

I recognized the street. "This is it," I called up to Kade as we approached Lee's house. I scrambled out of the car.

"Rayna," Kade called, but I ignored him. He could catch up if he wanted to, though I doubted he'd try.

Light beamed from the front-room window. That was a good sign, right? With newly restored hope, I gathered up my nerve and splashed up the front stairs. The doorbell chimed against the sound of the rain.

"Yes?" Lee's mom peeked through the window on the door, squinting without her glasses.

"Oh, thank God. Mrs. Kyon, it's Lee's friend, Rayna. I know it's late." Actually, I had no idea what time it was, but the night sky meant it had to be after six. "But I need to talk to Lee."

"I'm so glad to see you." She opened the door and waved me in. Dad obviously hadn't told her where I'd been these last few days, otherwise she'd be pulling the shades and calling the mental hospital. Which gave me hope that he hadn't told Lee either. "Lee hasn't been doing well."

Not doing well? How? I stepped over the threshold, wiping my ridiculous shoes on the doormat in the foyer. "I would've been here sooner but there was a … family emergency. Where is he?"

"In his room."

I glanced down the first-floor hallway, spotting four doors and a grand staircase. "Which room is his?"

"Upstairs. Third door on the left." I took off up the stairs and heard her add, "That's quite a costume."

I followed Mrs. Kyon's directions to Lee's room and opened the door, not bothering to knock. "Lee?" I was almost afraid of what I would find, but pushed down the coward in me and stepped forward into the dark room, feeling blindly for a light switch.

A lamp flicked on in the corner of the room before I found the switch. A soft, yellow haze washed over my best friend. He looked so pale, sitting up in that big bed, a fog clouding his usually bright, brown eyes. A pained smile tugged up the corners of his lips.

He was alive, but definitely not well.

I raced to his side, leaning forward to take his face in my hands. His glasses slumped off his nose and fell into his lap. "Lee, are you okay?"

"I … I did something bad, Ray." Even his voice was weak. I didn't breathe until he spoke again. "I took some pills." He reached behind his pillow and shook an empty prescription bottle.

I sank to my knees. "No." It left my lips in a whisper. "What were they?"

He shrugged with more of a smile than I liked. "I dunno." His words slurred together. "Something of my mom's."

Damn you, Az. I'll kill you for this.

I glanced at the nightstand for a phone, but found none. "Mrs. Kyon! Call nine-one-one!"

I took the bottle from him. Sleeping pills. "How many?" The date on the bottle was less than a week ago, which meant he'd probably taken at least twenty. Lee's eyes drooped closed. "Where's the bathroom?" I shot up and threw the covers off him. "Show me."

He pointed a weak finger to the door on his left.

"All right." I tugged him up. He wobbled, but I managed to get his arm around my neck and pull him into the bathroom. I lifted up the toilet seat. "I need you to stick your finger down your throat."

"But why?" he asked, still dazed.

My voice roared inside the tiny space. "Damn it, Lee! Do you wanna die?"

He looked up, heavy eyelids fluttering, and dropped his mouth open. He slouched against the white-and-black tiled wall behind him, and for a moment, I thought he was going to pass out. "Um. I ... thought I already did."

"Mrs. Kyon!"

Where the hell was she? I lowered my voice, trying to stay calm for Lee. His eyes rolled back in his head.

I crouched in front of him and slapped his cheek as hard as I could. His eyes snapped open, only to roll around his head wildly. "Listen to me, if you don't get those pills out of your system right now, that's what's gonna happen!"

Mrs. Kyon ran into the bathroom, phone in hand. "What's wrong?"

"Call nine-one-one. He took a bottle of pills." She didn't move, but the horror that reached her face would never leave my memory. "Now!"

I heard the echo of the phone buttons and turned back to Lee, who was slouched over the toilet. His breathing had slowed. "Lee!" I grabbed a spiky tuft of his black hair. His eyes were closed. "Wake up, Lee. I need you to do this for me. You're my best friend, and I love you." The salty taste of tears touched my lips. "I can't do this without you. He can't have you. C'mon Lee, please!" I kissed his cheek, and his eyes fluttered opened.

He stared blankly at me, a sliver of himself peeking through the empty shell that his body was fast becoming. I grimaced and shoved two of my fingers down his throat. He emptied the contents of his stomach into the toilet bowl.

"Lee, I know you're sad and you feel like it's all a waste, but it's not." My voice shook, and I didn't know why I was talking while he threw up. But I felt like I had to say this, had to tell him. "There's so much out there to live for, so much more to life than this. I want you to experience everything this life has to offer, all the good things and all the wonders." Tears poured from my eyes.

He gripped the edges of the toilet bowl.

"Nothing would ever be the same without you. This world doesn't deserve to lose you, and neither does your mom."

Mrs. Kyon collapsed to the floor beside Lee and gathered him close. "The ambulance is on its way."

Fissures of relief ran through me. I pulled myself up and washed my hands, locking my knees so I wouldn't go down. I pressed my back against the wall beside the bathroom door and rallied to hold myself together.

A glimpse of shadow skulked across the wall in Lee's room.

I blinked and it came again, circling the walls like a vulture overhead.

The menacing voice from my dream chuckled, and wings flapped in the shadows.

The room was fully lit now, with one bedside lamp on as well as the overhead fixture. There wasn't a corner to hide in. But Az was here. I could feel him in the chill that raised the hair on my arms.

The trail of tears on my face suddenly felt like ice. Fury cut the fear in my gut with a hot knife.

"You snake," I said before thinking to whisper so Lee and his mom wouldn't hear me. "You stay away from him."

I glanced over my shoulder. Mrs. Kyon wasn't watching me, too busy comforting Lee to worry about me. I moved deeper into Lee's bedroom and farther from her panicked stare.

That menacing laughter swept across me again. His shadow draped the wall beside the window, narrowing for a split moment. It took me a moment to realize it was glancing outside.

"I have a different game in mind, seer." A short movie clip of Luke dancing among other students flickered on the walls of Lee's bedroom, as if played by an old movie projector.

"Why Luke? Why now?"

"He's in the right place for our conversation. Why not come along? There could be more surprises." I had no idea what he was talking about. Come along to where? Az's shadow landed in the bedroom, his larger-than-life wings projected on the gray walls. His mouth and eyes were hollow, the gray paint shining right through them, moving when he spoke.

"And if I don't?"

"I'll take his soul and never stop coming for the ones you love most." The shadow grew, stretching across the length of the room before it disappeared.

My shoulders touched the wall, and I slid to the floor. A wild wanting split through me, one that sought to end all of this, to ignore the way Azriel used Luke as bait and stay with Lee instead, to pretend none of this was happening and angels didn't exist.

I paced the room to ward off my bone-chattering fear. My stilettos sank into the plush carpet. I concentrated on it, relishing the feel of soft fibers bowing beneath my shoes, and watched Lee and his mom huddle together on the bathroom floor. Voices sounded from downstairs. Authoritative voices.

"We're up here!" Mrs. Kyon shouted, rocking Lee in her lap. He was clinging to her, watching me pace.

Two uniformed EMTs pounded up the stairs and stormed through the room, medical supplies in hand. I waited until they announced they'd be taking Lee to the nearest hospital before I left.

Deserting Lee was the last thing I wanted to do. I would've loved nothing more than to ride in the ambulance and sit by his side at the hospital, but I couldn't, not with Azriel's sights set on Luke and him threatening my family.

Kade leaned against the purple car, still double-parked in front of Lee's house. "Your friend?"

I motioned to the ambulance. "Hospital." I nudged him aside to open the door, and slid into the back seat.

He followed my lead by getting in and starting the car. "Is he gonna be okay?"

As we pulled away, I turned to watch the EMTs remove a gurney from the back of the ambulance. "I hope so."

"Where to?"

I thought back to the picture Az had shown me. It was dark, but lights swirled all around. The way the bodies in the background swayed, it could only have meant one of two things: a party or a dance. "My school. There's a dance tonight."

Chapter Thirty-Seven

The rain had subsided into lighter drops, for now, but darker clouds still shielded the stars. Kade drove fast. Either he sped up because the rain had slowed, or he felt the same urgency that was strangling me.

"How'd he do it?" Kade asked, then clarified. "Your friend."

I swallowed back the feeling of needles in my throat. "Pills." My voice was even weaker than I felt.

"They'll pump his stomach. If he's still alive when the ambulance gets to the hospital, he's got a fighting chance."

"Az was there. He did some strange projection thing on the walls." I leaned forward. "What else can Fallen angels do, besides fly? And influence us."

"Depends on the Fallen One. I'm about as useless as they come. That's the price you pay when you skirt alliances." We sped around a corner. The engine roared. I watched the little white dial move up the speedometer. The steering wheel groaned under the pressure of Kade's grip. "Let me guess, he was an animal or a shadow, right?"

"Shadow." I exhaled the answer, feeling the punch of Kade's words. "How did you know?"

"Shadowing is a gift granted to those allied with Lucifer. He's his servant now. Besides, if he was at Lee's house in his own body, I would've sensed him."

I stared at the nape of Kade's neck. "Lucifer? Like *Lucifer*, Lucifer? King of the underworld, ruler of hell? *That* Lucifer?"

"Yeah." The dark edge in his voice seared me. "Lucifer's been working his last connections to get the Fallen on his side, promising near limitless power. My guess is the suicides are a stepping stone, a way to grow their army before they make their next big move."

"Cam thought they were working on some huge weapon."

He glanced at me before returning his focus to the wet city streets. The rain slapped the pavement, insistent now, and I wished he'd slow down. "No way I'd help kill one of my own kind under normal circumstances, but now that we know he's allied with Lucifer, I'm in. That devil bastard won't get his way. Lucifer and Az are one bad mix, and they'll both get stronger from here on out if they remain linked. If they're after you, finding Az's body and killing him is the only way to stop them. Alone, Lucifer has no power on Earth."

"Okay—geez this is real—so what should I do, while you look for Az's body?"

"Keep the kids at the dance alive. You saved your friend. Do it again. Do whatever you can to keep him from hurting anyone else. Just not at the expense of your life." Those dark eyes flashed off the road and into the rearview. "Promise me."

I couldn't argue with him, not now. "Fine. I promise."

Kade said nothing for the rest of the drive, didn't even glance at me in the rearview mirror.

We pulled up to Stratford Independence. With the rain pounding on the front steps, several giggling students huddled in the glass doorways. I pushed the front seat forward.

Kade's hand wrapped around my arm. "Remember what you promised."

"You can stop with the grab—" The grim look on his face stopped me. Almost like he cared. I looked away, everywhere but at him. "You just … need to find Az's body, not worry about me." I slipped through his grip and stepped up onto the curb.

The rain hit me immediately, soaking into the cloth over my wounds and battering the uncomfortable amount of leg my skirt failed to cover. Classmates I recognized from a few different classes eyed my costume, some already starting to whisper. I kept my head low, wrapped my arms around myself, and took my first step toward the stairs. My ankles wobbled beneath me.

Suddenly, Kade stood in front of me, his hands beneath my elbows, steadying me. "I *am* worried about you. That's the problem."

Don't do this. Not now.

I batted at his arms and walked around him.

He sidestepped in front of me again, this time flaring out his wings, becoming an immovable wall. His face was filled with conflicting emotions. Hard-pressed jaw, tight mouth, but soft, round eyes and peaks of worry across his forehead. He was the sexiest wall I'd ever seen.

"Kade, don't—" I tried to push him away again.

He pulled me to him, his strength unyielding, and forced me to look into his eyes. "You do whatever you need to do in there to survive. You hear me? No stupid shit."

In these heels, I was eye level with his lips.

Raindrops rushed between us. And then it happened. A spark ignited inside me. Heat warmed my belly and trailed up my spine. I rested my palm on his chest.

He tilted his chin down and leaned into me, slowly, giving me plenty of time to pull away. But I didn't. I no longer wanted to. I let my eyelids drift closed, but didn't move toward him. The rough stubble on his face brushed my chin and my cheek. His heart beat beneath my palm.

His heart. He had a heart.

I jerked back and my eyes flew open.

Today when his shirt was off ... the scar on his chest. Kade had a heart, and Cam didn't. How did that happen? What did it mean?

Rain continued to pour, blurring the distance between us. "Why didn't you tell me?" Of all the things he hadn't told me and the stuff he'd purposely kept from me, why did the fact that he had a heart when Cam didn't seem so important? Maybe because it made him human—well, more human.

"And give you another reason to be scared away? I don't think so."

A crack of thunder rattled my eardrums. I hadn't even seen the lightning. I hadn't seen a lot of things, including the mistake I'd almost made, and the time I'd wasted.

Whatever I was walking into, I needed to focus: on Luke, on the other students, not Kade. Not now.

"I have to go."

Kade closed his wings and stepped aside for me.

"Find him, Kade. I'm counting on you." I made my way up to the top of the stairs and pushed through the now-empty glass entryway.

I looked back at him and mouthed, "Be careful."

I moved as fast as my heels would allow down the first floor hall, leaving a wet trail of drops behind me.

A colorful poster stopped me. *Halloween Dance: October 30th in the Gymnasium.* Music boomed down the hall. The closer I got to the back of the building, the louder it became.

I turned the final corner and found students lining the halls, paired off against the lockers, some making out, others no doubt hoping to do so soon. I passed them, wishing again that I could take a deep breath in this damn corset, and made my way into the gym. The colorful lights blinded me, flashing off the crystal-encrusted corset. Once the burning-retina thing cleared, I stood on my tiptoes, scouring the dance floor for Luke. I waded into the horde, pressing my way across the dance floor, when someone grabbed my arm and pulled me through one of the side exits.

I fought, pushing off the grip. Arms spun me around, pulling my back into his chest and trapping my arms.

"Rayna!" A familiar voice said into my ear. *Cam.* I stilled.

He released me, and I spun around. My heart jumped, but I didn't know how to feel. I pushed away from him, waiting for the conflicting emotions raging inside me to settle into one, definable thought. I waited for something concrete inside to tell me how to act around him.

He'd asked for my help, and against everything I wanted, I'd given it to him. I let him suck me into all the winged stuff I thought I had left behind; I let him drag me into the center of their ongoing conflict. And when it all came crashing down, he abandoned me.

He'd abandoned me. Left me alone to face the aftermath when he could have helped. He'd done nothing to help. But Kade did.

I bit back all the emotion I could, hoping nothing

would leak out, and swallowed the tremors I still felt from his touch.

"Rayna." He looked like he wanted to hug me, but the ever-restrained Cam kept himself in check. His hair was different, spiked up a little at the front, and he wore a varsity jacket, dressed up for the dance. He leaned in close to my ear, speaking loud so he could be heard over the base-pounding song. "When did you get back?"

"Less than an hour ago."

His gaze trailed down and his brows perked at the sight of the too-small costume, then narrowed on my wounds. "What happened to your arm?" He took my wrists in his hands and turned them upward. The cuts burned more fiercely at his touch. Kade's shirt strips were drenched in my blood. Cam brushed his fingers over the back of my injured hand.

"Azriel happened." I kept my voice flat so that he wouldn't know just how much his touch was affecting me. "Where's Luke?"

Cam's hands tensed around mine. Small tremors worked their way up my arms. He stared too long at my hand and arm, several beats passing before he answered. "He's inside with Gina, near the back door."

That was all I needed to know. I opened the door to the gym and pushed my way through, the damn fluff of the tiny skirt catching twice on other costumes.

Cam caught up with me. "Did they release you?" He had to shout now to be heard over the music.

Did we have to talk about this now? A flutter tickled my insides. I wanted to kill the little butterflies. "Kade broke me out. So we might not have very long to fix this before they come looking for me, if they aren't already."

Behind me, Cam's steps faltered. A tiny, biting smile tipped up the corners of my lips.

Finally, I spotted Gina, standing alone near the back door, arms crossed over her stomach and anger flushing her cheeks. *Damn it.* I pushed past her and through the door, Luke's quickest possible escape after getting into another fight with his girlfriend.

The ground outside was mucky. The gym was on the first floor, and the school sat on the lowest part of a hill. The emergency exit led up a flight of stairs and into the alley between the school and a large office building. Tiny droplets of mist fell from the roof's overhang. I stepped out and ran to the stairs. Luke wasn't there. No one was.

A bright flash lit up the sky, the walls, and the angel beside me.

"I was crazy with worry," Cam said.

The sincerity on his face meant bad things. Bad things for both of us.

"I ... ," he started, but the thunderclouds above rumbled.

I shuddered and checked the sky to see if it had actually cracked open. It was too dark to tell.

"I missed you," Cam continued, shouting over the rain and the buzz of music inside.

I shook my head. This was not the right time for this. I grabbed the rail and blindly climbed the stairs until I reached the alleyway.

Around a metal banister, another door led into the school. I opened it. Cam was right behind me. The rain dripped from my hair and stung my eyes. I swiped the water away and saw a figure standing in the hall.

"Luke?"

He disappeared around the corner.

I stepped out of the borrowed heels. My bare feet turned out to be a blessing, gripping the floor better than wet stilettos could have. I rounded the corner as a classroom door near the end of the hall opened and closed.

The front of the door had a poster of the human skeleton and muscles. Mr. Ratchor's Anatomy class.

"He's in two-fourteen," I said to Cam and rushed down the hall. The small, square window on the door was covered, reminding me of the SS Crazy. My fingers shook, but I turned the knob and stepped into the classroom.

Chapter Thirty-Eight

D arkness cloaked the classroom. Another sky-splitting flash of lightning illuminated the walls and rows of desks. The answering clap rolled through the tight confines.

Luke's shaved head was bone dry. Tears streaked the black paint under his eyes. Sunshine-yellow spandex hugged his thighs, and a cobalt-blue football jersey hung off his lean shoulders.

Awareness prickled along my arms as someone stepped behind me. I didn't look away from Luke, figuring it was Cam—until something cold and threatening pressed against the right side of my skull.

"Don't move, Rayna," a girl's voice said sharply from behind.

My stomach sank. It definitely wasn't Cam.

The door clicked, opening and closing. "Cassie," Cam warned gently as he entered, his wet shoes squeaking across the floor. "You don't want to do this."

"Oh, don't I?"

Cassie Waters, the girl with the blue-black hair and blunt bangs who sat next to Cam in history class. She must have been hiding in the shadows.

Between the sound of Luke sobbing and what I had to assume was the barrel of an honest-to-God gun pressed against my head, I couldn't focus. "Put the gun down, Cassie," I said.

A hush fell over Luke, so suddenly it was as if someone had flicked the off switch. His gaze locked on the gun beside my head. He walked up to me. The barrel of the gun was the only thing keeping me from running out the door.

Luke stopped in front of me and reached for something. The cold pressure of the barrel dropped away. When Luke pulled his hand back into my line of sight, there was a revolver in it. Az's influence was apparently much stronger than we'd thought.

"Get back!" Luke commanded, pointing the gun over my shoulder. Toward Cam. Fear barreled into me.

Wet shoes squeaked behind me, but it was impossible to tell if they were following orders, or clearly not.

With a dead smile on his lips, Luke lifted the gun to his own temple. Another flash of lightning lit up the classroom. His arm shook. The blackness invading his eyes pulsed, then faded as Az's hold on him weakened. Az might have been able to invade and completely control two people at once, but my guess was he couldn't hold them forever. "Evans?" The fear in his voice spiked.

"Yeah, Luke, it's me," I said softly. "Put down the gun, okay?"

"No way. This is my out. Gina's pregnant. Did you know that? Of course you know. Everyone knows. Everyone but our parents. Soon there'll be no hiding it."

"But you're going to have a baby. That's amazing, Luke. And that baby will need a father."

"I'm seventeen. I'm not ready to be a dad!" he shouted.

"Keep him calm, Rayna," Cam softly urged.

"Luke," I tried, unable to keep the desperation from my voice.

"We could've been something, Evans. We could've had something. You're smart. Smart enough not to forget to take your birth control. But now my life's over." And then the black fog rolled over his eyes again, and I knew I'd lost him.

The moonless night flashed and boomed again, gleaming off the silver revolver. I had to stop this. "Az?" I called.

"Rayna, don't."

Sorry, Cam. It's the only way I can see an end to this without anyone else getting hurt.

"Azriel!" I called again.

Something shifted in the darkness. He was already here.

The shadows grew. "You do not disappoint, seer." Az's cold voice clawed at the exposed skin on my arms and chest. "I knew you'd come to me. I just had to get rid of that pesky Fallen angel of yours."

I shook off the unpleasantness of his voice. "Let Luke go."

"It has been too long since we've had a good, old-fashioned mass-slaughter." He drew a shadowy finger down the side of my skirt, and I shivered in revulsion. "I like the idea of having the next at a Halloween dance. Fitting, don't you agree?"

He didn't give me time to answer before he tore through my head, showing me exactly what he had in mind. Luke fired three shots into the gym's crowd, then turned the gun on Gina, shooting her twice in the stomach. Finally, he turned the gun on himself. The pain of each shot burned like a fire poker, ripping through every nerve in my body. I dropped to the floor, huddled over in horrified agony.

After a while, the acid sting eased. I crawled to my

feet, using a desk for support. "No. No, that's not what you want."

Az's shadow circled me, glancing toward Cam every few seconds. I watched him, realizing he was curious about him.

Cam sneered at Az's shadow, tucking his wings tightly behind him.

Then I remembered what he and Kade had said. They couldn't see each other's wings. Az didn't know Cam was an angel.

Az swooped from Cam to me. "Very smart indeed. Tell me what it is I want, then."

"Rayna, don't." Cam warned.

"Me!" I shouted, just short of dropping to my knees and begging him to release Luke and Cassie. "You want me." Though I didn't know why I meant so much to him, gift or not.

"Then give me what I want. You for his life."

This was what Kade had warned me about, what he made me promise I wouldn't do. I hesitated.

"Or I could always make a trip to the gymnasium," Az breathed into my ear while he circled me. "Pour chemicals in the punch."

I shoved back my fear enough to remind him, "But that would only add to your body count, not help you collect their souls, right? You won't be able to create your weapon."

"You're fishing, girl. And so very, very wrong." He tapped a finger on his chin. "Either way, it will be a great tribute to our Lord."

His Lord. Lucifer.

"Though, what I don't finish, one of my brothers will. Nothing would make Him happier than you and that sight of yours. What do you think, seer, one hundred of your dearest classmates, or you?"

Was I destined to be tribute for the devil, my soul

writing in hell for all eternity? My head swam and spun all at once, lost.

"You can't have her." The flare of Cam's wings punctuated his words.

My hair blew into my face. Luke's finger tensed on the trigger. I lunged toward him, but Cam grabbed my hand, pulling me back, as he ran for Luke himself. He made it halfway before Luke pulled the trigger. The empty click of the gun dropped my throat to my feet.

Luke quickly pointed the gun at Cam, stopping him in his tracks.

I didn't know if Cam could be killed, but my stomach turned at the sight. I tried to speak, but my lips moved around like rubber bands with no elastic. My throat made an awkward, whining noise. Cassie, still under Az's control, hooked an arm over my shoulders. I jumped, but she held me steady. Her pleather nurse costume squeaked as she leaned into me. She wore blood-red lipstick and white, patent-leather boots that zipped halfway up her thighs. My legs quaked, but I tested Az's hold on her by taking a step toward Luke. Cassie pulled me back.

"No more games, Az," I yelled.

"But Russian roulette is one of my favorites," he said with a pout.

Cam reached for Luke. Luke cocked the gun, holding it steady at Cam. "Stay back, angel. You *are* an angel, aren't you?"

Az had figured it out.

Cam. Not Cam too.

Az wanted me in exchange for Cam, Luke, Cassie, and everyone downstairs.

I leaned on Cassie for support. I was going to die tonight.

"That's enough!" I took a rickety breath. "Fine. Yes, okay. I agree. Just let them go."

Chapter Thirty-Nine

A z sank back into the wall with a smile, his shadow hugging the corner. In front of him, Luke jumped at Cam, knocking them both to the floor. The gun flew from Luke's hand, skittering to the other side of the room.

Cassie scooped up the gun. "Follow me, Rayna." Her voice mimicked Az's like a weird echo, and she ran out the door. Az's shadow slid along the back wall, then disappeared after her.

Luke punched Cam, knocking his head to the side. "I saw you kiss her. She could've been mine. My easy way out of this mess with Gina. If I had cheated on her, with Rayna of all girls, she never would have spoken to me again. Baby or not." Ouch. I knew Az was intensifying his emotions, making him say those things, but I still couldn't help but wonder if he'd really intended to use me like that.

I watched them fight, frozen between helping Cam and going after Cassie and Az. Az was baiting me away from the fight, trying to separate me from another angel. I hated that he was manipulating me, but I had to go.

"I still have a way out." Luke stood and kicked Cam in the side before he ran for the window. His eyes were consumed in black, still under Az's influence. Cam clawed up to his feet, dodging the desks and lunging for Luke.

They tumbled to the floor together, a tangle of desks and bodies. Cam pulled back, securing Luke's arms and legs with his own.

"Rayna," Cassie's voice carried in from the hallway. "Come fiiiiind me."

Luke would be safe with Cam. I had to believe that. "Don't let him out of your sight," I told Cam and bolted out the door.

"Rayna, no!" I heard Cam shout before Az's shadow swung the classroom door closed.

As much as I wanted to, I couldn't go back to him, and I didn't have the time to tell him anything else.

I scrambled after Az and Cassie, my bare feet slapping down on the wet tile floor. Cassie stopped at the end of the hall, in front of the stairs. She turned toward me and smiled that same ghostly dead smile Lee and Luke had given me. Cassie wasn't home.

Above us, the fluorescent bulbs snapped out, one by one. I took a step toward her, wading blindly through the darkness. Cassie could be anywhere. Waiting around a corner, or standing in front of me, with that gun pointed at my head. My heart drummed in my ears, the thought of all my former classmates downstairs pressing me forward. I stumbled down the hall, following the click of Cassie's heels up the stairs.

I swallowed down the lump of fear in my throat. It didn't go anywhere, but I had to. Forcing my steps one at a time, I finally reached the top landing that led toward the roof. I fought the shaking in my chest, squared my shoulders, and pushed the door open.

An icy wind bore through me. The rain outside had subsided, but the air was still heavy with its threat. The sky was almost as black as the stairwell had been.

"Cassie?" My voice traveled weakly into the open air. I stepped forward. The wet rocks sliced into my bare feet.

A soft whimper—a sob?—carried over on the wind.

There wasn't enough light to cast Az's shadow, but he had to be up here. "Az, let her go! I'm here now. Let them all go." Fear made me choke on my words. "But whatever you think I am, I'm not."

"You are gifted with the sight." My heart stopped. In the next breath, it raced faster than it had with any of Dr. G's pills. "You are the weapon I have been searching for."

"Weapon? I thought the souls you were taking were going to create a weapon."

"There is no better weapon than the one who can see our enemies. Identify them when we cannot."

A sour taste rose in my mouth. I swayed, digging my nails into my palms to ground myself. "Why kill anyone then? Why not just come for me?"

"I'd heard tales about a girl who saw wings, and her history in the loony bin. But no one could verify if she really saw them or if she was crazy. So I came here to find out for myself, to watch you. Imagine my surprise when you followed my clues and found the girl in the basement. Forcing the children's hands, then pulling back just in time does make their death a sin, and brings a new friend to my Lord. Collecting souls and keeping an eye on you. Two birds. One stone."

My body shook with anger. Allison, Tony, Caroline, they'd all died because of me. "Az, if anything happens to Luke, or Lee, or any of the people down there, the deal's off." I pointed to the roof, where the music pumped below us.

"Understood." From the sound of Az's voice, he could have been anywhere. Everywhere.

A breeze cut through the soaked layers of my

costume and shifted the clouds from the moon. Under the new light, I spotted Cassie only a few feet from me. The gun glinted at her side.

"Let Cassie go, too."

I took one step toward her. A thick blackness clouded the outsides of her vacant eyes. She blinked as the dark fog expanded, swallowing the whites of her eyes. A soft smile touched her lips. She raised the gun, pressing it against her temple. A single tear leaked from her eye. "I wasn't part of the deal," she said absently, that empty smile still on her lips.

Darkness swallowed the moon.

I ran for her. A loud explosion echoed, deafening me. Something wet and warm splashed across my face, chest, and shoulders. I caught Cassie as she fell. Cradled her lifeless body in my arms. The weight dropped me to my knees. Rocks dug mercilessly into my skin, but it hardly mattered. Nothing did, except that I could have saved her, and I hadn't.

"No, Cassie, no." My hand shook as it stroked what was left of her hair, avoiding the bullet hole. My tears mingled with the thick, sticky wetness leaking from her. Blood. So much blood. She was gone.

I was suddenly grateful for the darkness; I didn't know if I could survive seeing what was left of her.

I held tighter to the dead girl in my lap. The girl I'd failed to save. My fault. All my fault. It should have been me, lying there in someone's arms. She was sweet. Smart. Funny. Dead. And what was I? Too dumb to include her life in my bargain. A disappointment to everyone I knew. And alive. I was alive, and she wasn't.

Someone said my name. I ignored them. Clutched her head to my chest, rocking her back and forth, back and forth. *I'm sorry, Cassie. So, so sorry.*

Laughter saturated the darkness.

I wiped the wetness from my face with the back of my bandages, then gently set Cassie down and stroked my hand down the curve of her cheek. *I'll see you soon, Cassie.*

My grief turned to fire the second I let her go. "How could you?" I tried to hold it back, knowing it would change nothing, knowing his evil soul would thrive on it, knowing I would never understand his reasons for stealing so many innocent lives.

"You cost me the football player. I had to find another tribute. As it is, our time has come." His arms encircled me, and he swept me off my feet, leaving Cassie there on roof, alone. His hold was iron-tight. This was more than just his shadow. Az was finally here.

I screamed, but the noise disappeared in a crack of thunder. Cold rain poured down on the city, blurring its lights. I shivered violently. Az's wings drove us up until the air thinned and my breath came too fast. My head grew light, and my eyes rolled back, taking my consciousness with them.

Chapter Forty

"You won't need sleep where we're going, dear seer." The snap of Azriel's voice filtered through my unconscious haze a split second before he slapped me across the face.

My eyes shot open. I looked down. And down, and down. My heart slammed into my throat. The orange structure—a bridge—loomed high in the air. White and red lights sped below us along its length. The Golden Gate Bridge. Below the bridge was complete blackness. Bright lights from the city twinkled to my right.

Horrified, I glanced at Azriel and scrambled back, my feet struggling for purchase against the cold, wet metal. The lights around us were bright; bright enough that I could finally make him out.

"Forgive the location, but this is the closest place to open the gate." He stood, no longer an empty shadow, but a sunken-faced man. His wings extended, the black feathers tipped with red where they shriveled and contorted in odd, broken-looking angles. "There will be no more flying from now on. We will only be falling." He reached for me, but I scurried away, crawling backward. "Don't go too far. I'd hate for you to leave without me."

His thin hand stretched toward me in offering. I

didn't take it. He didn't seem to mind as he took two steps back, extended his arms wide, closed his eyes, and tilted his head back. He chanted, repeating the same five or six syllables over and over again.

The wind kicked up and the clouds parted. I looked below and saw the white caps of the abysmal waves, churning and funneling into the obsidian depths.

Water. Since Mom's drowning, I hadn't been able to take a bath. Since we'd moved to San Francisco, I did everything I could to avoid even *looking* at the ocean.

I peered back at Azriel. He laughed and ripped open the front of his shirt. "First I need a marking, but you're lucky. You already have one." He pointed to my arm, where the demonic scratches hid beneath Kade's bloody sleeve. Then he drew a long nail across his chest. Something sizzled. The smell of burning flesh bit at my nostrils. There, in the center of his chest, a brand appeared. An inverted pentagram inside a circle.

"It's time."

His voice echoed off the nothingness in the night. He reached behind him and took hold of his crumpled wings. "Lucifer, my Lord, give me the strength to sacrifice the best part of myself, so that I may reenter your world and pay you tribute." His face twisted. The sound of snapping and popping overtook the rush of the ocean below, and then he screamed. Blood dripped from behind him and he dropped his wings beside me.

I scrambled away from the shredded wings, as close to the edge as I could get. I couldn't blink, could only watch his broken wings flop around like fish pulled from the sea. He picked them up, blood pouring from his back, and dropped them over the edge, into the ocean.

Seconds later, a green light bubbled beneath the surface. The water swirled until it opened up into a whirlpool. The green light burbled and black smoke wafted over the surface. He offered his hand again.

No. No. I couldn't do this. I grabbed the railing beside me, then took one last look at the water below. Oh, I wished I hadn't.

But I couldn't let any more people be hurt because of me. I couldn't let what happened to Allison, Tony, Caroline, and Cassie happen to anyone else. I could stop the killings right here, right now. I had to.

So I pulled myself up and locked my knees. Az wound his arm around my waist and pushed me to the edge. There was no railing, no hope, only the eternity of green lights and black smoke and swirling waters. An eternity of hell.

My heart slammed into my ribs, trying to claw free from its cage. I dug my heels into the iron tower, leaning away from everything unholy, only to have more unholy at my back. But Azriel's grip secured me.

I didn't think I could be afraid of anything more than angels or water. But something so much worse loomed below.

"You must make the decision and take the leap for us both. I will remain with you so I can act as your guide. It can be difficult finding your way if you're unfamiliar with the nine circles. You will remain as alive as you are now, but the sacrifice to enter *must* be yours, and not against your will; otherwise the fall will kill you. And we need you alive, dear girl." His grip locked around me, secure in the most insecure situation.

I swallowed, refusing to look down again. I said a silent goodbye to Dad, Laylah, and Lee, and stepped off the bridge.

Chapter Forty-One

T he wind came up fast. My stomach dropped as we fell, fear erupting in my every nerve. Azriel's laugh broke through the rushing air, and my scream piggybacked behind it.

A blur passed beside us. I tried to follow it as it circled, but we were falling too fast. Too far. Cam's face appeared in front of me, the wind disheveling his hair. I wanted to tell him to get out of my head, that he shouldn't be my last thought before I disappeared into Hell, but fear kept my mouth clamped shut.

He grabbed my hands and slowed our descent. His fingers were soft, warm. Everything about them felt real.

Strain twisted Cam's face above me. I held his hands as desperately as he held mine. *Cam, please. I don't want to go to Hell.* But I knew he was a hallucination, something I'd created to help me deal with my death. I also knew this was what I had to do to keep my family safe. His white wings flapped. I closed my eyes, hoping that image would help carry me through.

Az's arms cinched tighter around my waist. "Give it up, angel," he called out. "She's a willing sacrifice. It's already done!"

Az's voice startled me. I opened my eyes. "Cam?" Was he real?

Cam gritted his teeth.

"Cam!"

He was here. How? How did he find me? It didn't matter.

I held tight to him, trying to shake the shock. But what was he doing? "Cam, no. It has to be this way!"

"Rayna, I won't let you go. Az can't hurt anyone else in Hell."

No. There were too many lives at stake. I choked back a sob. "No. Let me go."

Az crushed my waist.

Cam looked down at me. "I won't let anything happen to them. Or you. Please, Rayna, trust me."

Trust Cam. With not only my life, but so many others. I'd never been able to trust any of them before. But Cam was different. He had … oh what the hell, if I couldn't admit my feelings when I was falling toward Hell, then when could I? He had my heart. There, I'd said it.

Tears spilled over my cheeks, and I shook my head. My sacrifice was the only way to end this.

Cam lifted us high enough to see the span of the bridge, the cars' headlights beside us. He continued to flap, but the horizon sank quickly. The car lights on the bridge disappeared as we dipped lower.

If I didn't do something, all three of us would end up in the green pit. "Let me go, Cam. It's all right." The churning oblivion closed in, so close I swore I could see a mound of bodies and outstretched hands waiting to catch us. In a last ditch effort, I pulled one hand free from Cam's grip. Azriel slid down a few inches, but held strong.

"This isn't the way!" Az called up to Cam from

around my hips. "Accept her fate, angel. She has cemented her alliance with us."

Sweat formed between my and Cam's hands. With Az weighing me down, my grip started to slip. I tried to relax my fingers, to let them slide out of his, but Cam dug into the cut on my hand. I kicked my feet, struggling to get free from Cam. "This is the only way," I called up to him.

Az slid down my tiny skirt, until his grip locked around my knees. The three of us continued losing ground, sinking farther in the air. Az tried to climb up my legs, grabbing the waistband of my skirt.

My arm shook. My fingers slid farther from Cam's, and I watched my life slip away. Cam grunted and readjusted his grip on me. He wouldn't let go. Even when the three of us were mere feet from the water.

Azriel jerked one last time. My hand fell away from Cam's.

"Hold on," another voice called.

"Kade?" Kade was here. Really here. He'd come too.

His black wings swooped under us, stopping our descent. Az's weight lightened, but he was still attached to me. Cam struggled to grab me again, but I fought him off, wriggling and keeping my arms tight to my body. The four of us rose higher into the air.

"Don't you dare drop her," Kade warned Cam as he tugged Az.

"Kasade, you're a traitor to your own kind," Az growled and dug painfully into my thighs.

"Kade, no. Let. Us. Go."

Cam snatched one of my wrists while Kade jerked Az again. Az's nails tore into my flesh as Kade pulled him off me. I screamed as pain flared around the new gashes.

With Az's weight gone, Cam used the distraction to

hook my other hand again, and he pulled me up. I squirmed against him. Az and Kade zigzagged uncontrollably.

"No. Cam, don't do this."

Az had a handful of Kade's wing, and Kade had a handful of Az's face. Az kneed Kade in the gut, and the two of them plummeted again.

"Help him," I pleaded to Cam. "And let me fall!"

"There's no way I'm letting you go down there." Cam flew us above the span and toward the top of the bridge. He peered over his shoulder. Kade and Az rose again, higher, faster. Too fast. And too close. Before we reached the top of the bridge, they slammed into us in a tangle of arms and legs.

Beside us, Az bent one of Kade's wings. The snap carried over the wind. Kade howled and fought to keep himself in the air.

"Kade!" I screamed.

Az kicked off Kade's back and latched onto Cam's. His eyes were black, teeth bared. Like a rabid animal. Cam, Az, and I plummeted.

"You two are coming with me," Az hissed while one of his arms snaked around Cam's neck.

Cam's face turned red. So very, very red. *Let go, just let go, Cam. Save yourself.* The wind whipped up between us. Another set of arms wrapped around my waist.

I screamed, but Cam nodded as best he could and released me. Kade's arms felt familiar around me. Familiar and so comfortable I almost forgot I wanted to be in that green hole. We hovered unstably in the air as we watched Cam and Az fall.

"No," I reached out to Cam. "Kade, you have to let me go. I made a deal, for my family."

Kade's injured wing faltered, and we careened toward the bridge. My stomach dipped with us. We spun and fell, the world turning with no sense to it. My leg hit something. A clang rung out. Pain shot through every nerve, a vast, unending fire. I tried to grab for whatever had caused the pain, but it was long gone.

Still falling, Kade curled his wing in, trying to glide us onto the bridge. A gust of wind changed our direction. We angled right toward the metal railing and the fast-moving cars. Kade jerked and hissed in pain. His hold on me slipped.

I free-fell alone for a second, then slammed into the railing so hard unconsciousness flirted with my brain. I growled and fought against the ache and breathlessness, then struggled to wrap my bruised, sliced arms around the cold metal, not giving myself the time to wonder if anything was broken. Azriel, I needed him with me when I did this. I steeled myself and looked down. The ocean still housed a green version of Hell. Azriel's scream echoed from below.

I tried to keep my hold on the railing, but my fingers were empty before I even realized they were slipping. The doomed feeling of falling returned. This time I didn't scream. Didn't breathe. Didn't move.

I slowed to a stop and gasped. Dared a glance below. A figure fell into the green, the whirlpool swallowing it. "No," I whispered. The mouth to Hell closed, the green fading to the bottom of the bay before disappearing, along with any guarantee my family would remain safe.

Above me, Kade held his shoulder with one hand and me with the other. Cam flew beside him, holding my other arm. They were all right. Both of them. Good. Because I was going to kill them.

The cold air sobered me, pulled me back from unconsciousness, as they flew me to the bright lights of the city.

Az. Az was gone. Back to Hell. Without me.

I would have sobbed, but I couldn't. I could only breathe.

Everything blurred. Everything hurt.

Kade's grip on my hand slipped. I clung tighter to Cam. No reason to fall to my death now.

"I'll take it from here," Cam said. He pulled my arm up, hand over hand, until he could hold me around the waist. His fingers rested half on my corset, half on my exposed skin. My blood boiled at his touch.

To our left, Kade's one-winged flight looked painful. He cringed, never letting go of his shoulder. His shirt hung in shreds. He weaved crookedly, hardly able to keep up.

Cam hadn't escaped the fray uninjured, either. His eye was swelling shut and his lip was split. "I'm sorry," Cam said to me. "I never should have let it go that far. I should have found a way to stop Azriel earlier."

I shook my head, unwilling to talk about what had happened without blowing my top and donkey-kicking him.

"Rayna—" Cam started, his fingers forming a fist over my stomach.

"Don't," I spat. "You have no idea what you've done."

I glanced over to find Kade's dark-brown eyes on us.

A feeling stronger than anger circled my mind. There was something important I needed to know. Something that happened before the bridge. But what—

Cassie. Lying dead on the school's roof. Luke. Reaching for a window to jump out of. Lee. Being loaded in an ambulance. All the students at the dance. Drinking the punch.

"Luke—the others. You didn't just leave them?"

Cam inhaled deeply, taking his time before answering. "I subdued Luke. When he wakes, Azriel's influence should be gone."

Subdued? I didn't think I wanted to know what that meant.

"The others are fine. Az didn't poison them. Poison wouldn't be suicide, not the way he wanted. It was a bluff."

But I knew in my gut his threat to my family wasn't.

We dipped down the hill, farther into the city, closer to the ground. It felt like forever before we finally landed. Another alleyway. Solid ground. I sank down to rest on the balls of my feet and closed my eyes.

I wanted to use tears to expel all the things I wished I hadn't seen, the things I wished I hadn't heard. But there were no tears. Shutting down, I wrapped my arms around myself, hooked my hands around my elbows, and rocked.

Cam closed in on me quickly. I didn't understand why until Kade stumbled down beside us, his rocky landing almost smacking him into the farthest building. He steadied himself and straightened up, his broken wing flopping sadly.

"You flew for her." The shock in Cam's voice caught my attention, then lost it as I dropped a hand to the wet, gritty concrete, relishing the feel of it beneath me. Especially since I expected to land in Hell.

Kade bit back a grimace as he folded his injured wing behind him. "So did you." He spat at the floor at Cam's feet. His voice was deep, darker than usual, but nothing compared to Azriel's. He walked around Cam to kneel on the other side of me. "Are you okay?"

Still rocking, I shook my head, too lost, too angry to speak.

"This wasn't the first time you've flown her, was it?" Cam said, fishing for something.

I blinked at Cam, confused.

His fists clenched and his lips pressed into a thin line. He'd caught what it was he wanted from Kade. "You have feelings for her."

I dragged myself out of my shock-induced daze. "I asked him to come the first time."

"The Fallen don't do anything unless it favors them." He broke his stare away from Kade, but frown lines still traced his forehead as he spoke. "And they're only given a limited number of times they can fly."

My brows drew together, and I looked at Kade.

He stiffened. "I could say the same for your kind."

Cam stood, towering over Kade, his fists clenched. "How did you know where Azriel would be?"

Kade didn't rise to the challenge. "As soon as the doorway to Hell opened, I figured there was a problem." Sarcasm dripped off his words. "I sensed him near the school when I dropped Ray off. But you think I had something to do with this."

The silence that hung between them left me cold.

Kade finally stood, his muscles tense, and Cam stepped closer to him, both their jaws clenched, their fists balled.

"You're not worth the cursed heart they put in you," Cam said.

Kade turned away from him and knelt beside me.

Cam blinked, his brow furrowing. "She needs time." He squatted beside me. "As soon as you're ready, I'll get you out of here." It landed somewhere above a whisper, one I got the impression he'd intended for Kade to hear.

I could feel Kade's frustrated breath on my bare shoulder.

That was all I could take. I pulled myself to my

feet, ignoring the shakes in my knees and the unbearable pain in my hand, legs, and forearm. "You two just *had* to save me. You couldn't let me go to keep my family safe, to keep more people from dying!"

Their angry stares turned to me, and both faces went soft in surprise.

"We kept you out of Lucifer's clutches. They wanted you for a reason. Your family can be watched, protected, but you seem to be the important—" Cam's eyes fixed in the glass behind me, and he breathed a warning. "Rayna."

I turned, my knee not liking this action much. My reflection shone in the glass and in the puddles of rainwater below it.

Cassie's blood smeared half my face, chest and arms. My own blood coated my hands, arm, and leg. And small, gray wings peeked over my shoulders.

I had wings. And they both could see them.

"Wha—what is this?" I stared at them, uncomprehending.

Kade cleared his throat. "I don't know."

Everything else fell away. "Does this mean I'm an angel?"

Cam and Kade glared at each other. "I don't know," Cam spoke up first, confusion clear in his words. "But I've never seen anything like those."

"I doubt it," Kade added. "Maybe it has something to do with you being able to see us." He leaned against the window, holding his shoulder.

"It's been a long night," Cam said, offering me his hand. "Come with me. I can hide you. You'll be safe. We'll rest, and in the morning we can work on figuring it out together."

Kade pushed off the window, stepping between us, getting in Cam's face until he had to take a step back. "Not happening. She's coming with me. *I'll* hide her.

You shouldn't interfere more than you already have. Besides, you think your side would tell you anything, even if they knew?"

"My side? So it was my side that just tried to toss her to Hell? What would you have to do for the same information, Kasade?"

"There has to be another way," I said.

They both turned to me with a firm, "no."

It was obvious they couldn't work together for more than five minutes. These two were nuts if they thought I'd just go off with one of them and hide, or disappear, or whatever. Why did I have to choose between them? And who could make me?

"No," I said.

They both looked confused.

"No?" Cam asked.

"I don't want to go with either of you. The suicides are over, for now. Az is gone, for now. But my family could still be in jeopardy. I just got my life back, and I'm not going to give it up now." My eyes started to water, saving me from seeing their reactions. "I want to live my life, be with my dad and Laylah and Lee, keep them safe." Even if I had no idea how I could do that after busting out of the SS Crazy. No way I'd be going back there; I wasn't crazy and I wouldn't let someone ever tell me I was again. I swallowed and watched them through blurred vision. I thought I could spy a sense of understanding behind those two sets of eyes. "So, I won't hide. I choose to live."

I closed my eyes. "So what happens now?"

"I don't know. With those wings, you may never be safe," Cam said. I opened my eyes in time to watch him exchange unhappy glances with Kade.

I shook my head. "What guarantee do you have that Az is really gone? That my classmates are safe? My family?"

"Why don't you go talk to your superiors and find out? I'll watch her while you're gone." A taunting half-smile slid up Kade's lips.

"The last thing you need to be doing is mouthing off right now," I scolded, then turned away.

I took another look at myself, those gray wings still there, taunting me. I squeezed my eyes shut, blocking them out. God only knew what kind of repercussions they carried.

Everything I'd ever wanted—a normal life, not being singled out as a crazy freak, and any chance of returning home to my family, keeping them out of harm's way—disintegrated. My breakout from the SS Crazy and my shiny new wings pretty much guaranteed that. My dreams didn't only burn, they turned to ash.

"I ... I need time. To process. To think. Just make sure no one else gets hurt." My knees threatened to collapse, but instead of giving in, I ran. Truthfully, it was more of a limp.

Neither of them followed me. I was glad. So glad.

The farther I ran, the more time I had to think. I cared for them. Both of them. I knew that now. But I couldn't help hating them, too. I understood why they wouldn't let me go, but neither of them seemed to understand how much my loved ones meant to me, or how much I would sacrifice for them.

Eventually my anger faded, clearing my head and allowing me to better weigh my options. I couldn't go with either of them. They both wanted to hide me away from the world, away from any angels or Fallen. It was no different from being at the SS Crazy. I was done being locked up and told what to do.

Cam would probably Fall to protect me. That was an option I couldn't live with.

And Kade? He was either hot or cold, starting trouble or being sweet. I didn't even know who he really was. Except damn annoying. Plus, he'd dated Mom.

It didn't take long for the rain to start again. I pushed on, having no clue where to go, walking until my throbbing knee wouldn't take me any farther. I couldn't go home; Dad would throw me to the crazy police as soon as he saw me. The moment I escaped the mental hospital had guaranteed that. Knowing that didn't make it hurt any less.

I made my way to Lee's house and spent the night soaking wet, tucked into the front porch's alcove, hidden away from the world in my own little dark corner, where I could weep to my heart's content.

Chapter Forty-Two

I n the morning the sun came out, and I woke to find my own, smaller version of angel wings wrapped around my shoulders. The streets had been empty last night, thanks to the rain. No one had seen me. But what if today, in the light of day, my gray wings betrayed me? I wasn't an angel. What if my wings weren't a secret?

A white car stopped in front of the house and both doors opened. Familiar voices sprang from the car. I peeked around the niche and nearly blinded myself as the tips of my wings shimmered too-bright sunlight into my eyes.

Great. Not just inconvenient, but shiny, too.

I readjusted my position, scooting back to keep them out of the light. Every part of my body was sore and wet and cold. My throat ached, my knee was swollen, my cuts throbbed, and my eyes were puffy and tired. At the curb, Lee's mom stepped from the car and walked around to help Lee out. His skin was so pale. His eyes had bags beneath them, and a Band-aid covered his hand. But he was alive. *Alive.*

A relieved squeak squeezed from my throat. Forgetting myself, I stepped from the porch's shadows.

Lee and his mom reached the bottom of the stairs, looked up, and gasped.

They could see them.

I froze, wracking my brain, trying to think of a way to explain the wings. Wait. The Halloween dance. I decided to go with the costume thing.

"Ray!" Lee smiled. "Wow. That's some costume."

I glanced down, my entire top half stained dark with Cassie's blood.

"Rayna, it is so good to see you," Mrs. Kyon said in her soft way, her eyes quietly conveying their gratitude.

I pressed a hand against my stomach and sighed in relief. They couldn't see them.

"What happened to you?" she asked.

One forearm was slashed, the other swollen and an ungodly shade of purple. The same shade as my knee. My thigh ached where Az had scratched me. I wondered how much of Cassie's blood was still on my face. "I decided to take the costume a little further." I hoped the excuse was believable.

Lee did the zombie shuffle, and for once, I knew he wasn't joking. He leaned against the rail for support as he climbed the porch stairs. I helped Mrs. Kyon get Lee inside, up the stairs, and into bed.

Then I borrowed a washcloth from Lee's bathroom and scrubbed Cassie's blood off me. For good measure, I splashed rubbing alcohol on all the cuts. Each one stung more than the last.

"I'll go make some tea," Mrs. Kyon said, but she took her time, stroking Lee's spiky hair back from his forehead.

"I heard you saved my life," Lee said after his mom's footsteps faded down the stairs.

I shook my head. "Right place, right time." I took a breath, using what felt like newborn muscles to tuck my wings back behind me. "How are you feeling?"

He shrugged. "Eh, can't complain."

What would a normal person say in this situation? I didn't know. I wasn't one of them. Feathers tickled my back, reminding me I never would be. I dropped to the bed next to him, suddenly tired. "They released you pretty early. What were the conditions?"

"Yeah. I almost forgot to tell you. Cam put in a good word for me."

"Cam?" The word fell from my mouth before I could control my tone.

"Uh-huh." He didn't try hiding that triumphant smile. "He volunteers at the hospital, so he talked to the doctors, got my sentence reduced."

Cam didn't work at a hospital, at least not that I knew of, but I could imagine he had a few angel tricks up his sleeve. I steeled myself, remembering the decision I made last night. He wanted to lock me away from the world, keep me away from my family. If I let myself be weak or stumble just once, I could easily forget my reasons for saying no and end up back in his arms. As much as I wanted that, I wanted a life more. And I wanted him to have a life without me screwing that up for him. "Did he say anything?"

"Just that he had to say goodbye. He's moving again."

I crumbled a little, clutching my stomach. He was leaving, had probably already gone. With Az back in Hell, I guess that left Luke safe. And my family. For now. But he'd reassured me he could keep them out of harm's way. How could he do that if he was gone? In the back of my mind, I couldn't help thinking I didn't even get a chance to talk to him again. I'd probably just screw up a goodbye, anyway.

"You okay?" He draped a hand over my head, his fingers flopping into my face.

"No. Not with that, but what can I do, right?"

"Sorry, Ray. I never would've pushed him on you if I'd known he'd only be around a few weeks."

I had to change the subject. The thought of Cam gone forever hurt too much. "What else did the doctors say?"

"I have to see a therapist." Lee's gaze darted to the open door, but the hallway was empty. "But don't worry. I won't tell him what I really saw."

"What do you mean? What did you see?"

"That dark guy with wings you were talking to."

My jaw nearly hit the floor. *No, no, no, no!*

"I've seen the *Doctor Who* episodes with the angels, and I've been glued to ghost-hunting reruns." That wonderful, light-up-the-world smile tilted his lips. "We don't have to talk about it now. Besides, you look like you've had one hell of a night yourself."

I pulled myself together and hugged him, crushing him to me in case I had to leave, never to return. It still felt weird, but didn't suck too much. Thanks to these damn wings and Az's determination to use my sight for evil, I had a feeling I'd never be safe.

Though it was a relief to know someone else had seen Azriel, I'd never know how to explain it to Lee. Luckily, I didn't have to worry about that. Yet.

I stayed with him, deflecting questions about where I'd been the last few days with bad jokes, until Mrs. Kyon insisted he get some rest, per the doctor's orders. On my way out, I promised his mom I'd return soon. I didn't know if I'd be keeping that promise.

I closed the door behind me and descended the front stairs, limping, careful not to do further damage to my knee.

A familiar purple Acura was double-parked next to Mrs. Kyon's car. Kade's strong nose, sharp cheekbones, and unshaven face hadn't changed, but the dark rings of fatigue around his eyes were new. His injured wing was hanging a little straighter.

I thought about running, but I had nothing left, so I fiddled with my skirt, clenching and unclenching a layer of the red tulle in my palms, and said, "Hey."

He looked at my new additions. I tucked the wings behind me as best I could. "What happened last night, none of it was planned."

Sure, you had no idea you and Cam were stopping me from saving my family, even though I tried to tell you.

I took a deep breath, wriggling slightly in the corset, wishing I could take the damned thing off already. "Is that what you came all the way here to say?"

He pushed off the car and stalked toward me, invading all my senses. His skin radiated heat, and he smelled like soap. Like he was fresh from a shower. The smell had me wishing for the same: a long, hot shower. "I don't know what's going on with your wings, but I'm sure Cam'll find out. If I could … change what happened, I wouldn't. You don't belong down there." He reached behind me, his fingers tracing the tips of my wings. A phantom caress skimmed over me.

I jerked back from him, warning in my eyes. "Don't touch those. Ever."

He dropped his hand to his side and took a deep breath. "I know you can't go home. And I wanted to offer you a place to stay. With me."

His words knocked me back a step.

"I don't want you out on the streets," he said. "I've lived that life. It's not fun."

I pushed down the lump that rose in my throat at the reminder that home wasn't an option, not anymore. I had no place to go. There were no other offers on the table. Lee and his mom didn't know anything about my situation, and I'd like to keep it that way. Where else could I go? What else could I do?

Living with Kade. I couldn't even grasp it. Maybe I could buy a bus ticket to L.A. and throw myself at the mercy of Aunt Nora. But the first thing she'd do would be to call Dad. Then I'd be back at square one, locked away in the SS Crazy.

"I won't be hidden away like some …" Somehow, reminding Kade I was crazy didn't sound like a great idea. "I—I deserve to make my own decisions."

"You're right. Last night, when your," he nodded to my wings, "showed up, my reaction wasn't exactly a shining moment of clarity. It would be safer if you weren't seen, especially after both sides hear about what went down with Az—and they will—but you're right. It is your life."

So this was what a real apology from Kade the Fallen looked like. I scoffed, releasing my anger. "Boy that must have chapped your ass to say."

He looked up at me with a half-smirk. "You know it."

I considered his offer. It wasn't perfect, it wasn't home, but it was a place and a roof—neither of which I currently had.

I was too proud for a lot of things, but I knew when I was down. And baby, I was in the gutter.

If it didn't work out, I was no lower than before. I sighed. "Fine."

He opened the door for me without a word. The front seat of the stolen car was free of glass, and clear tape acted as a makeshift window. I curled my wings against my body as best I could and slid in.

"I thought we agreed you'd report the car stolen," I said when he settled into the driver's seat.

"I did one better. I called the guy. Told him I

wanted to buy it. Sent out a check first thing this morning."

"What is that?" I asked, eyes squinted, head tilted, as he started the engine. "Is that a ... conscience?"

A smile loosened his mouth and he chuckled softly. "Don't get too excited. One decent deed does not a conscience make." *Doing the wrong thing is so much more fun*, I imagined him adding.

He steered the car onto the street with one hand, driving as smoothly as if he'd put all ninety-seven thousand miles on it. The two seemed to belong together.

He drove much slower this time, and in only a few minutes, we stopped outside a dumpy blue apartment building in the Tenderloin, one of the worst neighborhoods in the city, but it was close to Roxy's diner and my old school. We got out of the car, stepping over a person sleeping in the doorway. He unlocked the front gate and then the door. "Top floor."

The hallway was dark, and there was no elevator. By the time we reached the fourth and final floor, my knee nearly gave out. The door to apartment four hundred wasn't locked when he opened it for me.

I stepped inside and looked around. A queen-sized bed sat against the back wall. Heavy blue curtains concealed a bay window. A small kitchen took over the left corner wall. The bathroom was beside the kitchen. Clothes littered the bed, the chair beside the window, and lay in a small pile on the pink carpet. Messy. It was so messy. My instant urge to scrub the entire place clean lost out to my exhaustion. I could clean another day.

My attention snapped back to the nonexistent bedroom. One bed? He couldn't be serious. "Well, this is ... something." A studio apartment in a bad neighborhood was exactly the opposite of what I expected. Kade was full of surprises.

"When people are looking for you, the best place to live is the last place they'll look." He rubbed the back of his neck.

I spun toward him, wondering who might be looking for him.

"Obviously, we can move. Give me a few days to find a better place."

"It's okay. If you clear some space for me, I can sleep on the floor."

"That's not necessary."

"Oh, yes it is."

"I don't sleep much, and when I do, it's mostly during the day. We can share the bed, at different times. For now. But I can find us a bigger place."

I plopped down on the bed. I'd never felt more tired. "Can I use the shower?" That would be my next step. I couldn't think of anything beyond that.

Chapter Forty-Three

I awoke later, after more nightmarish images than I could count. Sweat tacked the sheets to my legs. I kicked them off and sat up. The curtains were drawn, but afternoon light peeked through rips in the blue fabric. My head pounded, and every muscle in my body ached like I'd been torn in two, then sewn back together. At least I could move my knee without too much pain.

I lay in bed, listening for the sound of Laylah giggling with her Musketeer friends, or one of her obnoxious songs pounding from the bathroom speakers, punishing me for sleeping in. When there was nothing, I looked around again. I wasn't at home. I was at Kade's. And he wasn't here.

Home. Laylah and Dad had no doubt heard of my escape by now. The last thing I wanted was them worrying. I checked the alarm clock by the bed, then the calendar over it. Friday afternoon. I'd slept for a day and a half. I gathered all the courage I could find to leave the bed and showered. At the bottom of the bed was a bag of clothes. I pulled out a pair of jeans and a white sweater, the tags still attached. Kade had gone shopping. A smile touched my lips as I fingered the soft fabric, picturing Kade in a women's clothing store.

I looked down at my cuts. They felt tight, like they were healing. He must have used some kind of liquid bandage on them. Thank God. I didn't think I could handle stitches.

I got dressed and walked to Laylah's school, glad the inflammation and pain in my knee had faded to a dull throb. I waited outside the parking lot, my fingers laced through the chain-link fence. Waiting even after the parade of parents picking up their kids from school had long gone.

I'd begun to wonder if she'd left before I'd arrived, when I spotted her hair shining in the sun.

Okay, you've seen her. She's okay. I swallowed, but couldn't look away. She waved bye to her friends and headed for the exit in the fence. *Now would be a good time to move.*

I dropped my gaze and tried to convince myself to move, or leave.

"Ray?" Laylah's voice carried over the yard.

I looked up. She stomped toward me. I was too late.

"What are you doing here?" she screamed at me, doing something weird with her hands where she stretched them out toward me, then dropped them again. Like she was trying to decide whether to hug me or strangle me. "You're so dumb. If I was you, I'd be a thousand miles away right now." She crossed her arms in front of her chest in that stubborn Evans way. "Your Kade, the one you sent me to the diner for, he got you out, didn't he?"

"I just wanted to make sure you're okay. You weren't supposed to see me." I tapped my fingertips against the liquid bandage in my palm. All I wanted to do was kiss that little brat on her forehead, but I knew if I touched her, she'd probably snap.

Laylah drummed her fingers on her arm. "You ignored the question, just like Dad does." It seemed we'd both picked up a few of Dad's traits. "You seriously need to get out of here. That detective's been around."

Her words stopped my tapping. "Detective Rhodes?" Did that mean I was still a suspect? Breaking out of a mental hospital wouldn't make me look super guilty or anything, right? Holy hell. I covered my face with a hand and grasped onto the fence for balance.

A familiar voice came from behind me. "From what I hear, he's been to the school, your house, Roxy's Diner, and the mental health clinic."

I turned toward the unbelievable sound of that angel's—my angel's—voice, but standing there, I couldn't find reason to trust my vision. "Cam?"

Holy Father, what is he doing here?

"Yeah," Laylah said, "he's been walking me home almost every day since you went back."

Heat trailed along the inside of my stomach. He was here. Still here. I'd let my heart break, tried to make myself accept that he was gone, that he'd returned to Heaven. Why hadn't he?

A familiar ringtone cut through the thought. My old cell phone. Laylah retrieved it from her back pocket and checked the screen. "It's Dad. He'll want me home."

Poor, Dad.

"Please don't tell him you saw me."

"I'm beyond pissed at you, but if I tell him, he'll tell that detective, and I guess I'd feel guilty if you went to jail or something."

"I won't let that happen." Cam said from behind me.

I stepped back, stretching my lips into a half-smile. "Go. Before Dad starts to worry."

She nodded and turned, but Cam stood his ground.

"Laylah, would you mind if I stayed behind, to talk to your sister?"

"No. I think she needs that."

I watched her get smaller and smaller, until she turned a corner and disappeared.

"Thank you for keeping an eye on her when I couldn't." The next thought occurred to me late. "Wait, are you protecting her?" My heart slowed to a crawl as I waited for his answer.

"Not officially, no. Just watching out for her."

If he didn't, then who would?

A long silence stretched between us. Cars blew by on the street. I turned to him, the fence still in my left hand, holding onto it so I couldn't float away with Cam. "What did you do to get Lee out of the hospital early?"

His blooming smile brought attention to his healed eye and lip. "I can be very persuasive."

"Is that a … Protector thing? Part of the white-wings-only club?"

"You could say that." Cam bit down on his bottom lip, melancholy digging lines between his brows. "I'm sorry I couldn't help you the day they took you. It broke me to stand there, watching."

It hurt to remember those moments. "But you did. You just stood there and … did nothing." And when he did finally do something, it was to stop me from taking the plunge with Az and ensuring my family's safety.

"It's complicated."

"Complicated? You don't think things were complicated for me, Cam?"

"I wasn't supposed to get involved, and couldn't risk developing more human emotions without Falling."

Oh. So Kade hadn't exactly been lying. There must have been more than one way to Fall. But that didn't make it any less fair that Cam could keep an emotional distance from me while I was stuck with these confusing, frustrating feelings. "Locked away in a mental hospital for talking to you and Kade—for helping you. And that day in the hallway, you kissed me. I thought it could have meant something to you, but I guess it was just another—"

"Please, Rayna!" The sadness in his eyes threw a bucket of cold water over my searing anger. "Part of being what I am means doing what I'm told. I broke so many rules when I kissed you. And the mental hospital, it seemed a safer place for you. As far as dragging you away from Azriel, I won't apologize for that." He swallowed, taking his time before speaking again. "I'm not asking for your forgiveness, because I know I don't deserve it. But please, don't ever insinuate our kiss meant nothing to me."

It was hard to be mad at that, but damn it, I tried.

He cleared his throat. "I spoke to my superiors. They're as surprised by your wings as we were. One day I'll have answers for you, but that day isn't now. The rules apply differently to you, though no one understands why."

Great, so we still knew nothing. I gripped the fence harder.

"With Azriel back in the circles of Hell, your school is safe. For now." He paused. "With Luke no longer in danger, that means my job is done here and I have to leave."

I nodded. "Lee told me. But you promised me you'd keep my family safe. How can do you that if you're gone?"

"I'll be watching them, from above."

"But …" I searched my mind for an argument that could keep him near, but nothing I came up with would have been fair. He was an angel; I was a human with wings I might never be rid of. I knew this all along, should have braced myself for this, but nothing could have braced me for the pain of losing him. This was so much worse, saying goodbye, than it was when I'd thought he'd just left.

I shook my head, remembering the other night, reliving it like I had in my nightmares.

Anger twisted his face. "But what? Would you rather I stay and Fall? Become one of them? Come back as your enemy? Because that's the alternative."

"What kind of question is that?" I snapped. "The last thing I want you to do is Fall. But if you did, you'd have a choice, right? You wouldn't have to be Lucifer's minion. Look at Kade."

"He is the exception. The Fallen who fight for eternity, half-in and half-out of the pits, very few of them turn away from the promises of power. Driven by revenge, cast out by their creator, their father. In all honesty, I don't know if I'd be able to withstand the temptation."

"Cast out by their father? No, I couldn't understand that at all." Bitter dryness singed my tone.

Cam winced. "I've said the wrong thing again."

I looked away. He took a deep breath. If he was leaving, the last thing we should do was argue. When the warmth of my anger had left my cheeks, I looked up at him. It reminded me of the day he pulled me back from the driveway, when I was almost flattened by a van. The first time he saved my life. Of the time we'd spent at the park, in class, and our moments in the hallway. It reminded me of the other side of Cam, the side that was almost human. It also reminded me of what could never be.

"What will you do?"

I shrugged. "Can't go back home, can't go back to school, but I need to be here. Even though I won't be able to see them, I have to stay close to Lee, Laylah, and my dad. Just in case." Nothing in this world was certain.

If anybody knew that after the chaos of the last few weeks, it was me. And if anything happened to either of them, I would be there. No matter what the cost.

"This isn't fair to you." He came too close and slid his hand into mine.

I held tighter to the fence with my other hand, steeling myself against brushing closer.

His hand left mine to brush the tip of one of my gray feathers. I shuddered through the half-touch. Cam looked skyward. "I don't have much time."

A fire burned in my chest. Why did goodbyes have to hurt so bad?

I placed my hand on his chest, not knowing if I wanted to feel a heartbeat or not. Nothing ticked beneath my fingers. I looked him over, memorizing everything. The white wings, the golden hair, and those too-infuriating controlled stances. This was probably the last time I'd see any of them.

His lips parted, but I placed my hand over his mouth. No good could come of anything else he had to say. "Don't. Don't say anything. I want to remember you like this, just as you are now."

This was it. Say goodbye and walk away.

I kept my hand over his lips, feeling the soft warmth of them. Complexities ran through his gray eyes. I couldn't look at them anymore for fear they might undo me. I stood on my tiptoes and kissed the hand still over his mouth. He closed his eyes, straining against my hand. He didn't want it to be over, either. My heart sped. I took two steps back, fighting against each one. "I'll never forget you, Cam."

But I never actually said goodbye. If there was one thing the SS Crazy taught me, it was that no situation, no matter how good or bad, was permanent. Unless it was death. To avoid being drawn into the gray pools of his eyes again, I dropped my gaze. A patch of orange poppies grew beneath the shade of a small tree beside us. The same orange flowers from the dream I'd had of Cam. I picked one and handed it to him, watching his hand brush mine. "To remember me by," I took a few more steps back. "If you want to remember me."

Tears burned behind my eyes. Before they could show him how much I'd miss him, I turned and headed for the nearest corner. I glanced over my shoulder.

Cam and the flower were already gone.

I walked back to Kade's, determined not to shed a tear until I reached the shower, where it was private. But when I went upstairs, Kade was already there, sitting on the edge of the bed.

"You've got angel stink all over you."

I couldn't dredge up enough anger to be mad at the casual, unthreatening way he said it.

"Want to talk about it?"

I looked toward the bathroom, then at Kade again. Curling up in a ball on the shower floor sounded really good right now. But what good would that do? I wasn't mentally ill, at least not as much as I'd been led to believe the last three years. Instead of being nuts, I had gray wings ... like that was any better. Not to mention Cam was gone, and I was stuck living with Kade. All these things meant I had to find strength I'd never had before.

"I don't, not now. But I could use a friend."

He leaned forward, resting his elbows on his knees, eyes on the floor, as far away from me as they could be. My wings vibrated, picking up an odd tension filling the room. Strange. I wondered what else they could do.

"A friend, huh?"

"Yeah," I glanced sideways and spotted one of my gray feathers. Right now, I didn't think I could handle anything else.

He sighed and pushed his hair back with both hands. Then he slouched back and looked at me. "Don't know how long this can last, but … I'll give it a shot." He patted the spot beside him.

I took a seat on the other end of the bed, keeping as much space as possible between us. The sensation in my wings eased, and they reverted to simply foreign, unwanted things. "Then it'll be a trial, for both of us. And Kade … thanks." It didn't seem enough, those small words in exchange for everything he'd done to help when he didn't have to. But I couldn't give him anything more. I didn't have anything more in me. At least, not today.

"No problem, Ray. I don't plan on letting you forget that you owe me. Twice." Kade turned those dark eyes on me, a playful glint softening them. "You up for pizza and a movie?"

"Only if the movie isn't about angels or Hell." I didn't like the idea of owing Kade, but I couldn't deny that I did. I owed him my life. "And you're paying for the pizza." I softened a little, grabbing a pillow from behind me and twisting to see the TV better, eventually relaxing a little more, propping my feet up on his lap.

I could push Cam's absence to the back of my mind for two hours, but probably not much more.

"Fine. Dinner's on me. But you won't always get off so easy." His hand landed gently on my ankle, then trailed up my calf. Shivers ran beneath his touch. "I won't wait forever." The hard smile he shot me sent my wings aflutter with warning.

I swallowed back a shaky voice, determined to be stone when I said, "Knock it off and pick a movie."

He changed the channel and picked up the phone. Before he dialed, he patted my bruised knee harder than he needed to. "Just don't say I never warned you."

Lisa M. Basso

Lisa M. Basso was born and raised in San Francisco, California. She is a lover of books, video games, animals, and baking (not baking *with* animals though). As a child, she would crawl into worlds of her own creation and get lost for hours. Her love for YA fiction started with a simple school reading assignment: S.E. Hinton's *The Outsiders*. When not reading or writing she can usually be found at home with The Best Boyfriend that Ever Lived and her two darling (and sometimes evil) cats, Kitties A and B.

For more on **A SHIMMER OF ANGELS** please visit www.month9books.com.

Sidekick: The Misadventures of the New Scarlet Knight

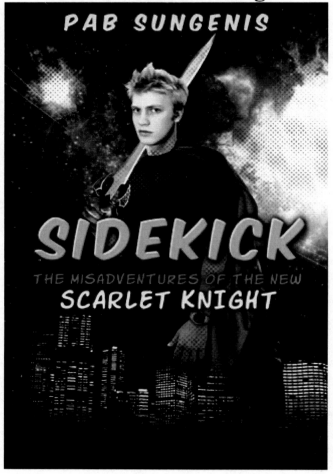

Available from Month9Books in
March 2013
www.month9books.com

Pretty Dark Nothing

Available from Month9Books in
April 2013
www.month9books.com

Praefatio

Available from Month9Books in
May 2013
www.month9books.com

My Sister's Reaper

Available from Month9Books in
May 2013
www.month9books.com

A Slither of Hope: Book 2 in the Angel Sight Series

Available from Month9Books in
January 2014
www.month9books.com